STEVEN MOORE

THE FEATHERED SERPENT

Quetzalcoatl

**In ie tlecujlixquac,
in ie tlamamatlac.**

Already at the edge of the fire,
already at the stairway.

Vinci Books

vinci-books.com

Published by Vinci Books Ltd in 2025

1

Copyright © Steven Moore 2019

The author has asserted their moral right to be identified as the author of this work in accordance with the Copyright, Designs and Patents Act 1988. This work is a work of fiction. Names, characters, places and incidents are the product of the author's imagination or are used fictitiously. Any resemblance to actual persons, living or dead, places and incidents is entirely coincidental.

All rights reserved. No part of this publication may be copied, reproduced, distributed, stored in any retrieval system, or transmitted in any form or by any means, including photocopying, recording, or other electronic or mechanical methods, nor used as a source for any form of machine learning including AI datasets, without the prior written permission of the publisher.

The publisher and the author have made every effort to obtain permissions for any third party material used in this book and to comply with copyright law. Any queries in this respect should be brought to the attention of the publisher and any omissions will be corrected in future editions.

A CIP catalogue record for this book is available from the British Library.

Paperback ISBN: 9781036706821

The EU GPSR authorised representative is Logos Europe, 9 rue Nicolas Poussion, 17000 La Rochelle, France contact@logoseurope.eu

Printed and bound in Great Britain by Clays Ltd, Elcograf S.p.A.

By Steven Moore

The Hiram Kane Archaeological Thriller Series

The Condor Prophecy
The Tiger Temple
The Feathered Serpent
The Samurai Code
Of Curses and Kings
The Shadow of Kailash
The Oak Island Enigma
Killing Koreana

Prologue

Cañada de la Virgen, San Miguel de Allende, Mexico

Flames flickered from a series of rustic torches that hung on ancient stone walls. Shadows danced wildly across those fine-hewn stones, their haunting silence only heightening the child's burgeoning terror. One shadow in particular leapt and danced, its wings jerking in crazed, untamed directions, though their owner stood statuesque before her. The gargoyle mask was terrifying. The creature's lack of communication was even more so.

The little girl, Rosa, had lost track of how long she'd been strapped to the cold stone plinth. A few hours? Days? It mattered little. Rosa was only nine years old, yet, somehow, she innately knew what was to come. The creature... was it a man? The *thing* before her had said only a few words since that man horrible had snatched her from her house and delivered her here. She had fought, she had scratched and kicked, and she had tried to scream, but the hot, sweaty hand clamped over her mouth kept her from uttering a word.

And then that gargoyle, that monster, had loomed out of the darkness.

"Un sacrifice digno," it had whispered as it towered in front of her. *A worthy sacrifice.*

Rosa understood she was a bright kid, though she definitely wasn't the smartest girl in her class. She wasn't even the brightest girl in her family... That honour went to Flor, her younger sister. But she was smarter than Juanito, her fourteen-year-old brother. Now, Rosa was glad Flor had gone to the store with Juanito when the man came and took her.

The torch flames flickered higher. The shadow wings danced on.

And now the unsaid words echoed around her terrified mind...

Un sacrificio digno.
Un sacrificio digno.
Un sacrificio digno.

A worthy sacrifice.

Rosa knew she had to be brave. She couldn't give up hope yet, despite everything.

There was one man who might yet be able to save her. She couldn't remember his name, but his face pulsed in her mind as those terrifying words of sacrifice and death rang in her ears.

Chapter One

Kenny's Place, San Miguel de Allende, Mexico

Three Days Earlier

Kenny Peters looked up from his local newspaper, *Atencion*, at the sound of footsteps echoing up the stairs to the rooftop terrace of his neighbourhood bar in Colonia Guadelupe. No need to wonder who that might be; the imaginatively named 'Kenny's Place' had become a kind of sanctuary for his visitor over the last few months, as it tended to become to many long-term guests to this corner of his adopted city. Kenny reached behind him and pulled down a bottle of Los Siete Misterios Doba Yej Mezcal. His visitor had been coming to the bar long enough that Kenny knew exactly what he would be drinking, just as any good bar owner should.

Kenny's charming yet low-key bar sat nestled on the fringes of the Historico Centro district of San Miguel de

Allende. The small though beautiful Spanish colonial-era city in central Mexico's high desert region had proven to be the perfect place for Kenny to live a low-profile existence while still being surrounded by stunning art and architecture; the perfect climate in what was known locally as the city of eternal spring only added to the perfection, along with a steady stream of thirsty expats who gave Kenny all the excuses he needed to indulge in a few adult beverages himself.

San Mike, as the expats called it, had been recommended by a friend, and the city's beauty and peaceful atmosphere had bewitched Kenny from the moment he'd first arrived a decade ago.

His guest arrived at the top of the stairs and, shielding his eyes from the bright sun, hesitated a moment, as though suddenly unsure if he should make his presence known after all.

"Hey buddy... the usual?" Kenny was already pouring the mezcal.

The man hesitated, then muttered, "Yeah... no... alright, yes, thanks... make it a double."

"Double it is, coming right up." Kenny finished pouring the large mezcal and placed it before the man now sitting in his usual seat at the rooftop bar, then Kenny stepped back and leaned on the counter. *Bit early for a double,* he thought.

"Everything alright, bud? You usually at least wait until the afternoon before hitting the doubles. It's eleven-fifteen... guess it's happy hour somewhere, right? Wanna talk about it?"

The man looked up at Kenny Peters, who immediately knew everything was not okay with his friend.

"It's those dreams again, isn't it?"

Danny nodded, then offered the hint of a smile. It soon faded.

Kenny poured himself his preferred early drink, *a little beer*, which wasn't a beer at all, but a shot of the Mexican liquor, *Liqor 43*, and a splash of thick cream. Kenny had a distinct notion it was going to be one of those days.

He stepped from behind the bar and took the stool next to his friend. Though Kenny knew hardly anything about the man's backstory, they'd forged a pretty tight bond over the last few months. Kenny liked Danny for many reasons, not least the amount of money he spent in his bar. More than that, the guy was quiet, thoughtful, never any trouble and, perhaps best of all, in a town full of people who had little better to do than whine about their lives and about getting old, especially the wealthy retired gringos and gringas from north of the border, Danny didn't spend his hours at the bar moaning. And, compared to those estafadores out to make a quick buck or peso, whether by legitimate means or otherwise, this guy was honest.

"So, it's the dreams?"

"Yep. I'm having them more and more often. Darker, too, and so real, Kenny, almost as if it's actual reality, and not a dream at all. Except, as always, it's not me that goes missing, it's… well, you know…"

"You mean your brother?"

"Yes." Danny had never spoken to Kenny about his brother directly, but occasionally referred to him in relation to other glimpses into his past.

Kenny didn't know the truth, and he would never ask. Yet from the bits and pieces he had learned, and short snippets and anecdotes Danny had revealed, usually when drunk, Kenny gathered that Danny had left his native England a long time ago, and put simply, had been living in hiding ever since. He knew nothing more than that, other than sensing a deep regret in his friend, perhaps even some vestiges of remorse and shame. One thing he did know without doubt was that a deeply troubled soul now sat beside him at his terrace bar on that otherwise bog-standard sunny Tuesday morning in paradise.

"Look, Danny, I know I suggested it before, but… well, why don't you see a doctor? Maybe even a shrink? Get some help. Surely they can give you something, you know, help you sleep a little better. I can talk to Doc Carlos… strictly off the record…"

His friend glanced sideways at him then, and raised his mezcal. "Thanks Kenny. I appreciate your trust and friendship. But I know what I need to do. I've always known it. I just can't." A long pause followed, then Danny said, "I never can."

Each man took a long gulp and finished their drinks at the same time. Kenny then stood and returned behind the bar to pour fresh ones. Once he'd sat down again, he asked, "You mean, contact them? Your family in England?"

Danny nodded, then looked up, his brown/green eyes wet with usually suppressed emotion. "Yes. Yes, that's what I know I should do. Just make contact. Tell them I'm sorry. Sorry for what I did, what I put them through. But… but it's been so long now, Kenny…" There was another long pause. Then Danny downed his new drink in one long gulp, and swivelled to face Kenny, hot tears now flowing unabashed.

Kenny spoke softly, not wanting to disturb Danny, or scare him in any way. He was clearly fragile, close to some unseen edge, and Kenny feared a single wrong word from him might have disastrous consequences. But Kenny knew he had to say something, afraid what Danny might do if left to dwell too much longer.

"Surely you can contact them, Danny. Don't you think they'd be relieved to hear from you after all this time, no matter what you think you may have put them through?"

"No." Danny stared at his friend with haunted eyes. "I can't do that. I am sure now that they believe their grandson, son and brother is long dead. That Danny Kane is dead." He slammed the glass down on the bar, cuffed away the last few stray tears and added, "So Kenny, my friend, let's drink, and raise our glasses to the dead."

Kenny Peters sighed and stood up. He had been right. It was definitely going to be one of those days.

Chapter Two

Kenny's Apartment, Barrio Aldea

Kenny awoke just before dawn after a night of fragmented, troubled sleep. That was normal. Kenny rarely slept well, but this was different. Something in particular had caused his unrest. He trudged across his cozy apartment to the bathroom, and splashed cold water over his face to wake himself up. After letting his dog out for his morning business, he took a coffee to the balcony and gazed out over the beautiful city of San Miguel as it too roused from its slumber.

He thought about last night, the drinking the two men had done, the stories they had told to each other and to the revolving door of various revellers. Yet, however much they talked, Danny always managed to avoid the subject of his family, and whatever it was he had done that tormented him so much.

Kenny finished off his coffee in one long gulp and placed the cup on the balcony rail.

"Danny," he said to no one. "What's your real story?"

Kenny wasn't the kind of person to sit around doing nothing. 'Restless is my middle name,' he'd say to clients at his bar who found his perpetual-motion effervescence comical. Right now he needed to take action of some kind.

He grabbed his phone and hit Contacts. A quick scroll down the contact list brought him to the Ls, and he paused at Stephy Loren. Stephy was a beautiful, talented singer and musician from Colombia, living in San Miguel and wowing the punters in a range of bars across the city with her stunning voice and sultry ebony skin. The fact she performed alongside her husband, Nelo, didn't deter most members of the audience from focusing on Stephy's many considerable talents. Noticing the time was still before six he put his phone down and made another coffee, then managed to show impressive self-restraint and waited until the far more respectable time of 6:57 before hitting call on Stephy's contact.

"Hola Stephy, ¿cómo estás?" *How are you?*

"Kenny? It is the middle of the night... ¿Qué pasa?" *What's up?*

Kenny continued in English. "Yeah, sorry it's early. Hey, you know Danny, the perma-wobbly guy from my bar? You guys are friends, right?

"Yeah," Stephy said then Kenny heard her yawning. "Yeah, we are friends. What's up, Kenny? Is everything okay?"

"To be honest Stephy, I'm not sure. He's been acting a little strange lately. I'm getting worried about him. He's drinking even more than usual, and he's having more and more of those damned dreams... I'm worried he's gonna do something stupid."

"No. He won't, I'm sure of it." To Kenny, Stephy didn't sound sure of that at all.

"I hope you're right," Kenny replied. "Anyway, does he ever talk about his family to you? Or mention his past?"

Stephy didn't answer for a long moment. Kenny knew that both she and her husband Nelo had become close with Danny over the last year. He'd often help them transport their music gear, setting the equipment up before shows and taking it down after. The couple were his only real confidants in the city. Kenny doubted he'd told them much, but like him, they knew enough to know he had been depressed lately, and that he had a lot of skeletons buried deep in his closet.

"Listen, Kenny," Stephy said, "Danny trusts us. I don't think I should say too much. I—"

"I get that, I really do, and I appreciate why you've said it. But I think we should do something. He mentions family to me occasionally, but I know nothing at all about them, or their relationship with him, if any. Maybe… I don't know, maybe we should contact them?"

Another long pause. Then Stephy said, "I don't know. He… he once casually told me that his brother was kind of famous? Like, some kind of explorer? I can't be sure. He has mentioned the word Vilcabamba a few times. Does that mean anything to you? Is it a place?"

It did mean something to Kenny, and yes, it was indeed a place. Since moving south to Mexico in order to escape the freezing Canadian winters twenty years ago, first to Acapulco before that lifestyle got too crazy even for him, Kenny had taken a keen interest in the culture and history of Central and South America. Though he hadn't done it yet, hiking the Inca trail to Machu Picchu in Peru remained high on his bucket list to tick off before he died... or in truth, before middle-age had its wicked way with his joints.

But Kenny was well-read on the histories of pre-Colombian cultures, such as the Aztecs, the Mayans and the Incas. Thus, he knew well about the exploits of perhaps the most famous ever explorer to the region, Hiram Bingham. He knew Bingham was the man who had rediscovered the fabled lost Inca city of Machu Picchu, high in the Peruvian Andes. What he also knew was that despite the fame Bingham received for finding Machu Picchu, it wasn't the true lost city. No, the real lost city of the Incas was known as Vilcabamba, and if his memory served him well, according to a National Geographic article he'd read a while back, that had been found by Englishman Hiram Kane only a couple of years ago.

Kenny leaned back in his chair and shook his head; something was slowly dawning on him. Scratching his stubble, he suddenly sat upright. "No way," he muttered, startling his dog, who rolled over in disgust at the rude intrusion to his nap. "Vilcabamba. English explorer Hiram Kane. A famous brother?" Kenny placed his phone back against his ear and quickly said goodbye to Stephy. Then he Googled the name Hiram Kane, and clicked on an image.

"I'll be damned," he said to his dog, who showed no interest at all and was already snoring at Kenny's feet. "I'll be damned," he said again, "no doubt about it. They could be twins."

It seemed Danny did have a brother. And yes, he was famous. Very famous indeed. Hiram Kane had received an enormous amount of recognition worldwide for being the first man to find that elusive, long-lost Inca city in Peru, Vilcabamba.

And now Kenny knew Hiram Kane also had a long-lost brother.

His name was Danny, and he was Kenny's best customer.

It was time to send a letter.

Chapter Three

The Kane Estate, Ringsfield, Suffolk, England

The darkness dragged him down like quicksand. With clawed fingers he reached for safety, something to hang onto, anything to pull him up. His hands grasped nothing but thin air.

Hiram Kane opened his mouth to scream. The black void, somehow a physical, sinewy thing, flowed into his mouth and down his throat, smothering him with an evil force so powerful he knew he could not escape.

And yet still he fought it, refusing to give in, battling against the inevitability of it all. He had to. This was not a choice. This was his life; Kane was a man who's will would simply not give in, even when debilitating odds were piled against him.

His muscles burned with exhaustion. His stomach cramped at the black void settling inside his body and his soul. Then, finally, Kane could battle no more. The darkness had won.

And yet, as his strong muscles went limp and his eyelids twitched, a chink of light sparked in the black. The darkness began retreating, and hope fluttered to life in his chest.

Only to be extinguished once more when he saw what lay before him…

Kane snatched at the bedclothes, gripping the sheets as if they were a lifeline thrown to him in a storm-tossed sea. Sweat dripped from his face and his hair felt damp against the pillow.

Something had startled him, snatching him from his tormented sleep. Hiram Kane was highly attuned to his environment, wherever in the world that might be, and he knew with certainty something had awakened him.

Thin beams of sunlight pierced the chink in the curtains of his bedroom. He rarely slept late, if ever. Today he'd slept late again, which was never a good sign.

Kane pushed himself up onto his elbows and quickly scanned the surroundings. Something had woken him up; Kane suspected it had been the sound of movement.

There was an intruder in his bedroom.

Whoever it was, they were being careful to keep hidden in the still dark room. They had to have been quick to hide themselves; Kane had switched from sleep to wakefulness in an instant.

Danger and excitement were close bedfellows with Kane, even though that was not his choice. He would much rather have lived a peaceful life, exploring far flung corners of the world and indulging his natural curiosity for people and places.

Yet Kane had one big weakness in his life; he could not stand by and see others suffer injustice or persecution. This weakness of his had led him down dangerous paths where he had often come face-to-face with the very worst of humanity, and battled it.

"It's not a weakness," Alexandria Ridley, his fiancée, had often told him. "It's your strength."

Kane's thoughts were interrupted by a scuffling noise. He had been right... there was someone in his room.

Kane clenched his fists, his body a wound-up ball of tension, ready to explode into action.

Later, he would ask questions. Who the intruder was. How they had got access to his room on the Kane Estate. How they had even found out where he was. Most importantly of all, why.

There was a sudden blur of movement in the gloom as something hurtled past him. Kane was ready to take this intruder out, no matter their size or strength. Yet... now he was puzzled. Whatever had made its way into his room was too small to be human.

In fact...

The thing landed on the bed, its green eyes almost glowing in the gloom.

Kane burst out laughing. "Hemingway! You absolute bast... Jesus, you scared the life out of me!"

Kane reached out and ruffled the cat's head, and scratched it behind the ears. This was Hemingway's favourite thing in the world, apart from eating and sleeping, and tormenting his brother-from-another-cat-mother, Fitzgerald. He rubbed his head against Kane's hand, purring in appreciation.

Kane realized he'd been clenching his teeth, and his jaws were aching with the exertion. His nerve endings were crackling with tension, as though filled with sparks of electricity.

"Okay, Kane, you can relax now," he told himself. "No one is after you... at least not today."

As his breathing at last slowed to its usual rate, Kane knew Hemingway had woken him from another nightmare, though if he were honest with himself, it wasn't just a nightmare; it was a painful memory, seared into his unconscious forever.

A light knocking on the bedroom door interrupted his thoughts.

"Hiram?" The voice was soft, and caring. "Is everything alright? I thought I heard...?"

"I'm alright, Grandma," Kane called back. "It was just Hemingway, causing trouble as usual."

"If you're awake..."

Kane frowned. His grandmother sounded unusually hesitant.

"Yes?"

"Your grandfather and I would like to see you in the drawing room when you're up."

"Of course," Kane said, deciding not to question his grandmother on what might be wrong. He would find out soon enough.

Kane swung his legs off the bed and looked down at Hemingway. The cat had already curled up on the bed, and looked settled in for the day.

"Thanks for letting me sleep in your bed, Ernest, old boy," Kane said, smiling and shrugging into his clothes. "Now where's that much nicer brother of yours?"

"You'd better take a seat," said his grandfather, Patrick, his strong, charismatic voice unusually weak and seemingly laced with doubt.

Kane was used to his grandfather's playful dramatics. He'd been that way ever since Hiram was a boy and he hoped he'd never change. The only question was, what was the latest joke?

"Okay, Gramps, here we are. What is it this time? Finally found Atlantis?" Kane grinned.

Patrick Kane would normally smile at this point, his eyes twinkling, unable to continue the ruse. But this time the wise old eyes didn't sparkle. Instead, they blinked rapidly several times, then locked on Kane's. The old man didn't smile.

That in and of itself unnerved Kane, but something in the air unsettled him more, though he had no idea what it was. Fear? Hope? His own grin faded away.

Kane remained silent as his grandparents sat either side of him on the couch. Hemingway, apparently having decided not to spend the day asleep on the bed after all, jumped onto Kane's lap and immediately began purring. Fitzgerald, a more sensitive soul, hadn't yet made an appearance.

Patrick Kane looked at his wife. They shared a subtle nod, then Patrick's eyes settled back on his grandson's. After a moment's pause, as if mentally checking with himself once more whether or not to say what he was about to, he spoke.

"Hiram, we... we've received a letter. It says..."

Kane gulped. This wasn't normal. Out of character. Something was wrong.

"A letter? From whom?"

"It's... It's anonymous." It was Kane's grandmother who'd spoken, and she continued. "It says... well, it says that your brother... Danny... well, whoever sent the letter claims to be his friend, and says that he lives in… he's in Mexico. This letter says Danny is alive."

Kane's heart leapt into his throat as his body sunk back into the couch.

Patrick read the letter aloud:

To the Kane family.

I realise this letter will probably come as a major shock to you all, but I can assure you that I am writing it with the utmost integrity and sincerity. I'm sorry it is so out of the blue, but please read on, and you will understand why.

I know nothing of your family history, other than what I have recently found out after a simple Google search. However, I write this with the utmost confidence that someone dear to you and whom for many years you feared lost is in fact here in this little city of San Miguel de Allende, in the state of Guanajuato, Mexico.

There is a man here who I have become friendly with in recent months. He doesn't say much, but I can confirm his name is Danny. He has never told me his family name, nor anything of his history. But what little I do know has inspired me to write you this letter. And the main reason I'm writing is because I'm worried about him. The thing is, he drinks a lot. A LOT! And he sometimes says things that concern me. I believe he is depressed and becoming a little unravelled. I am sorry if this is tough to read, but I hope that by writing you this letter you might come to Mexico and, for want of a better phrase, save Danny from himself.

I hope you'll understand why I want to keep this letter anonymous. I don't want to interfere in another man's life. But Danny is a good man. A genuine man. I just think he needs help. I don't want to be the one to get Danny into trouble, because as I said, I know nothing of his history or what he might have done before coming here. But he is clearly running from something. I see pain in his eyes, and hear it in some of the things he says. My gut instinct is that he wants to be found, which is why I have taken the liberty of writing you, the Kane family, this letter.

The city is San Miguel de Allende, 3 hours north of Mexico City. The nearest airport is Leon, also in the state of Guanajuato.

I hope you take this letter in the spirit it is meant, written by someone who cares and who is simply trying to do the right thing.

Regards,
A friend of Danny's.

Chapter Four

"I have to go immediately," Kane said to Alexandria Ridley, his long-term, on/off partner. Mostly on, these days, but Kane still wanted more. Ridley had just returned from a few weeks away on holiday with a friend, and was dozing on the couch at the annex of Kane's grandparent's home in Suffolk, England.

"Huh? Go… where?" Her voice was slurred, the jet lag obviously weighing heavy on both her mind and her body. Ridley rolled over, but as soon as she saw Kane's face she sat up. "What is it? Darling?"

Kane paced up and down the room, clenching and unclenching his hands into fists.

"I have to go. Right now. I'll get the next available flight from London."

"Slow down, Hiram," Ridley said. "Whatever is it?"

"I'll have to leave the estate now and head to the airport…"

"Hiram, please—"

"I need to pack a bag first…"

"Hiram..."

"And my passport... where the hell did I leave my passport?"

"Hiram Kane!" Ridley yelled and stood up from the couch.

Startled, Kane spun around to face her. "What?"

"Hiram, come here and sit down. Then tell me what the hell is going on."

Kane stared blankly at Ridley for a moment, then, as if coming to his senses, he exhaled a breath he hadn't realised he was holding. "Yes. I'm sorry, yes, of course." Kane took a seat on the couch next to Ridley, who had sat again, though he couldn't settle and fidgeted like a kid in school the day before summer holidays. He stood up again, then turned to face an increasingly alarmed Alex. "It's... I just can't believe it," he said, and turned and paced over to the huge window offering an expansive view out over the Kane estate.

"Hiram? Can't believe what?"

"It's..."

"It's what, love? Please, Hiram... please calm down and tell me what's going on."

Kane stood looking out at the beautiful scene stretching out before him. He took a few slow, deep breaths. This vista always had a calming effect on him. Today it wasn't working. He forced himself to breathe deeply and compose himself. He turned and went to sit back beside Ridley.

"I'm sorry, I didn't mean to panic you," he said, forcing himself to remain calm. "I've... we've just had the most incredible news. We received a letter. I mean, the family... we got a letter. It was anonymous, and it... well, it came from Mexico. It said..."

Ridley leant over and hugged Kane. In his ear, she said,

"It's okay... Take your time. I'm here. You can tell me whenever you're ready."

Kane held the hug for a few seconds longer, and when he finally eased himself from Ridley's arms, tears had dampened his cheeks.

He cuffed them away with a sleeve, then said, "It's Danny. The writer of the letter claims Danny's alive and living in Mexico. I... I... well, it has obviously come as a massive shock to us all. I... I always feared he had... well, we all believed Danny was no longer with us. But now, well, this letter... I have to go, Alex. I have to go to Mexico. Tomorrow. Danny might be out there somewhere, alive. If that's true, then I need to find him."

Ridley stood from the couch, her own eyes wet with obvious emotion. She pulled Kane up and wrapped him in a tight hug. "Go to your family now, and pour us each a large G'n T. I'll go and book us flights and a hotel."

"Us?"

"Yes, us," she said. "Of course I'm going with you."

Chapter Five

Colonia Los Mesquites, San Miguel de Allende

All across the city, both in Historico Centro and throughout the outlying colonias—the neighbourhoods—of San Miguel, families and tourists alike were enjoying the beautiful weather. Local fathers played football with their sons and daughters in the darkening streets and beneath the lights in the parks, while mothers hung out with their sisters and friends and gossiped about how much beer their husbands drank. The expats either joined in with their Mexican neighbours, or gathered at each other's homes or bars and restaurants downtown, making the most of the *happy hour* shenanigans and the never-ending 2-for-1 mojitos and margaritas. Even the street dogs revelled in the building excitement, innately knowing that there would be plenty of discarded food left strewn throughout the streets once the upcoming Alborada festivities had finished.

The light-hearted atmosphere everywhere was infectious, and it seemed as if the whole town was having fun.

The annual Alborada Festival was a highlight of the city, and the excitement was growing.

Lurking in the shadows of those bustling parks and streets, another group of people waited. They numbered seven, though one man alone was in control of the others. It had always amazed their leader how easy it was to convince people to do something they wouldn't normally have done, under any circumstances. He knew it was because he was smart and they were not. In fact, this man understood he was a genius, not that anyone had ever recognised that trait in him. Instead they focused on his awkwardness and his aloof manner. In fact, the truth was, no one ever really noticed him at all.

But that would soon change. As the puppetmaster, he would make sure if it.

Months ago he had conceived a plan, and he knew it was a plan so ingenious... so brilliant and beautiful... that no one would ever be able to ignore him again. Only one other person knew exactly what his scheme entailed. Like himself, that person had been shamed in the same incident a year ago. It was a moment that had ended the man's career once and for all, and the future career of his 'companion'. It was that loyal companion who had helped him come up with this wonderful scheme. He wouldn't be directly involved in carrying out the plan. If it went wrong, neither wanted him to be implicated. He was to help from afar however he could. If it went well, he'd been promised that his rewards and recognition would come later.

The gang of seven men had arrived at the arranged meeting place, a shady cantina on the outskirts of downtown not far from the city's main bus station. The leader had spent the last couple of months recruiting them, each man individually, from their native city of Guanajuato, ninety minutes from San Miguel. He had coaxed them in initially with petty chores to gain their trust, such as stealing a car, or robbing a grocery store. However, he had also promised them each a huge final pay off for one final duty. He hadn't yet told them what that last duty would be. But he understood the simple mentality of these... these kinds of men, and knew without doubt that once they got a taste for the easy money, they would not refuse him. As a genius, he understood it well... some people were just plain stupid.

All of his chosen minions had proven his instincts about them right when they had arrived on time. Once they had all arrived independently at the specified cantina, most arriving on the intercity buses from Guanajuato and surprised to see other men like them gathered at the meeting place, the leader had explained exactly what it was he needed from them. Initially, only a couple of the men had baulked. That was, until he had shown them the stack of pesos they were soon to receive once the mission was complete. He knew that in the state of Guanajuato, the average local worker got paid just one hundred pesos for an eight-hour shift (five US dollars), so he also knew that not a single one of them could afford to turn down twenty-thousand pesos (a thousand dollars), eight or nine months' work for a normal working man in Guanajuato. Not that these were normal working men. The leader had chosen them because that's exactly what they were not. These men were an unsavoury collection of low-level criminals, drunks and junkies, all desperate for an easy payday... and to hell with the consequences. They were perfect for his needs. He was a genius, so of course they were perfect.

The men obviously didn't know the whole truth of what

would happen once they had completed their tasks. The leader had only told them the first part. When one or two of the more conscientious of them had questioned the leader, he had simply insisted, "Do not worry. No one will get hurt. You have my word." The leader knew he was a good liar.

Each man's task was simple: kidnap a young girl. Then, once he had taken her to the prearranged destination, he was to go to the next colonia and kidnap another one. It was vitally important the girls were young, the leader stressed to them, no more than twelve or thirteen years old. Emphatically insisting again that no harm would come to these girls, the leader explained the simple yet strict instructions of what to do when they had secured their two girls.

The leader felt certain that not all the men would succeed in their individual task. One or two of them would probably lose their nerve, he believed, and another one or two he guessed were just too useless to pull it off. That was okay. He ideally wanted twelve girls in total. If he got half that amount, it would still be sufficient to carry out his plan.

The leader knew it was time the world started turning in his direction. And he would make sure it turned full circle.

He glanced around the faces of each of the recruits to his mission, holding the gaze of each for a moment until he was sure they were as ready as they could be. He inhaled, and looked up into the night sky. Some of the more localised festivities had already started, as fireworks whizzed and banged overhead. Despite the noise and modest light-show, the leader knew it was merely the calm before the almighty storm of the Alborada to come.

He turned and looked back at the men. Next he checked his watch and inhaled deeply, savouring the intoxicating aromas of sulphur from the fireworks and burning flesh from the taco stand nearby.

Finally, he turned back to face the gathered men, and nodded. "Go," he stated calmly, "and fulfill your missions."

As each man trotted off in different directions to the various colonias, he looked once more to the sky and said into the void, "Fulfill your missions, so I can at last fulfill my destiny."

Chapter Six

It was a long and restless flight from London's Heathrow Airport via Mexico City to the tiny Guanajuato International Airport, in the state of the same name.

Kane had grabbed a couple of hours of fitful sleep on the first and longest leg of the journey, while Ridley had slept almost the entirety of both flights, waking only occasionally and briefly when a bout or two of turbulence had shaken her from her slumber. Kane knew she was still exhausted from the exertions of her recent trip, and also knew Ridley could sleep anywhere, even standing up. But not him. Kane was a terrible sleeper.

Even when he had managed to doze off, the nightmares made sure his sleep gave him no rest.

So it was a weary yet determined Kane that hustled from the plane to the immigration line, which was thankfully short. "Bienvenido a Mexico," the immigration officer said in the same mirthless monotone of all immigration officers anywhere in the world. *Welcome to Mexico.*

They waited just twenty minutes to snag their modest

baggage of one backpack each from the carousel, before Kane and a decidedly lively Ridley marched to the car rental section of the small airport. While Kane rented a car, Ridley purchased two large coffees and a few stale-looking pastries from the cafe opposite, and soon they were racing off towards San Miguel de Allende, some sixty-five miles east, on what Kane hoped beyond all hope wouldn't turn out to be a wild goose chase.

Modest hills stretched out in all directions, and scattered across those hills were flocks of goats, the occasional farm shack, the even more occasional hacienda-style mansion, and of course the ubiquitous cacti and mesquite trees synonymous with central Mexican landscapes Kane remembered from his last visit to the country a decade earlier. It was beautiful indeed as the sun sank lower in his rearview mirror, and if it were not for the seriousness of their visit, Kane would have slowed down to enjoy the sweeping scenery.

But Kane was not there to admire the vistas, as stunning as they were. He had an altogether more important mission; find his long-lost brother.

As he drove his thoughts drifted to Danny. The brothers had been close, and despite the few years' age gap between them, they had always hung out a lot as if they were friends rather than siblings. Hiram was older, and the more outdoorsy of the two. Danny was a quieter, more timid kid. The truth was, Kane knew he outshone his younger brother both in the classroom and on the sports fields, a fact that hadn't sat well with him and one he'd always played down wherever possible. He was the bigger, stronger and apparently even the more academic of the two, at least according to their respective school reports. The one area Kane knew Danny had always had the edge over him was in the humour stakes. Danny had been a sharp and witty kid, and was a great practical joker, whereas Hiram's natural shyness gave him a more aloof countenance, often confused as arrogance by those who met him as he got older. Kane didn't believe he was arrogant. He tried to be thoughtful and mindful, so that when he did give an opinion it was measured and considered from all angles. He understood some people didn't always 'get' his shyness, and he accepted that. *We are what we are*, he would remind himself often.

He glanced over at Ridley, who had somehow managed to drop off to sleep with her head crunched against the window, and Kane grinned, trying to focus on Danny's sense of humour as he sped east on his brother's trail. As usual the smile didn't last long.

The day Danny had gone missing was a day Kane would never forget. At first he thought it was just another of Danny's practical jokes. They had bunked off school that afternoon. Danny had been reluctant at first, but with a little gentle cajoling Kane had convinced his brother to go with him to the Old Rectory, a well-known but deserted old building just half a mile from their childhood home.

They fled from the school on their bikes, and twenty minutes later were standing at the boundary fence to the Ol' Rec. With some trepidation, they left their bikes behind and scaled the fence, and against both of their better judgments, five minutes later they had broken in. It was harmless. The building had been abandoned and derelict for so long that no one they knew could ever remember a time when it was occupied. But rumours of ghosts and creepy goings on had persisted among the kids of their village for years, and ultimately, Hiram's curiosity had gotten the better of him. He simply had to go inside and find out for himself if the rumours were true. What he shouldn't have done was take his little brother with him. Danny had never been seen since…

"You okay?"

"Huh?" Kane blinked and snapped back to reality. He looked with alarm at the road ahead of them and thought of the miles he must have covered driving on autopilot. *Holy shit!* Kane resolved to not let himself be distracted like that again.

"Hiram? Are you okay?"

"Um, yes… Yeah, sorry… I'm fine." He paused and took a breath to clear his mind. "I was just thinking about Danny and the day he… you know, disappeared."

Ridley reached across and placed her hand on Kane's forearm. "Of course. I'm not sure how anyone could ever get over that… Despite what you have always thought, no one blames you." She squeezed his arm tighter, and Kane appreciated it, yet he had always carried that guilt with him since that fateful day all those years ago, and knew nothing would ever change it. Even if the letter was true, and Danny was alive and well in San Miguel de Allende, the guilt would still exist.

What the letter had done was give him hope. Hope that Danny was indeed alive. That he hadn't been kidnapped that day. Had not been murdered. Hope that Kane himself might at last find some form of redemption for what he had long considered his greatest mistake.

They fell sient again as Kane drove on, and a little more than an hour after leaving the airport, they passed a road sign that read:

San Miguel de Allende 4km

Kane glanced at Ridley in the passenger seat, very glad she was there. He knew why; they were getting close now, and Kane realised he was nervous. If the anonymous letter was true, and it was leading them to Danny, then what? Maybe Danny didn't want to be found? Maybe he would be angry and resentful? Maybe he would tell his brother to disappear and leave him the hell alone? Or maybe he would embrace him like a long-lost brother would, and everything would be okay forever...

"Almost there. And what a pretty town." Ridley almost purred with delight as they curved round the roundabout and entered Calzada de La Estacion, the main road from the west running into town, and beyond onto Umarán, a gentle hill that took them into the Historico Centro.

The colonial architecture that lined each side of the cobbled street was stunning. No buildings were over two storeys high, and the colourful facades and the ornate doors and windows were truly something to behold. Kane somehow already felt an innate peace about the place, as though the pace of the lifestyle hadn't sped up in decades, maybe hundreds of years.

Ridley pulled out her phone and hit the Google Maps app, and punched in The Rosewood Hotel, her choice of accommodation for the duration of their stay. Kane steered them up into the Historico Centro, directly towards the main square known as El Jardin, or The Garden, where they caught a glimpse of the magnificent seventeenth-century Gothic Parroquia de San Miguel Arcángel, resplendent in pink marble as it towered skyward into the darkening sky above the square.

The Rosewood had already confirmed there would be a room available whatever time they arrived, and within five minutes, after negotiating several more narrow cobbled streets and heading south on the Ancha de San Antonio, Kane pulled into the arrival bay of the impressive Rosewood Hotel, apparently the prime address for wealthier visitors to San Miguel de Allende.

At the check-in desk they were greeted by a smiling young man. "Buenas noches," he said. "Good evening, and welcome to The Rosewood San Miguel."

Kane and Ridley smiled and returned the greeting. The man who took their passports stepped over to a photocopier to make copies. Kane sensed the man seemed to dwell over their passports for a few extra seconds before returning, an odd look on his face that was somewhere between awe and surprise. But Kane, who was used to being recognised due to his unwanted flirtations with fame in recent years, ignored it, and the man quickly regained his composure. After being given a brief rundown of the amenities and facilities of the fancy hotel, a porter escorted them and their modest baggage across the lobby and into a lift.

The porter led Kane and Ridley to an expansive suite on the third floor, and after dumping their gear and splashing water on their faces, they immediately made their way back down to grab some food in one of the hotel's several dining rooms.

"What a place," said Ridley as they stepped into the lift. Despite their reasons for being there, Kane had to agree and turned to Ridley.

"It really is… it's a beautiful hotel. Listen, Alex… thank you."

"For what?" she replied, though he knew she was just teasing.

"For coming with me, and for arranging the flights and this hotel so quickly. I truly appreciate it."

"Of course. You're my soulmate, and I'm here to help

in any way I can. And Hiram?" She paused and looked earnestly at him. "I hope... I truly, truly hope, more than anything, that we find Danny."

They hugged. "Me too," Kane whispered. "Me too."

Just seconds after the new arrivals had followed the porter out of the reception area, the young receptionist excused himself from his colleagues and disappeared into a back room. Pulling out his mobile phone, he made a call.

"Buenas noches, Professor," said the receptionist.

"Bueno, Rafael. What is it?"

"You will never believe who just checked into the hotel!"

Chapter Seven

Having let the arm holding the phone receiver drop to his side, the man stood there, stunned, and for a moment, he was unable to move. Then, he sat heavily on his bed. He remained silent for a few further moments, as if trying to comprehend what this could all mean, before something like a grin crept onto his face.

"Professor?" enquired Rafael on the other end of the line. "Are you there, Professor?"

Finally, the man raised the phone and said, "Si, Rafael. I am here. Thank you for telling me. You have given me... given *us*... an excellent advantage for my... for *our* plan to work. As you know, I do not much believe in fate or luck. But destiny is an entirely different beast. And for whatever reason Mister Kane is now in Mexico, and on our doorstep, no less, it means my destiny... *our* destiny, is as good as guaranteed."

"Si, Professor. But I... I do not understand. How is this so?"

The man exhaled. "Rafael, as you know, Mister Kane is

someone I have admired for a long time, and equally, I admired his grandfather before him. Mister Kane, like me, was once an archaeologist. Then he became an explorer, and also like me, he found something rather extraordinary. Do you recall what that something was?"

"Si, Professor... how could I forget?"

"Yes, indeed. Yes, Rafael, Mister Kane discovered a lost city in the jungles of Peru, while I... well, you know what it was I found."

"Si, Professor, I know. But those... those selfish bastards... they denied you the glory you so rightly deserved."

Then man nodded to himself and sighed. "Si, Rafael, they did. But no one has ever denied Mister Kane *his* glory." Unbidden, his eyes narrowed as a tidal wave of jealousy swept over him, and for a moment his hand clutched the phone a little too tightly, his knuckles turning white with the strain.

"Professor?"

Then he relaxed again and closed his eyes, gathering his thoughts. "Rafael, we must make the most of this golden opportunity. Are you still committed? Committed to me? You know... you know how I feel about you?"

"Por supuesto, Professor. Siempre." *Of course. Always.*

"Good. Will you do anything I ask?"

"Si. For you, professor... I would do anything."

The man opened his eyes and said in a more stern, authoritarian voice, as a wise older professor might say to an unruly student, "Then you must quit your employment immediately, and follow Mister Kane. And you must report back to me what he is doing at all times. Why is he in Mexico? Who is he with? What is he doing here? When is he leaving? Can you do that, my protégé?" he asked, softening his words once more.

"Si, Professor. Consider it done."

The man... who was once known as Professor Palomares... exhaled and put down the phone. He knew Rafael would not fail him, and for the first time in a long time, he allowed himself to believe the world was at last turning the right way.

Rafael Cortes was so happy in that moment he was almost overcome with emotion. He had idolised the professor since he'd first started taking his archaeology classes at the university in Guanajuato several years ago. But his feelings ran deeper than that. Much deeper. He felt responsible for the scandal that had cost Professor Palomares his job and his reputation—one of the many scandals. And though both men had been willing participants, now... now Rafael had a chance to make it up to the man he admired and... make it up to the man he loved.

He would not waste this opportunity, and he repeated his words that now only he could hear. "For you, professor... I would do anything."

Chapter Eight

San Miguel de Allende was named after Saint Michael, now the Patron Saint of the city and hence why many expats had come to refer fondly to is as San Mike. The city itself lies within a vast natural bowl, surrounded by the mountains of the high desert and the semi-arid plains of the state of Guanajuato. The undulating hills around the city, dotted with a range of cacti and ancient mesquite trees, some centuries-old, are beautiful. In and of themselves, the hills and their myriad hiking trails are worthy enough reasons to visit the region. And yet they do nothing to prepare first-time visitors for the magnificence of the city itself. The steep, charismatic cobblestone streets lined with colourful buildings—none more than three stories high, most just one or two—simply beg to be explored. An early morning stroll around those quaint, uneven streets immediately transports a visitor back hundreds of years in time, and it is perfectly normal to see old men riding around on mules or horses, and clusters of brightly clad women and girls selling hand-made arts and crafts and spectacular arrays of flowers on the sidewalks.

San Miguel's charm lies in its tranquillity, more or less untouched by the more unsavoury aspects of society found occasionally in other parts of modern Mexico. The pace is slow, and its local inhabitants are mild-mannered and calm. There isn't even a single traffic light in the city. Both residents, and taxi drivers in their immaculately clean, ubiquitous white and green vehicles, are more than willing to allow pedestrians to cross, and let cars proceed from narrow junctions on a one-by-one basis, their gratitude given in the form of a smile and a gentle nod, or the casual flick of a wrist.

It is undeniable that the influx of tourists and expats since the dawn of the new millennium has added a new dynamic to the city, but almost all of those infiltrators try their best to retain the beauty and tranquil charms that once lured them there in the first place.

San Miguel is renowned across Mexico and beyond for its amazing array of cultural and religious festivals, and one of the most famous of all is the annual Alborada. Alborada —dawn, in Spanish—is a festival that celebrates the Archangel Saint Michael's victory over Lucifer, and as the story in the Book of Revelation goes, it was down to that epic battle that ultimately saw the Devil cast out of Heaven.

As they always do and have done for many decades, the Alborada festivities begin in the early hours of the morning. A vast procession comprising thousands of men, women and children carry a life-size effigy of Saint Michael to various churches around the city for the ritual blessing. The brass and string-wielding mariachi bands, resplendent in their black and silver outfits, along with the giant papier mâché mojiganga dancers—usually men on stilts in a variety of hilarious costumes—follow the crowds from one church to the next.

The culmination of this massive party is an extraordinary firework display, which is a visual representation of the fire and fury in the battle between Saint Michael and Lucifer. It happens at dawn, hence the name alborada —dawn—at the moment light eventually overcomes the darkness, and when good overcomes evil.

As sunlight floods the Principle Jardin, the main square in the historic centre, the faithful haul themselves back to their homes, exhausted but joyous after a long night of drinking, dancing and often wild partying. And then, just a few hours later, those same weary revellers resume the festivities, starting with the burning of Judas.

That's what usually happens…

Chapter Nine

"What time is it?"

Kane turned away from the window to gaze at Ridley stirring in the bed. As usual, he hadn't been able to sleep much. "Almost five."

"Really?" Ridley sat up and rubbed at her eyes. "What's all that noise?"

Kane turned back to look out of the hotel window. "It looks like San Miguel is getting ready to throw a massive party."

"Getting ready?" Ridley tried but failed to stifle a yawn. "It sounds to me like they've already started."

Ridley joined Kane at the window. As always he was comforted by her physical closeness. His love for her transcended all else in his life, though it sometimes felt unrequited and that was a constant thorn in Kane's side. Still, whether she said it or not, he felt sure that deep down she did feel the same way about him. It was enough. For now. She was definitely a soulmate and he would always cherish that knowledge. It was true their lives often took them on separate paths, and that was something they both understood, but Kane always clung onto some hope that their major life journey would be one they shared.

"I think you might be right," he replied.

"If we weren't here on such... for such an important reason, I'd be tempted to party with them."

Kane drew Ridley close and gently turned her head to face him. "Thank you again, my love, for coming with me. It means the world to me. *You* mean the world to me."

Ridley kissed him gently on the lips. "And you mean the world to me. Whatever happens next, we will face it together. And we will find Danny, I know we will."

Kane hugged Ridley tight. "Thank you."

"Neither of us is getting any sleep now, not with all that noise going on," Ridley said. "Why don't we head outside and join them? We might as well start looking for the mysterious bar from the letter right now. Let me just have a quick shower."

Kane stretched out his arms, relieving the tension in his muscles which were knotted up from the long flight to Mexico.

"You're right," he called out to Ridley, now in the bathroom. "If we can't sleep, we're just wasting time. I'll make us a coffee, then we'll head out." Hope blossomed in Kane's chest that today could just be the day he might be reunited with his brother, a brother he had long feared was no longer with him. He flicked the coffee machine on and returned to the window.

It was six in the morning, and still dark, when Rafael watched Hiram Kane and Alexandria Ridley leave the hotel and cross the street. Despite the party atmosphere, he noticed both wore expressions of determination.

Rafael slunk back into the shadows as they walked past him, oblivious to his presence. From the moment he had first learned to walk, Rafael had been good at hiding; it was a skill he'd had to learn fast to avoid the constant beatings administered by his stepfather. And once the beatings had stopped, after Rafael, at the tender age of twelve-years-old, had slid a knife into his stepfather's guts and carved him open, the young man had realized this skill was a transferable one. Hiding in the shadows gave him access to all sorts of information and tip-offs he never would have had otherwise.

Kane and Ridley disappeared into the colourful crowd of excited locals and tourists. The Alborada drew sightseers and explorers from all over the world. They were like flies buzzing around a spilled pot of sugar; detestable, horrid pests, worthy of nothing but extinction. Rafael was grateful to have made the acquaintance of the professor. His brilliant mind was like a beacon of light in Rafael's life, and when their plan had reached its conclusion, the rest of the world would see that brilliance too, and the professor would finally get the glory he had already been robbed of.

Rafael left his hiding place and followed Kane and Ridley into the crowd. The professor had told him to keep an eye on them and, if possible, find out what the one and only Hiram Kane was doing here on the very day the professor's plan was finally swinging into action. *Is it just coincidence?* Rafael mused. It was impossible to imagine how, but Rafael wondered, *Does Kane know something?*

Surely that wasn't possible. Nobody but the professor and Rafael knew the true extent of their plans. Those men who had been hired to kidnap the girls, even they knew little of what was planned. They had their purpose to serve, and their gains to make, and that was it.

Rafael had to quicken his steps to keep up with Kane and Ridley, who kept disappearing amongst the crowds of people, before reappearing, then disappearing again.

He wasn't too worried about being discovered by Kane in the midst of the celebrations; after all, Rafael was just a friendly local out and about and joining in with the festivities…

Even so, Rafael liked to keep his distance and practice his talent for remaining out of sight. That's what made it more entertaining, too.

And then when the girls started disappearing, that's when the fun would really start.

Rafael could hardly wait.

Chapter Ten

"This is amazing!" Ridley exclaimed as she watched a group of men, women and children dancing down the street, her eyes shining with excitement.

Kane couldn't help but smile, despite the seriousness of their reasons for being there. It wasn't just the festive dancing that was lifting his spirits a little; seeing Ridley happy always made Kane happy too.

Fireworks lit up the night, oranges, reds, yellows, and blues dazzlingly bright against the black sky above. The crowds cheered.

Maybe looking for Danny, or even the mysterious author of the letter, was a mistake right now. There were too many people, too many distractions. But it felt good to be outside; better than being cooped up inside their hotel room, failing to sleep while all this excitement took place out here. Even so, despite his heart being lightened somewhat by the happiness and joy exhibited all around him, Kane couldn't fully escape the sense of foreboding and doom that hung over him.

Would they really find Danny, here, alive, after all these years? Or were they on a wild goose chase? The victims of a practical joke, perhaps. This sudden, new thought chilled Kane's heart. In the rush to get here, Kane hadn't even considered the possibility this might be someone's idea of a joke. If so, it was a nasty, unimaginably sick act, yet Kane knew there were plenty of people out there who would enjoy pulling off an elaborate hoax like this.

"Relax a little," Ridley said, squeezing Kane's hand. "You're all tensed up."

"I know. Sorry. I can't help it." Kane rolled his shoulders, willing himself to unwind, and dismissing his doom-laden thoughts. But it was pointless; his stomach was knotted up, and his eyes darted through the crowd, constantly searching for that familiar face of his brother.

How much would he have changed by now? Kane wondered. After all, they had been children when Danny disappeared. Would the years, and possibly all the drinking, have taken their toll as well? Kane knew he would recognise his brother the moment he saw him, no matter how much he might have changed.

Kane froze.

"What is it?" Ridley said, instantly attuned to Kane and his emotional shifts. "What's wrong?"

"Over there, look," Kane said, pointing.

Standing at the edge of the crowd, his back to Kane and Ridley, was a man holding hands with a little girl.

But the girl was struggling, yanking at the man's hand in an obvious effort to pull herself free. The man dragged her closer and began walking away, his head bowed as though he might be talking to her.

"Could be her father, but…" Ridley's voice trailed away, her tone uncertain.

"You're right," Kane said, "he could be."

"He needs some parenting lessons if he is."

"Parenting's not exactly in our wheelhouse though, either, is it?"

"No, it's not. On the other hand, he might *not* be her father."

"In which case that young girl is in trouble, and someone should do something to help her."

"And if that's the case, that is exactly in our wheelhouse, right?"

"Right," Kane said. "Let's go find out what's happening."

The man disappeared into the crowd, dragging the girl along with him. No one paid them any attention, as almost everyone's attention was fixed on the magnificent fireworks display above.

Kane and Ridley pushed their way between the onlookers. The crowd of locals and tourists all had their heads tilted back, expressions of wonderment on their faces.

"Where's he gone?" Ridley hissed. "I can't see him anymore."

"I don't know." Kane paused for a moment, scanning the crowd. Someone bumped into him and muttered an apology.

"I've got a bad feeling about this," Ridley said.

Another round of fireworks exploded above them, and the crowd gasped in astonishment and appreciation at the magnificent display.

"There you are..." Kane muttered as he spotted the man dragging the little girl down an alleyway in a brief opening between the masses of people.

Ridley had spotted him too. Together they pushed their

way between the packed bodies, ignoring the half-hearted shouts of protest aimed their way.

In the narrow cobbled alleyway they were free of the crowd. Kane picked up speed, accelerating from a walk to a run. Up ahead, in the gloom of the alley, the man glanced back over his shoulder. When he saw he was being pursued, his eyes widened and he picked up his pace.

Away from the noise of the festival, Kane could hear the little girl crying. That was enough for him to know that his instincts had been correct; this was almost certainly a kidnapping attempt.

Followed close on his heels by Ridley, Kane narrowed his attention down to that helpless little girl and her kidnapper ahead of him. When he caught up with them, and if it was how it appeared to be, Kane would make that man pay for his despicable actions.

The man was trying to drag the girl along as fast as he could, but she was slowing him down. Not only could she not run as fast as him, but she was fighting against him, struggling hard to free herself from his vile clutches.

Good for you, Kane thought. *Fight him with everything you've got.*

And with that final notion, Kane sprinted down the alley and threw himself at the man's legs from behind in a rugby tackle. Their two bodies tumbled to the ground, smacking into the hard cobbles. The man yelled out in pain, pinned against the stone cobbles by Kane's weight.

Ridley was quickly down on her knees, comforting the little girl. "Hey, you are okay now, nobody is going to hurt you."

Whether she understood Ridley's English words or not, the girl nodded, her breathing ragged and tearful.

"Get off me, you idiot!" the man yelled in Spanish.

Kane got the gist. "I'm not doing anything. You... you attacked me! Help! Somebody help me!"

Kane stood up and dragged the man to his feet, then shoved him hard up against a wall.

"Really?" Kane said, doing his best in Spanish. "Do you want to explain to the police what you are doing with this little girl?"

The man smiled, revealing dirty chipped teeth. "La policia? Why would the police want to interfere in a family matter? This is my daughter. I am taking her home to her mother."

"Why was she fighting you so much?"

The man shrugged. "Her mother is very angry with her. The girl knows she is in a lot of trouble."

Kane twisted to look at the girl. "Is he telling the truth? Is this man your father?" Kane said. Ridley's arm tightened around the girl's shoulders as the girl seemed to shrink away from the perpetrator. "Don't be scared of him," Kane encouraged. "You can tell us. We will look after you."

With moist, wide-open eyes, the girl gazed at the man pinned against the wall. She shook her head.

Kane turned his attention back to the would-be kidnapper. "Where were you taking her? What were you going to do with her?"

The man's smile had slipped somewhat. "The girl is lying. She is a naughty little bitch, and she deserves a slap when she gets home."

Kane saw red and slammed the man against the wall, the back of his head crashing against stone. "Say that again and you will be the one getting slapped. Except I will use my fists. Now, I will ask you again... what were you going to do with this girl?"

"Nothing!" the man spat. "I was going to do nothing."

"That is not good enough," Kane said, leaning in so his face was mere inches from the perp's. "You're going to have to try harder than that."

Suddenly Kane was distracted by a scream from the alleyway entrance.

"Rosa! Rosa!"

In that moment of distraction, the villain wrenched himself free of Kane's grip and before Kane could make another grab for him, the man punched him in the side of his head then turned and ran down the alleyway and was soon out of sight.

Kane stumbled, a sharp pain shooting through his skull.

"Hiram?"

Ridley was there in a split second, hands on his shoulders, supporting him.

"I'm... okay," Kane said, grasping his head in both hands. "I'm going to have a killer of a headache though."

"Rosa! Rosa! Oh, my precious baby!"

A woman had bundled Rosa into her arms and was smothering her in kisses. Rosa had wrapped her arms around the woman's neck and was snuggling in close.

"I don't think we need to ask her if she's Rosa's mother," Ridley said.

Kane glanced back down the alleyway into the gloom. "Dammit! I just wish I could've kept hold of that bastard."

"Rosa's safe now, that's all matters," Ridley said.

Kane shook his head. "Yeah, but what the hell did he want with her? And if he can't have her, what's stopping him from kidnapping another little girl? I should have... I should've taken him down."

Kane was still looking down the alleyway into the darkness as he spoke. He felt Ridley place a hand against his cheek and gently turn his head so that he was looking at her.

"Hiram, you can't be there for everyone. You saved this little girl. Remember that at least."

Kane's lips twitched but instead of the usual wry smile, he just inhaled and looked away. He knew he could be hard on himself sometimes, that whatever he accomplished he always wished he could have done that little extra. That the things he achieved were never quite enough.

"I want to thank you so much for rescuing my baby," the woman said in her native Spanish, her eyes glistening with tears. "How can I ever repay you?"

Kane said, "My name is Hiram, and this is my… friend, Alexandria. You don't need to repay anything. Rosa is safe now, and that is payment is enough."

"I am Mariana, and I am in your debt. Please, at least come home with us and let me make you breakfast."

"Oh, no. Thank you though, but we couldn't possibly —" Kane began in his best Spanish.

"We would love too," Ridley cut in. "It would be our pleasure, Mariana, thank you."

Kane looked at Ridley and nodded, then translated as best he could. As always, Ridley was right; they risked offending Mariana by refusing her gratitude. And if he was honest with himself, Kane was more than ready for a good feed.

"Gracias, Mariana," he said. "Breakfast sounds lovely."

From his hiding place in the shadows, Rafael watched Kane and Ridley leave with the Mexican woman and her daughter.

Now I have an opportunity to impress the professor, he thought.

The idiot who had tried to kidnap Rosa was obviously one of the professor's men. He had failed in his mission, as the professor had suspected some of them would, yet he had given Rafael a chance to prove once more his utter devotion to his master.

The young man followed Kane, this time keeping his distance. For what he had planned now, Rafael knew he had to stay hidden.

Luckily, remaining hidden was what he did the best.

Chapter Eleven

The Principle Jardin, San Miguel de Allende

After a filling breakfast of eggs, homemade corn tortillas, fresh mole and black beans, washed down with a couple of strong coffees each, Kane and Ridley expressed their gratitude to Mariana, said goodbye to Rosa, and headed the 15-minute walk back to the Rosewood hotel. There they refreshed themselves with quick showers, and then set out again, renewed in their mission to find Danny.

When they first arrived, they'd had no contacts in town, and no real idea where to begin their search. The anonymous letter had only mentioned a bar, but Kane had already surmised there were plenty of bars in San Miguel de Allende. So, with no better plan, Kane figured the best thing to do was to simply set out for the Jardin and commence from there. With a little research, they had learned San Miguel was a popular city for expats and wealthy Mexicans to retire to—partly due to the wonderful year-round climate, and partly because of the cheap margaritas—so they felt sure that by asking around they would eventually find someone who could lead them to the right bar.

Besides, thanks to Mariana they had an advantage now, a possible contact in town who might be able to help them.

At Mariana's humble home, Kane and Ridley had met Rosa's siblings, Flor and Juanita. Flor was younger than the nine-year-old Rosa, and Juanita was eldest of the three children at fourteen years of age. They were a delightful family, and their home was filled with joy and laughter, a perfect environment for Rosa to forget her terrifying experience at the hands of the cowardly bastard who'd tried to abduct her.

"I'm learning karate!" Rosa had said at one point, dropping into a fighting pose.

"Wow," Kane said, taking a step back and raising his hands in mock fright. "That's amazing."

Rosa pivoted on one foot and kicked out in Kane's direction. He actually had to dodge the kick.

"Whoa, you're pretty good, aren't you?"

Rosa scowled at Kane and lowered her voice into a growl. "If anyone tries to take me again, I will be ready for them."

"I bet you will," Kane replied, laughing, though it was anything but funny. He tried hard to keep the mood light. "Here, let me teach you a move."

Rosa approached him, eyes wide with eagerness to learn. "You know karate?"

"I do... a little." Kane smiled at Rosa. "This move I'm going to teach you will help you escape if anyone ever has hold of you from behind, okay? I think it's called Koshi Suriyoku, or something like it. It's Japanese." Rosa rolled her eyes as if everyone knew that simple fact. Kane chuckled again, then said, "Here, let me show you."

He gently turned Rosa around so that he was behind her and then wrapped his arms around her so that she was pinned in place.

"Hey!" Rosa yelled, giggling.

"Now try and get free."

Rosa wriggled and squirmed, but to no avail. "You are too strong."

"You think so? You can get free, if you want."

"But how?"

Kane kept his grip on Rosa. "Okay, this is what you do. First of all, go into a slight squat. That's good. And now take a step to your right, while tensing your arms and your shoulders, and place your left foot in between both my feet. Okay, that's it. Good. Now hook your foot behind mine and lean—"

Kane suddenly tumbled to the ground. Rosa leapt into the air, cheering.

Kane grinned up at her from the simple concrete floor. "You are a quick learner, aren't you?"

Everybody laughed, none more so than Ridley. "That was amazing, Rosa! Girls kick ass, right?"

Kane was going to translate, but Rosa high-fived Ridley and Kane assumed with a grin he didn't need to.

It was only when the conversation turned to Kane and Ridley's purpose for visiting San Miguel that the mood turned serious.

"I think I might be able to help you," Mariana said, after Kane had finished telling his story. "It might be nothing, but then again…"

"Any and all help is very much appreciated," Kane replied.

"I have a friend, an American woman who now lives here, and she…" Mariana paused for a moment. "Well, this friend of mine, she seems to know everyone and everything." Mariana threw her hands in the air in a pantomime of astonishment. "How she does it, I do not know!"

Kane leaned forward, all of his attention now on Mariana. "And you think she might know Danny?"

"Might she even be the one who wrote the letter?" Ridley asked.

Mariana shrugged. "I don't know the answers to any of this, but I think Vicki Allen will know someone who knows something, at the very least."

"Thank you, Mariana," Kane said. "Now it is I who will be forever in your debt."

Chapter Twelve

San Miguel sits in Mexico's high desert at a lung-busting altitude of 1,900m (6,235 feet), an uncomfortable altitude for those not used to it. Despite Kane and Ridley's supreme fitness, they took a while to catch their breaths as they headed uphill towards the Jardin. They paused occasionally to take a deep breath and admire the city's quaint streets and colourful colonial architecture.

It was almost ten in the morning now, and the streets were starting to fill with wide-eyed tourists and locals going about their business. Just ten minutes' walk after leaving The Rosewood they entered the Jardin, and after a couple of laps of the tree-lined main square to get their bearings, they took a seat on a bench and sat admiring the magnificent Parroquia.

Both the square and the church were obviously a photographer's dream. The beautifully landscaped gardens in the centre of the square, perfectly framed by the Spanish colonial-era buildings, were stunning by themselves. Add into the picture the soaring spire of the Gothic masterpiece before them, resplendent in pink stone, and they could soon appreciate why San Miguel was such a hot topic among travel magazines, such as Conde Nast and Travel & Leisure. In fact, Ridley had read that for several years now San Miguel de Allende had been voted the world's best city in which to live... high praise, but it wasn't hard to see why. They grabbed another coffee from a hole-in-the-wall cafe just off the square, called Ventanas, or The Window, and wandered back into the now bustling crowds in the Jardin.

After another twenty minutes or so of wandering a few of streets that ran adjacent to the square, Kane checked the time.

"Should we head back?" Ridley said.

Kane nodded. "Yes, it's time."

They threaded their way through the throngs back to the Parroquia de San Miguel Arcángel, and took a seat in the square once more.

Mariana had told them that Vicki liked to visit the square outside the church every morning.

"She can be a very private person," Mariana had said. "She will probably appreciate you meeting her there, rather than visiting her home. At least until she gets to know you better."

Now Kane and Ridley sat in the warm sunshine, waiting for, based on Mariana's description, a short lady with a shock of short, cropped white hair, and clutching a tiny dachshund, to arrive.

Ridley slipped her arm around Kane's shoulder. "Are you nervous?"

Kane turned to face her. "A little, yes," he said. "More than anything else, I want this to be a solid lead, since it's the only one we have."

The Feathered Serpent

"If this one doesn't work out, we will find other leads and avenues to explore," Ridley said, leaning in a little closer.

After only a few minutes of waiting, Ridley pointed. "There she is; that's got to be her!"

Kane looked where Ridley pointed, and had to agree. The woman fitted Mariana's description perfectly.

As one, they rose from the bench and walked across the square. Kane's stomach churned with a mix of anxiety and excitement at the thought of this woman potentially being a step closer to him finding his brother.

"Excuse me, miss," Ridley said, having agreed with Kane beforehand that it might be better for her to introduce them first.

The lady with the dachshund looked up. "Yes?"

"Sorry to bother you. Are you Vicki Allen?"

"As it happens, young lady, yes I am, and very glad about it I am too."

"Do you mind if I ask you a question?"

"I certainly do not mind, but I can't guarantee to know the answer. Fire away," Vicki Allen said, before adding, "But please, before we get to the asking and answering questions part of this conversation, may I ask who is doing the asking?"

Ridley smiled. "Good morning, Vicki. I'm Alex and this is my, um, partner, Hiram."

"Well, Alex and Hiram, it's very nice to make your acquaintances."

"And you too," Ridley said. "We were given your name by a friend of yours, Mariana, and... Well, we are... we're here in town looking for someone very special to us."

Vicki nodded, and said, "Come with me. Let's find somewhere with a little shade where we can sit down and have a proper conversation. This sounds like a conversation that's too important to be having in the middle of the Jardin being scorched by the sun and without the proper refreshments."

Vicki led them to a bench beneath the tightly manicured laurel trees, the perfect place to escape the rising heat of the day, then checked her watch and with what to Kane appeared to be mock surprise, she seemed to reconsider. "My my, it's already eleven o'clock," she stated with a wink, "so why don't I buy you guys your maiden San Mike margarita while you tell me why you're here in our fine city."

Vicki, along with little Henry the dachshund, who Ridley suspected went everywhere with his charismatic human, led the two newcomers just north of the square to an expat hangout by the name of Hanks New Orleans Oyster Bar, which at just eleven fifteen in the morning was already well stocked with retired expats getting their morning buzz on.

They took a seat at the bar, where a young barman—Mario, according to his name tag—greeted Vicki as if she was a regular. By Vicki's rosy cheeks and twinkling eyes, Kane guessed she probably was.

Kane scanned the bar's interior, searching for his brother. *Of course he isn't here. It couldn't be that easy, could it?*

Vicki ordered their drinks... Kane opting for a beer and Ridley a coffee... and Vicki listened with intent and growing curiosity as she sipped her margarita and Kane told her everything, including about the mysterious and enigmatic letter.

"Well, son," Vicki said, her Dallas drawl unmistakable, "I think I could narrow it down to perhaps three places where you might find what you're looking for. This place is

The Feathered Serpent

one of them." She smiled, and it was the heart-warming smile of someone content with life.

Vicki then began asking the staff if they knew anything about a man named Danny Kane. No information was forthcoming, however, and Kane already feared the worst, his spirits sinking once more.

But then Mario held up a finger, as though he'd had a thought. "How about Kenny's? Have you tried Kenny's Place?"

"Kenny's? You mean down in Guadelupe?" asked Vicki.

"Si. That's the one."

"Ah yes, I know it. Gracias, Mario." Vicki turned to Kane. "I'll show you there next. I know Kenny a little too. A good guy, Canadian. Got a big heart. And if I'm being honest, Kenny's the kind of guy I imagine writing an anonymous letter."

They finished their drinks, then Vicki guided Kane and Ridley out of Hanks and down Hidalgo towards Kenny's Place in Colonia Guadelupe. She pointed to the rooftop terrace they could see from a distance. "I do hope you find what you seek, Hiram," said Vicki.

"Thanks very much," Kane replied, then turned to Ridley. "Shit... I'm so nervous."

"Do you want me to come in with you? Of course I'd understand if you'd rather go in alone." Ridley leaned in and hugged Kane close, a hug he seemed reluctant to release her from. After a long minute, he eased out of Ridley's arms.

"No, but thanks. I think I... well, I need to do this alone."

Ridley smiled and stepped back. "Good luck, my love. Meet you back at the hotel later?"

"Yes. And thanks again... to you both." Kane took a

couple of deep breaths, then turned and entered the downstairs door to Kenny's Place.

"Come on, Alex. Let me buy you a glass of wine or two," Vicki said." "If I'm right about Kenny, your guy could be up there a while."

Chapter Thirteen

Kenny's Place, Colonia Guadelupe, San Miguel de Allende

Kane stepped up onto the single concrete step into Kenny's Place, and stood rooted at the threshold of the bar. Frozen to the spot. Chilled to the bone, despite the heat of the day.

He didn't believe in ghosts. But one sat before him right now.

He took a step forward, then stopped, the weight of three decades of guilt too much to bear in that moment. A light-headed feeling wobbled him a little and his stomach tightened in knots.

It's... impossible, he thought. "Impossible," he whispered.

Another step forward into the bar. Then another.

The man sitting at the bar shifted in his seat. He leaned back a little, stretching his shoulders, his gaze never leaving the glass sat on the bar in front of him. It was nearly empty. His elbows slipped off the edge of the barstool's armrest, suggesting to Kane there had been many full ones in the last couple of hours. Years, possibly. Kane shook his head a little, as if to remove an unwanted thought from his mind. He edged sideways a fraction to get a glimpse of the seated man's face in profile and noticed the hint of a smile cross his lips. Then it was gone. But there was no longer any doubt who this man was and a quiver of excitement caused Kane's mouth to go dry and his fingertips to tingle.

Then the man in the seat who he believed was his long-lost brother called over to the girl behind the bar.

"Otra ves, por favor." *Another, please.*

"Okay, Danny," she replied, smiling.

Kane's legs felt like jelly, and he leaned against the doorframe to prevent himself falling. *Is it… possible? Danny?* Suddenly, two strong arms grabbed his, and guided him to a nearby seat.

"Hiram Kane, I presume?"

No answer.

"Hiram? Are you Hiram Kane?"

"Huh? I'm sorry, what?"

"You're Hiram… You are, I know it. I knew you'd come."

"It was you? The letter, I mean. You… it was you who sent the letter?"

The man who Kane was slowly realising must have sent the letter smiled. "Yes, I did. The name's Kenny. Kenny Peters. Should I… should I give you guys a moment?"

"I… Yes, please. I…"

"It's okay. I'll close the bar for an hour. I'll take the girl with me." The man left Kane and approached the bar. "Flaca, let's go. We've got us some errands to run." Kenny put his hand on Danny's shoulder. "I'll be back in an hour, buddy. And buddy?"

Danny glanced up at his friend, seemingly oblivious to

the conversation just now taking place behind him. Kenny's position was blocking any view of Kane. "Yeah? What is it?"

Kenny looked down at Danny, and Kane saw the mix of joy and concern in his blue eyes. "Just take it easy, okay?" He turned to Kane. "You too," he said, but smiled. "And help yourself to drinks."

"What do you mean, take it easy?" Danny asked.

But Kenny led Flaca—*Skinny*, in Spanish—by the arm, and they were gone.

Danny looked back down at his newly refreshed double Bombay Sapphire and tonic, no rocks. And then he looked up again. Kane watched on, his heart racing as, very slowly, Danny turned his head towards him, his eyes widening in evident shock. Then they narrowed again in confusion and he turned back to the bar and reached for his gin and downed half the glass in one swift gulp. Then he polished off the rest. Kane stepped forward and to the side of Danny and watched as he screwed his eyes tightly shut. It wasn't tight enough to prevent a tear escaping onto his cheek, glistening under the lights of the bar. Another soon followed it. Then a third.

Danny stood up, cuffing away the tears on his shirt sleeve, but then his arms fell to his sides as if he lacked the strength to hold them up and he slumped back into the seat, exhaling loudly then sucking air back into his lungs. Then he braced his arms against the armrests and tried to stand, but his legs seemed unable to function, and Kane wondered if it was from the quantity of gin in his system, or from the sudden, overwhelming flood of emotions he probably felt that echoed his own; for Kane they ranged from love to fear to regret and, finally, to hope of forgiveness. He suspected they were shared.

Finally, Danny managed to force himself out of his seat and he turned to face his brother, eyes now open. He stepped forward a little. Then a little more. The brothers were now only six feet apart. It wasn't far; closer than it was before today. Kane edged forward another two steps, his own tears now falling. Danny did the same. Kane lifted his arm, extending his hand towards his brother. Danny tried to do the same but failed, his body betraying the commands of his brain, now in turmoil. He tried to speak, but failed again.

There was to be a reunion. Kane understood it would be made in silence.

Two feet now, and Kane grabbed Danny's hand in his own. They locked eyes, held the gaze for long moments. They shared no words, but in their eyes, the question and answer were clear.

Kane wanted to know, Why?

Danny wanted to say, I'm sorry.

And then the Kane brothers hugged.

Chapter Fourteen

The look in his older brother's eyes left Danny Kane in no doubt at the question he needed to answer: Why?

Why did you leave me? Why did you disappear? Why did you never contact us to say you were okay? Why did you let us believe you were dead?!

They were fair questions. Tough questions. Impossible. And now that Danny was face to face with his brother for the first time in thirty years, he honestly didn't know the answers.

Had he truly believed his family had ignored him in favour of Hiram? Did his family really love his brother more than him, as he had always assumed? Had his childish jealousy really been justified? Warranted? Delusional?

Now, he simply didn't know. For three decades Danny Kane had remained an enigma. An awful, recurring nightmare for his entire family and his many distraught friends. A ghost.

He had put them all through what must have been unimaginable hell, just because he had felt inferior to his brother. Less, even, than that. Not inferior at all. Pointless. Worthless.

He had felt like nothing.

And it was because of those terrible feelings that, as a ten-year-old boy, he had fabricated his own disappearance; a probable kidnapping… his likely death.

In the more recent years, two decades after the dust of his disappearance had settled, according to the news and his discreet inquiries, Danny had never expected to be found. In many ways worse than that, in the early days, months and years, he'd never even expected to be searched for.

Yet they had searched for him. Incessantly. He knew in his heart and in his soul.

Now, they had found him. His brother Hiram had found him.

And now that he had, Danny had to confront both his brother and perhaps, more importantly, he had to confront himself.

But Hiram was first. Face to face.

Right now.

Danny Kane had never expected anything in his life.

He had never expected this.

Chapter Fifteen

"Shall we sit?" Kane motioned to Danny's barstool.

Danny nodded and retook his seat at the bar.

"Drink?" Kane asked.

"No, thanks. I think I've... I know I've had enough."

Kane grabbed a beer from the fridge behind the bar, as offered by Kenny. "I think I need it," he said, motioning to the beer, then, upon seeing the sadness in Danny's eyes, he thought better of it and wordlessly placed it back in the fridge before taking his seat. They sat in silence for a minute, each seemingly coming to terms with the bizarre fact that their brother sat next to them. It was something Kane suspected they had both believed would never happen, though their reasons for that belief were almost certainly very different.

From Kane's point of view, quite simply, he had believed his brother was dead. And if not dead, then at least missing without a trace. In other words, he had no idea what had ever happened to Danny, but whatever it was, he had never expected to see him again. It was more than surreal that he was sitting beside him now, and in truth, he didn't know how to feel about it. Obviously, there was immediate joy to have learned that his brother was still alive. That was by far and away the most important thing. The only thing. Yet, now that realisation was beginning to sink in, other emotions were coming into play. And not all of them were as joyous, as he sat there quietly, pondering all that was unfolding.

Danny had never even imagined that one day he would find himself sitting in a bar with his brother. He was the one who had left his family behind. He had thought at that time he was unwanted by them. A burden. He had always believed himself inferior to his brother, and in many simple ways, he was. He was younger, and had been naturally smaller, but not just because of the age difference. He was what in those days was considered a weak kid, somewhat sickly, and not naturally athletic like Hiram. His brother was braver than Danny, and was more adept at almost all subjects in school. Hiram excelled at virtually everything he did, both in the classroom and beyond, on the sports field and with his friends, whereas Danny excelled at almost nothing. He was witty and funny, but otherwise he felt as if he paled into insignificance alongside his brother.

At least that is how he had felt.

He had the misfortune once of overhearing a conversation between his brother and their grandfather, Patrick. It had been one summer holiday, when the two kids were staying at the Kane estate in Suffolk, England. Danny had sneaked up through some bushes to where Patrick and his brother sat chatting in order to play a prank on them. Danny had overheard his grandfather say to Hiram, "I wish your brother Danny was more like you. He's weak, he's not as good in school, and he's not as adventurous as you are." His heart had immediately sank. He then also heard Hiram's reply, which was something along the lines of, "I don't think Danny is weak. He *is* good in school and he's just like me." That had meant a lot to Danny, that his older brother was sticking up for him. But his grandfather had seemed disappointed with him, and the seeds of discontent had been firmly sown in Danny's heart from that day on.

That's what he thought he'd heard, anyway, though he had to admit to himself now that it was a very long time ago and there was a very real chance his emotions and sadness had possibly gotten the better of him.

Unfortunately for Danny—for all the Kane family—he had missed what they'd said moments before. Just before Danny had arrived within earshot, his grandfather had actually been saying how much potential Danny had, and that he just needed a little more encouragement to fulfil that potential. His grandfather had simply been saying that, whilst the more outgoing, naturally curious Hiram took after his grandfather, Danny took after the boys' father more. Their Dad had not followed in his own father's footsteps. He was not especially adventurous, and would rather stay home during his work holidays than explore the world. It had been a source of frustration to their mother, Melanie, and theirs hadn't been a particularly happy marriage. They had endured it for their childrens' sakes, and neither Kane son could have any complaints about their childhood, which was safe and loving, and with their grandparents around, a new adventure was never far away.

Danny was the quiet, more well-behaved of the brothers, which their grandfather had often declared was a good thing. "We can't all get ourselves in trouble all the time now, can we?" Patrick had said to Hiram on the bench that day, but it was meant as a compliment to both Hiram and Danny. The fact Danny hadn't heard it rendered it insignificant.

It was the following sentences that Danny had heard that had convinced him his grandfather wasn't proud of him. The things he'd missed from just moments before was what would shape the course of the Kane family for the next three decades.

Now as he sat beside his brother in Kenny's Place in a random small city in the middle of Mexico on the other side of the world from home, Danny didn't know how to feel. Yet, as the seconds of silence became minutes, it became clear what his overriding emotion was; regret.

Regret for leaving the way he did. Regret for letting his family suffer for all those years. Regret that he hadn't been strong enough to at least make contact and let them know he was okay, even if he had wanted nothing to do with them. Those were all weighing heavily on his slim shoulders now, as they had been for many, many years.

Almost worse than all that, was the regret he felt that he hadn't grown up alongside his brother, and that Hiram didn't know how amazingly proud of him he was and always had been.

Yet when it came to the crunch, in his heart of hearts, Danny suspected he had always been wrong about his family's feelings towards him. Of course they had loved him. They always had. He had seen on the TV how long the search for him had gone on after he'd 'gone missing', and that everyone involved had done as much as they possibly could to find him. Hiram had even gone on live television and appealed, with tears in his eyes, for any information about his brother. Hiram had been just twelve years old himself when Danny had left him. A child. And yet he hadn't given up on Danny.

Ultimately, life went on and somehow his brother had created an amazing life and career for himself, which Danny had followed from afar, and in secret, with great love and pride. There were many times he had almost made contact. In the end, he was too ashamed about what he had done.

Danny sat there now, desperate to speak to his brother, desperate to explain to him how and why everything had happened. But the words wouldn't come. Try as he might, he could not utter the two words he had wanted to say for close to thirty years. Bizarrely, a song came into his head. He didn't know who it was by or how the tune went, but he somehow knew a few of the words. *Sorry seems to be the hardest word? Is that it how it goes?*

Danny smiled, and turned to face his brother, who was already looking at him. Yet, what Hiram said to him then made Danny's tears flow freely for the first time in many years. His brother had said the words he should be saying but couldn't, and it shamed him even more, to the point of it breaking down the dam of self-preservation he had clung onto and hidden behind for so long.

They were simple words; hearing them from his brother was just too much.

"I am so sorry, Danny. I am so very, very sorry."

Danny's shoulders shook under the weight of thirty years' worth of shame and regret spilling forth, and he couldn't prevent the flow of tears and emotion even if he had wanted to.

His brother leaned over and wrapped his right arm tightly around Danny's shoulders. "It's okay," Hiram said. "I'm here now, and I will always be here. It's okay."

After a couple of minutes Danny regained some control of things and the tears at last stopped flowing. He stood up and faced his brother, and finally the words he'd been longing to say for decades came freely.

"It is me who should be sorry. I have been sorry my entire life, ever since I left you all. Just a few weeks after I left, I knew… I understood I had made a mistake. But I was weak then… I am still weak. I was nothing like you when we were kids, and I am nothing like you now. It is me who should be sorry. I left you all, and I never told anyone why. You did not deserve that. None of you did. But especially you, brother. I should never have left you. I hope… I hope… do you think you could…could you ever forgive me? Because with my whole heart, I am so very, very sorry."

Hiram stood too now and embraced his brother as tightly as if it was their last day on Earth. "There is nothing to forgive you for. And I could ask the same of you. Ask for forgiveness, I mean. I led you to the Old Rec' that day. I teased you into coming. And I couldn't find you. I could n—"

"I didn't want to be found. I thought nobody was proud of me, that nobody loved me…"

"What? Of course we loved you. You were my little brother, Danny, and I would've done anything for you. I would've died for you, and for all these years since, I wished it was me that had gone missing, not you. I would've done anything to have traded places with you, anything. You have to know that?"

Danny nodded and sniffed, cuffing away more tears with a sleeve. "I do. I have always known that, really. I have just been too weak and ashamed to tell you. But you're the greatest brother I could have ever had. I am sorry I have wasted all these years. Let me make it up to you?"

"You have nothing to make up for, I promise you. You are here now, and we're together. The rest is all history now. But…"

Danny took a deep breath, afraid of what his brother might say next. "But what?"

"Well… how did you do it? I mean, how did you give me the slip in the Old Rectory?"

Danny smiled now, and it was the smile of someone who felt as if he'd been given a second chance at life. "Well, brother… I think that's a story for another day."

Chapter Sixteen

Cañada de la Virgen, just outside San Miguel

Fear wasn't a strong enough adjective for how the girls felt. It was a mix of emotions really. Fear, obviously. But there was also confusion. Incomprehension. Some of them felt ashamed, though none of them should. Combined, the range of emotions equated total and utter terror.

Their captors hadn't actually harmed them deliberately, not yet, at least not physically. They had all suffered a few bruises during the moments they were snatched, but they were all so young, most of them thin, that they had been easy to handle. They had all been blindfolded moments after they were taken, and not a single one of the girls had any idea where they were. Almost all of them were kidnapped from poorer neighbourhoods in and around San Miguel, and most of them had never left the town before, so they couldn't even make a guess as to where they were.

And now they were each strapped down tightly against something solid, the straps digging sores into the skin of their ankles and forearms, their heads forced back against the cool stone and their bones aching against the unforgiving surface. No, they hadn't been beaten, but they were all in pain, and several of them quite understandably whimpered for their families.

The men kept two of the girls apart from the others, both of whom believed they were alone. Each of them was in a separate part of the complex, and having heard no other voices except those of a couple of men, they figured they were literally alone. That was the worst part; alone, tired, cold, hungry... they believed they had been left to die. At least the other girls had heard familiar noises, similar to the ones they were making; the same crying; the same screams. At least they knew there were others there like them. It offered a tiny amount of comfort to know they weren't completely alone. But only a tiny bit.

The man walked casually around the chamber, admiring the girls. Not in any sexual way, nothing like that. For a start they were children, and the thought of... touching them in that way was abhorrent, even to him. They were also girls. He didn't like girls. So, he was admiring them for what they represented to him, what they meant to him. And more importantly, he was grateful to them for the opportunity they would provide him. And he loved them for it.

Thus, he didn't want to have to hurt the girls. Yet, despite his aversion to violence, there were some things that just needed to be done. He wasn't looking forward to that part of his plan. *Needs must*, he told himself, and he had long since mentally prepared himself to do it. In fact, to do whatever needed doing.

And when the time came, the man knew he was ready.

With a last look at the final girl on his circuit of the chamber, the man left that dark space and walked the short distance to his office. It wasn't actually an office, but he had appropriated a closed off area of the chamber where, over the course of a few days, he had installed a range of high-tech audio and visual equipment. That was perhaps the most important thing he'd had to do in preparation for the main event. Except taking the girls, of course. However, without the filming and broadcasting equipment, he had little chance of success.

He had recruited an old friend from university—one of the few actual friends he had—and even those relationships were tenuous. But he had followed Alonso's career into broadcasting, and the two had stayed in touch. He needed someone on the inside of one of the big news channels, someone with the power to help him with his scheme. Yes, Alonso was a friend, but even friends weren't guaranteed to do everything you asked. Thus, a hefty bribe was paid. And it was necessary. Because, not only would Alonso lose his job if he was caught, but he would almost certainly end up in prison. This meant the sum of the bribe had to be enough for Alonso to escape the country and live out his years abroad, probably Nicaragua, he'd mentioned, where the weather was perfect, and the beer was even cheaper than in Mexico.

Luckily, finances were not a problem to the man paying, who was independently wealthy via both a series of sound financial investments, and money inherited from his family. Though no one had ever believed him—he'd never understood why—he was a descendent of a very famous and important man from Mexican history, and with that heritage came wealth. A lot of it. And he was more than happy to use that money now.

So everything was in place. He had his girls. He had his friend on the inside at the news station. He had his media equipment installed and tested, then tested again. Mentally, he himself was ready. He just had to get his timing right.

And the time was close. It was very, very close.

Soon, he would set in motion a chain of events that would not only shock the world, but elevate him to being one of the most famous people on the planet.

Chapter Seventeen

Principle Jardin

After Kane and Danny had spent some time catching up, they agreed to chat more later and for now, would meet the others at a cafe bar in the jardin, recommended by Vicki Allen.

Kane beckoned over the young waiter and ordered another round of coffees and pastries for everyone. Sitting with him at the table on the corner of San Miguel's main square were Danny and Ridley, as well as Kenny Peters, Stephy Loren and Vicki. They were all in good spirits, enjoying the lovely climate and the jovial atmosphere that was an almost permanent feature of Historico Centro. At the centre of their amusement were the Kane brothers, who were making up for almost thirty years of lost bantering opportunities. Danny in particular was excelling, his wit and humour as sharp as Kane remembered from when they were kids.

"So, bro, should I tell these guys about the time you

were riding your BMX home from school and somehow fell off, wrapping both yourself and the bike around that concrete bollard in front of all those girls. Didn't you... I mean, didn't you piss your school trousers that afternoon?"

It was a true story, and though Kane wasn't a blusher, he shook his head in acute embarrassment. "I, erm, yeah... I might have had to change my trousers when I got home, that part's true."

"Ew, disgusting," chimed in Ridley, teasing her man. "It's no wonder you like me so much... no other sensible girl would have you."

"And what about that time we were cycling to the playing fields, showing off as usual, riding with no hands while playing that old Casio keyboard? Want me to tell these guys what happened next, or will you?"

"It's okay... go ahead... you're obviously on a roll."

Danny grinned. He was clearly enjoying himself. "Well, my big brother here had borrowed the keyboard from his mate, and he was cycling to Tim's house to return it. But Hiram being Hiram, he attempted to play the thing while riding his bike—I have to admit he could," he added, to which Kane winked, "and instead of watching the road he was looking down at the keyboard and didn't see the convertible parked up ahead. Next thing I know, his bike slammed into the back of the car, and he's gone flying over the handlebars and landed in the back seat as the keyboard flew through the air and smashed into bits on the road. Absolutely brilliant, isn't he? What an inspirational man!"

This time Kane cringed a little as the others cracked up laughing.

The conversation and banter continued, and the late afternoon soon passed into early evening. Vicki was living up to what Kane had learned was a deserved reputation, which meant it was definitely time for cocktails. She summoned the waiter again and upgraded her white wine to a margarita. "Anyone else?"

"I'll have one of those, please," agreed Ridley.

"Me too," added Stephy, "though just the one. We have a show later tonight."

"Boys?" Vicki asked.

"Beer for me," said Kane.

"And me," added Kenny.

"Nothing for me, thanks," said Danny. "I erm… I want to take it easy for a while."

Kane clapped Danny on the shoulder. Kenny had mentioned Danny's drinking in the initial letter and had since confirmed it to him in person quietly over the last couple of hours. Kane didn't want to pressure Danny by asking him about it, but he was proud he seemed to be addressing the situation himself anyway.

The Principle Jardin was getting busy now as the beautiful early evening sunshine kept the tourists from venturing into the many artisan stores dotted around the square. Young couples walked hand in hand in the shade of the majestic laurel trees lining the square, while families and their effervescent children ran around and played with the balloons and other toys purchased from the street hawkers. The ubiquitous mojigangas—entertainers dressed in wild costumes and balancing on enormous stilts—paraded around, their riotous outfits a perfect match for the lively colours of the colonial architecture across the city. It was a stunning scene, and surrounded by good people, not to mention his brother, Kane felt as at peace with the world as he ever had.

The small flat-screen TV on brackets above the door of the cafe bar had been on, yet muted since they arrived, but Kane noticed as the waiter suddenly flicked on the volume, and stood staring at it, his mouth agape in apparent shock.

Kane glanced up at the TV, now alert to the wild change in the atmosphere of the café as everyone fell quiet and listened to the local reporter saying:

"So far we have had reports that ten children are missing in the city of San Miguel de Allende, Guanajuato, but authorities are warning this number might climb."

"What's going on?" Danny said, the last to turn his attention the television on the wall. No one answered, all eyes glued to the screen.

"A police spokesman has said that so far, it looks as if an organised gang jumped into action this morning as the annual Alborada festival wound down. The children, all believed to be girls, were apparently snatched in the early hours, some from their own beds. The police believe this operation was carefully timed to take place during the aftermath of the all-night festivities."

"That's awful," Vicki said. "Who would do such a terrible thing?"

Danny spoke up: "Sorry, could someone explain? My Spanish isn't that great yet."

Kenny briefly summarised what the reporter had explained to Danny and Ridley, who hadn't quite grasped the extent of the drama. Danny's shock was evident immediately, and his face paled, though Kane noticed Ridley's face harden, as if it was not that great of a shock.

Both Kane and Ridley had come face to face with evil in recent times, and had experienced some of the worst humanity had to offer. Unfortunately, depraved and evil people were not strangers to them.

"Hey..." Kane said, snapping his fingers as a thought occurred to him and he turned to Ridley. "I bet—"

"I know exactly what you're going to say," Ridley cut in.

"That man this morning? Rosa?"

Ridley nodded, her face grave. "Part of that same gang. No doubt about it."

Kane's heart filled with a heavy sense of loss that he hadn't been able to help more of the girls. Ridley seemed to sense his thoughts and placed a hand on his. "At least we helped one of them."

Kane nodded, and brought the others up to speed on what had happened early that morning.

"Is there anything we can do to help?" Danny said, asking the group in general.

Kane inhaled. "We should go and talk to the local police," he said. "Tell them what happened with Rosa, describe her to them, and offer to help in any way we can."

Before Kane could even rise from his seat, he was distracted by a cry for help.

"Hiram Kane!"

Kane looked around at the mention of his name.

"Hiram Kane!"

That voice sounds familiar. In fact...

Mariana rushed up to their table, shoving a customer out of the way without a second thought. Kane saw she was crying.

"What is it, Mariana?" Kane stood up. "What's wrong?"

"Oh, my Rosa, they have taken my Rosa!" Mariana wailed, throwing her hands in the air.

Ridley was on her feet now, and gathered Mariana in her arms.

Kane's expression, only moments earlier full of joy, now

turned grim. "Who has taken Rosa? The same man we saw before?"

"I don't know!" Mariana almost screamed. "But they have stolen my baby from me!"

A look of horror mixed with rage had fallen over Ridley's face, who to Kane appeared as if she was ready to rip someone's head off. But then she seemed to gather herself together, forcing the inner turmoil down and fixing a determined expression onto her face.

"Come and sit down," Ridley said, pulling out a chair for Mariana. "And then you can tell us everything you know."

Chapter Eighteen

Mariana almost fell into the chair as she covered her face with her hands. Kane and Ridley exchanged looks. Kane knew they were both thinking the same thing: Rosa had obviously been kidnapped by the same group of people who had snatched the other children earlier that morning.

Kane glanced back at the TV as he became aware that something else was happening.

The image of the news anchors flickered a few times, then went blank. The waiter stepped closer to the television and slapped it sharply on the edge as if it was a common problem. At first nothing happened, and he was about to slap it again, when the screen flickered a little more, and the images returned. Instead of showing the news studio and presenters, however, it showed an image of a dark, lamp-lit space, bringing to Kane's mind a cave. It could have been anywhere, really. The only discernible object showing was the lamp and a stone wall, which could have been a cave, the inside of a house or even beneath a bridge. It was all a little strange. Then the screen flickered again, and this time the presenters returned, though the screen was now split into two halves; the stone wall and a lamp on one side, the two presenters on the right.

In Spanish, the female presenter said, "Erm, yes, we... we are not sure what is happening. We seem to be having some, uh, technical difficulties. We... we are working on fixing them as soon as possible. We..." The pretty female presenter then put her hand to her earpiece, as if listening to her producer, and blinked twice in surprise. "We are... yes, what you are seeing are live scenes from an... from an unknown location. Somebody... someone has apparently hacked into our broadcasting system and is... is somehow overriding the feed. We have our best technicians working hard on this situation, and right now they are trying to understand what is going on."

Kane and Ridley once more shared a look. Something about this seemed sinister, and the hairs on the back of Kane's neck stood on end. Over the last few years, when danger had seemed to follow Kane around the world wherever he went, his senses had become heightened to anything slightly off kilter, and this certainly qualified. The presenter continued:

"In light of what has recently happened in the beautiful colonial city of San Miguel de Allende, in the state of Guanajuato, we now believe these... these scenes, have something to do with the missing girls. However, nobody has yet confirmed or denied this, nor have they let themselves be known to authorities... I—"

The presenter paused. Someone was again saying something to her via the hidden earpiece. "I... we have just been contacted here at the station by someone calling themselves... Quetzal? Okay, yes. He... he says he is responsible for taking all twelve of the girls, but he has... he says he has... an announcement? Well, I—" Another pause followed as the presenter listened to the voice in her ear, her face suddenly paling, as if in shock at what she was being told. "We... the man, Quetzal, has a messa—"

The screen suddenly flickered again, and the lamp-lit stone wall now filled the entire screen. After some audible crackling, a voice sounded:

"My fellow Mexicans, and all visitors to our... deeply flawed and corrupted country. You are listening to Quetzal, ancient Aztec God of wind and air, and of course, God of learning. Most of you will not know this. Yet, I know there are some of you out there listening who will understand. The archaeologists, art historians and explorers among you, for example..."

Kane suddenly turned to Ridley, his already alert senses now set to extreme. His muscles unconsciously tensed, and he spun around, on the lookout for any imminent danger. But he saw nothing or no one alarming. Just hundreds of people enjoying the sunshine or shade while milling about in and around the square. He took a deep breath, fighting to remain calm despite the burgeoning sense of dread he felt, certain it was evident in his eyes and across his face.

He glanced down at Mariana, who was sobbing into her hands.

Ridley grabbed Kane's hand; looking into her eyes, Kane was in no doubt she shared how he was feeling. He was an archaeologist and an explorer. She was an art historian. *Surely, he doesn't mean us?* Ridley had been with Kane during some of those terrible recent events, which had almost seen Kane killed. Others hadn't been so fortunate. Kane had a knack of encountering crazed gangsters and terrorists wherever he went, and Ridley knew this, yet stuck with him anyway. Neither of them could have anticipated what the man—*Quetzal?*—would say next.

No one could have.

"Yes, Mister Kane, I am talking to you."

Kane's knees almost buckled at hearing his name spoken from the TV, and he had to place a hand on the table to support himself for a moment. His skin suddenly tingled with apprehension and anxiety. He had only travelled to Mexico to find his long-lost brother. And now some madman had kidnapped young girls and was addressing him directly on live television? He stood up straighter now, staring at the screen and frozen to the spot, knuckles blanching white under the strain of his tightly clenched fists. *What the hell is going on?*

The unseen speaker's voice came through the television again. "Mister Kane, I, like you, am an archaeologist, And I, like you, have made some very important archaeological discoveries. The only difference between you and I, is that you are now a wealthy man, and world famous, and I... well, who I am can wait. For now. Now, you will know me only as Quetzal. And I advise you, and your friends, to listen carefully to what I have to say. That is simply because, if you do not heed my warnings... and make no mistake, they are warnings! Well, let me remind you, and all the listening world, that I have twelve innocent young girls hidden somewhere from where they will *never* be found. Never! And unless you do as I say... well, Mister Kane, I will leave that to your imagination. And from what I know about what has happened to you over the last few years, I believe you can imagine something very, very bad indeed. I suggest you keep your phone close by... I will be calling you very soon. And believe this, Mister Kane, you do not want to miss that call."

Suddenly the lamp-lit scene disappeared from the small screen, and the ashen faces of the young female broadcaster and her older male colleague came back into view.

"We, erm… it seems as if we have… yes, we have recovered our usual feed," said the male presenter, any semblance of control missing from his voice. "That… well, that was…" Another pause, and the presenter gave a subtle nod. "It is time for a commercial break." Then the screen flicked to an advertisement for Modelo Especial, one of Mexico's most popular beers.

Chapter Nineteen

Kane slumped back down heavily into his seat, his mouth open in horror at what he had just heard. What they had all heard. Ridley and Danny, and Kenny, Stephy and Vicki each looked at Kane now, all of them speechless. Neither Vicki nor Stephy really knew much about Kane, though Danny had hinted to Stephy in the past at having some kind of famous explorer brother. Famous or otherwise, now it seemed as if he was destined to somehow be involved in one of the greatest mysteries modern Mexico had ever seen.

Only Ridley truly knew what Kane must have be going through in that moment, and her heart ached for the man who seemed to be shadowed by trouble and danger no matter where he went in the world.

Kane, and Ridley herself, had been through so much trauma and heartache lately, and they had hoped they would never find themselves involved in anything like this ever again. Kane's most recent experiences on the Japanese island of Miyajima had left him both physically and mentally scarred, and only in recent weeks had Kane come to terms with that particular tragedy. Meeting Danny again after all these long years had finally helped put that event behind him, and he'd believed he had, finally, a calm and peaceful future to look forward to. It appeared now he was wrong. Horribly, horribly wrong.

"Okay, listen," said Kenny. "Let's go to my bar. It's closed right now, so we'll have the place to ourselves. We'll put on the news and, well, I guess we'll wait for whoever this madman is to call. Hiram?"

Kane remained silent, his face a blank mask devoid of emotion. Yet inside he was fighting to keep it together. *Why me?* he thought. *Why me, and why now? I've just got my brother back. I have my love Alex beside me. I've met some good people here, friends, and the future looks as bright as it ever has…*

Of course, he didn't say these things aloud. Whining and feeling sorry for himself publicly would not help the situation, whatever it turned out to be. But inside his heart raced with both sadness and rage. *Who the hell is this Quetzal character? And how the hell did he know I'd be watching TV right now?*

Kane stood suddenly, almost certain now that someone must be watching him, reporting back to this Quetzal psycho. He didn't notice anyone suspicious, just reams of locals and carefree tourists, all seemingly oblivious to the drama unfolding around them.

"Hiram? Kenny suggested we could go to his bar…" said Ridley.

"Huh? Yes, sorry. Yeah, okay… let's go. Thanks, Kenny." He placed his hand on Mariana's shoulder. "I promise you, Mariana, I will do everything I can to get Rosa back."

The Feathered Serpent

Mariana lifted her face from her hands and looked up at Kane, her cheeks stained with tears.

"Thank you," she said.

They all stood, and as Vicki paid the bill and promised to follow behind them in a few minutes, Kenny led them to his bar, each of them in stunned silence at what had just happened and what they'd learned about the abducted young girls.

Just twenty yards away, concealed behind a busy taco stand in the Jardin, Rafael nodded with satisfaction. Everything was going according to plan. Quetzal had been delighted with Rafael's delivery of another girl. The TV announcement had been timed to perfection. Hiram Kane had been tempted into the fray.

Now Rafael had to hurry, and get back to his master. He wiped a bit of spilled mustard from his shirt, and threw away the trash.

It was time to put the next part of the plan into action.

Chapter Twenty

Kenny hustled Kane and the others the short walk from the Principle Jardin down Hidalgo, then up the narrow, single flight of stairs to his bar and out onto the terrace. The bar had one of the best rooftop views in the entire city, with the colourful buildings and myriad church towers stretching out beneath a clear blue sky all around. For Kane, the stunning vista was the last thing on his mind, or anyone else's mind, he suspected, in that moment.

Kane sat gazing out at the vista, though he was oblivious to it. Instead, his mind raced with images from the recent past that flickered unbidden before his eyes. The deadly flood in Japan. The kidnappings in Bali and, before that, Prague. The brutal murders in Peru...

Ridley sat beside him and clasped his hand in hers, but remained silent. Kane knew she would give him all the time he needed.

Stephy sat with Mariana, comforting her, the poor woman's gentle sobbing a constant reminder to Kane that he had failed to protect Rosa after all.

Kenny poured a round of mezcal, declaring to those listening it was his go-to drink in times of crisis. Kane glanced up. This definitely seemed like a crisis.

"What the hell just happened?" Danny asked.

No one answered for a few seconds. Then his brother said, "I... I don't know." Kane's voice was low and fragile, as if he wasn't sure what on earth to say. He certainly didn't know what to think. "I... I—"

Just at that moment his mobile phone rang, startling him, and he looked quickly at Ridley sitting quietly next to him. Her eyes were as wide in shock as he knew his were.

"How the hell does he have your number?" Danny asked.

"It might not be him," Kane stated without conviction. He glanced at the others. They, like he, all knew it was. "Should I answer it?"

"You have to," said Kenny. "You heard what he said."

"But I... I..."

"Do you want me to answer it?" asked Ridley. "If you want me—"

"No!" he answered a little too harshly. "No, thank you though. It's okay. I've got it." The phone rang on, its simple tone taunting Kane to hurry. He dared not wait too long and snatched it from the table and answered.

"Mister Kane?"

"Yes... yes, this is Kane."

"Ah, Mister Kane. It is so nice to hear your voice. I am very glad you took the call, and believe me, you will be glad, too. I—"

"Who are you?" Kane asked, his voice a low, uncertain whisper.

There followed a long pause.

"I said who are you?" Now Kane's voice rose a little, anger creeping in alongside the fear.

"Who I am matters little at this stage, Mister Kane. Believe me, you will find out soon enough. Just know this; for now I am someone who you need to pay very close attention to. You have done the right thing answering my call. I highly recommend you continue to do so."

"What... what do you want from me?"

"You will also find that out soon enough. Adios, Mister Kane."

"Hey... what the hell do you want? Hello?" The phone line was dead.

Kane slumped back onto his chair. He screwed his eyes tight shut, fighting off a sudden wave of dizziness that threatened to overwhelm him. It was an uneasy sensation that had happened far too often in recent years, and for Kane it was a sure sign things were about to get messy. He glanced up at the cloudless blue void above, not yet ready to believe it was happening to him again.

Not long ago Kane was in Japan attending an adventure travel conference, where representatives had invited him to appear as a guest speaker. He was a reluctant speaker in public, but after his adventure company in Peru had taken off, he had become somewhat of a minor celebrity. Of course, being the great grandson of a legendary explorer helped, and the Kane family name was synonymous with adventure. At least, it used to be.

Unfortunately, that visit to Japan had resulted in Kane doing battle with two enemies; Mother Nature, in what had become the infamous and devastating storm of the century, and then psychotic Yakuza gangsters with an ancient vendetta to settle. He had narrowly escaped with his life on the island of Miyajima; others weren't so lucky. Japan was one of just a series of catastrophes to have hit Kane over the last few years. It seemed that no matter where he went or what he did, and no matter how low of a profile he kept, danger and death were always awaiting him with their arms wide open around every corner.

And now, here in Mexico, another psychotic madman had ensnared him into yet another nefarious scheme. What that was, Kane could not even guess at. Yet something deep in his gut, his innate and unwanted instinct for sensing danger, told him that without any doubt at all, by the time he left Mexico his life would once again be changed forever.

Kane opened his eyes and grabbed the untouched mezcal Kenny had placed before him. He took a deep breath and threw the shot back in one, wincing as the clear liquid burned his throat. He wasn't much of a liquor drinker; he almost always chose beer or wine. Right now the mezcal burn felt good. The second shot Kenny intuitively poured hit the spot and roused him from the deep-seated despair he had felt since he'd heard the unknown voice from the television. It had awakened in him a desire to put an end to whatever this was before it even started.

"Kenny? Could I have another please?"

Kenny nodded and poured them all a second shot and Kane his third. Kane thanked him and tipped that one back too. It felt good. He stood up, and Ridley looked at him. She made eye contact, and something seemed to stir within her too. She would know how he felt, know the wildfire he was sure was in his eyes and the wildfire returning to his belly, and would be feeling those things too.

After the shock of being called out in person by whoever this unknown perpetrator was—some criminal, maybe a terrorist—Kane could not sit back and do nothing. More than that, he would do everything in his power to stop whatever this fucker was up to. And it started now. He fixed his gaze on Ridley's, as if asking her for permission to start taking action. Ridley's inbuilt moral compass was always on point.

She stood up and stepped towards him, her gaze never leaving his, and nodded. "So, what do we do?"

Chapter Twenty-One

Kane looked around the terrace at those standing there with him. There was his partner, Alex. Kenny leaned on the bar. He didn't know much about the tough-looking Canadian, but Kane sensed he was a good guy who wanted to do the right thing. The anonymous letter informing the family of Danny's whereabouts testified to that. Then there were the ladies, Vicki and Stephy. He guessed Vicki's age to be around sixty, and while she was trim and sprightly, she clearly liked to drink... a lot. Kane thought she might be a liability to them and to herself, and would insist she stayed out of it. On the other hand, Stephy was quite the opposite of the ageing Texan. About five ten, and in phenomenal shape, Stephy appeared to be more Amazon warrior than sozzled Texan; she looked as if she could kick arse with the best of them. Kane had only just met her, but sensed in her the same qualities as Ridley possessed. Big-hearted, smart, kind, but tough, no nonsense and with the ability to go toe to toe with anyone. She'd be a formidable ally.

Finally there was his brother. After almost three decades

of believing Danny was missing, likely dead, and having only just reacquainted themselves over a wonderful few hours in San Miguel, the last thing Kane wanted now was to lose him again.

He could not involve him.

He *would* not involve him.

Kane would do all he could to make sure Danny stayed far away from whatever was about to unfold.

"Listen," Kane said, finally in control of his ragged nerves. "It seems I have once again found myself in the midst of a whole lot of trouble." The hint of a grin crept onto his face unbidden, but disappeared as quickly as it had appeared. "For whatever reason, this madman has learned I am in town, and has targeted me in some sort of awful plot. As you know, we do not yet understand what it's about, other than it somehow involves those innocent missing girls." He looked at Mariana and his heart panged with regret. He forced a half smile in her direction. "One of those girls happens to be very dear to us, even though we only met her a few short hours ago. So let's all put our heads together. What do any of you know about what might've happened to those poor girls?"

Stephy explained she had been out of town with Nelo, her husband, the last two nights, performing shows in the nearby towns of San Luis Potosi and Celaya. She was learning all of this for the first time now too.

Kenny and Vicki, the only two permanent residents of the city among them, filled Kane and the others in on the little they knew. Kenny said, "I think you pretty much know everything we know. It seems as if no one has any idea where those girls are now, or who took them. The Alborada festival is wild, and most of the city's men stay out all through the night, drinking and partying. I hate to say it, but whoever is behind this, they chose the perfect time to strike, and I'm sure that was deliberate. Think about it... fathers, brothers, uncles... ninety percent of the male population of the city were away from their homes around the time anyone noticed the girls were missing. Goddamned clever bastard," Kenny muttered, shaking his head. "Very clever."

"So all we really know is that twelve girls are missing, but no one knows who took them or where they are. And the police have no idea what to do about it?" Kane was incredulous.

"That's about the size of it, yes," finished Vicki, who Kane noticed had pushed away her full mezcal. "Other than that, no one seems to know anything."

Kane nodded. "But... Jesus, how the hell does he even know who I am? And that I am here in Mexico? And how the hell does he have my phone number? I hardly give my number to anyone, and no one here knows it apart from Alex, and now Danny. That's—"

"The hotel!" Ridley stated. "We gave the hotel our phone numbers at check in, didn't we?"

"Damn it, yes, we did." Kane shook his head. "But how does this guy... whoever the hell he is... how does he have it?"

"That's what we need to find out next?" Stephy set her jaw firm, and her stance left no one in any doubt she wanted to stick around and be a part of this.

"Right. Listen... I've only just met you guys," Kane said, looking around at Kenny, Stephy and Vicki, "and you're great people. Yet, whatever this is, it involves me, and has nothing to do with any of you. I insist you all leave and stay away from me. I... people tend to get hurt when I'm around. You should all go." He looked at his brother, sat quietly at the bar, his mezcal untouched. "You too, Danny." Kane knew better than to say anything to Ridley about leaving. She would stay by his side no matter what he said. Despite his regret about that, he was also encouraged. She was tougher than any man he had ever known... tougher than him. She was a warrior, and he was glad she was there whatever, or whoever, they faced.

Vicki stood up, placing her hands firmly on her hips. "You listen to me, Hiram. I may only be little, and I might be getting on a bit... but if you think you can tell me to step away from this when I know there're a dozen missing little girls out there, then think again. I'm a Texan woman, and I ain't going nowhere. Besides... you might need my car." Vicki seemed to sense Kane's doubts, probably about her drinking. "Don't worry... I won't touch another drop until this is over. You have my word."

Kane breathed out through his nose and nodded. A hint of another smile crinkled his eyes as he met Vicki's.

Next he glanced over at Kenny. The Canadian's shoulders were broad, and his chest was solid. His eyes locked on Kane's as if daring him to even try and suggest he stay away.

"Would I be wasting my time?" Kane asked.

Kenny nodded. "Totally. Look, I know the city better than anyone. I have wheels, contacts... yes, you'd be wasting your time. Goddammit, I have nieces... the joys of my life. I'm in."

"Me too." Stephy stepped close to Kane. "When I was a child, a friend of mine went missing. We helped the police search the streets around our district of Bogota for weeks, but we never found her. I have felt guilty about it ever since. Why her and not me? That's what I thought. Why her? Do you know what I mean?" Kane, more than anyone should, knew exactly what she meant. "So I am staying. Got it?"

Kane just nodded. He really did know. He knew it all too well.

"And for the opposite reasons," stated Danny, rising from his chair and approaching his brother, "I have to stay too. I—"

"No, Danny, you can't! You have—"

"Listen," Danny cut in, "like Stephy, I know a thing or two about kids going missing. I know how terrible it is for the family who get left behind." There was such despair and guilt in Danny's eyes that Kane had to blink back a tear. "I can never make up for what I put you and our family through, I know that. But if I can somehow help these girls, then... Well, you know what I mean."

Again, Kane did know. He understood Danny's point, and in helping, it might ease some of both his and his brother's guilt, if only a little, and only if there was a good outcome from whatever it was they were into.

The brother's hugged. "Okay, Danny," was all Kane needed to say. He eased out of the embrace and faced the others. "So, here we are. I think it's time we gave our unknown friend a call."

Chapter Twenty-Two

"Hello? It's me... it's Kane."

A few seconds of silence was all Kane heard, until the man who'd called himself Quetzal said, "Hola, Mister Kane. So nice of you to call."

His tone was mocking, and it drove Kane mad. He wanted to remain calm, remain in control, but he failed. "What the fuck do you want? Who the hell are you? Why—"

"Mister Kane, I suggest you try and calm yourself down a little. If you want to know more, then please be so kind as to shut your mouth and listen!"

"No, you listen to me first, you evil bastard! I have no idea what you're up to or why, but let me tell you this... If you harm one hair on any of those girls' heads I will—"

"You will what, Mister Kane?" Quetzal cut in. "Ha, you don't even know where they are. For all you know, they might be in another state by now... even crossing the northern or southern border. Do you know how easy it is to move little children around these days?"

Kane seethed, breathing hard through clenched teeth. Sadly, he did know how easy it was. In that moment Kane's calmness evaporated. *This mother fu—* "Your words are cheap. I will find you, and I *will* kill you. Do you understand me you sick fuck?"

Silence greeted Kane's words down the line. Kane forced out his breath through his nostrils, almost snorting, like an angry bull, and gripped his phone so tight he almost cracked the screen. He lowered the phone from his ear, letting his arm dangle by his side in an effort to once more try and calm himself. After a few seconds, he raised the phone again.

"Okay... okay, you piece of shit, I'm listening."

"That is better. Your anger will not help me, and nor will it help you. And it definitely will not help the twelve young girls I have at my mercy."

Kane inhaled again, trying to find some zen amid the chaos of his mind. "Go on," he said.

"You have no idea who I am. That will change. But I know exactly who you are. Hiram Kane; archaeologist turned expedition leader, the man who rediscovered the fabled lost Inca city of Vilcabamba, and..." Quetzal paused, savouring the moment.

"And what?" Kane hissed, not liking where this was going. "And what?!" he barked, momentarily losing control.

"... and you are the man who will be responsible for the deaths of twelve innocent children if he does not help me get what I want."

Kane's eyes shut involuntarily. *Déjà Vu? Fucking groundhog day?* Dealing with unhinged, dangerous madmen was becoming a recurring theme in recent times!

He clutched his prized possession, the gold Inca sun disc that had hung around his neck for more than twenty years.

It was a subconscious tick that happened when he was stressed. "What is it you want?" Kane asked, but no sooner had he uttered the words, he knew he had asked them before; the last time was to a crazed Neo-Nazi in Prague. That didn't end well. Didn't end well at all. More deep breaths followed, as he waited for the madman's response.

"It is simple, Mister Kane. I want what you have... Fame. Wealth. A reputation in the field of discovery... just like you. You see, I have been robbed of my greatest discovery, and along with the fame, I have had my reputation and career snatched from me. Now, I understand my career is lost. That, I can handle. I also understand and admit that some of my life choices have not been, how shall I say... the wisest I could have made? But in terms of my great archaeological discovery? That credit should have been mine... and it should be mine for all time."

Now Kane was intrigued as well as enraged. *What on Earth is this crazy bastard talking about? Archaeological discovery? Is he serious?* "What do you mean? Who the hell are you? If I knew who you were it might help me understand the situation better."

"All in good time, Mister Kane. You will know who I am soon enough. As will all the world. And believe me, when they know, they will never, ever forget."

Kane didn't like the man's sinister tone and was certain he was speaking with a deranged lunatic.

"But until then," Quetzal continued, "you need to do something for me. And if you do not..."

"If I do not, then what?"

Quetzal paused again, and Kane struggled with the silence. The man was toying with Kane, and although clearly insane, he didn't sound stupid. That, in Kane's experience, made him more dangerous. "Then what?" Kane pushed, unable to contain his frustration.

"Let me remind you of your previous record, Mister Kane. I seem to remember reading about an incident in Bali, when one of your friends was murdered. How about the old man in Japan, who died trying to protect you? And who could forget all those young boys in Peru, who died while working for you—"

"What the fu—"

"What did I say about anger, Mister Kane? I suggest you let me finish."

Kane raged, and paced around Kenny's terrace, ignoring what he suspected where the concerned looks of his friends. He knew full well that if he saw whoever this psycho was in person right now, he'd rip his damned head off. But… Kane had a dire hunch he knew where this was leading, and had to fight hard to bite his tongue.

"Good. Let me finish. Those boys in Peru died while working with you, did they not? Not to mention your close friend? A Mister Craft?"

Kane didn't answer. It was a burden of truth he'd had to bear since the expedition had ended with many innocent deaths, including that of one his oldest friends.

"And then of course there was the incident in—"

"Just make your damn point!" Kane yelled. "What the hell do you want?"

"Mister Kane, your anger will get you nowhere. Once you have calmed down, we will talk again. Until then, I'm afraid I will have to teach you a lesson."

The line went dead.

"Hello?" Kane hissed. "Hello!"

He raised the phone, ready to throw it against the

nearest wall and smash it to pieces. Ridley's gentle touch on his arm brought him back to his senses, calming him a little.

"He knows all about me," Kane said, his voice hollowed out with fear and anger.

"So he's done his research," Ridley said. "That doesn't mean he's really who he says he is… an archaeologist?"

Kane nodded. "You're right… as always." He exhaled, then inhaled deeply. "We need to know more about who the hell this Quetzal guy really is."

Chapter Twenty-Three

"I have a laptop downstairs... hold on." Kenny disappeared down the stairs and a minute later emerged with a battered old laptop. "It's old but works fine. What're we looking for?"

"Pull up a Google tab and search for disgraced Mexican archaeology professors, or controversial archaeological finds, something like that." Kane turned to Stephy. "Do you have a phone?"

"I do. What should I search for?"

Kane paused, then nodded and said, "Google recent archaeological discoveries in Mexico, in the last decade."

"Okay, I'm on it." Stephy snagged her phone from her bag and in a mad blur of fingers, she was soon searching for what Kane had asked.

Kane sat down next to Danny at the bar, and ushered Ridley and Vicki closer. "Look, the girls were all taken from in or close to San Miguel, right?"

Vicki answered. "That's right, and Rosa was taken, I don't know, maybe four or five hours ago?"

"Well, that means the girls could be anywhere by now.

Possibly near a border, as he said, but my hunch is that they're still close by, maybe even right here, still in this town, or somewhere on the outskirts. Let's assume it would've been difficult to move so many young girls, what with all the media coverage after their disappearance and the fact that they've only had a few hours to move them. It would be much easier to contain them nearby, right? So the question is, where? I need a map."

"I have one in my car... back in ten minutes," said Vicki, and she disappeared out the bar and down the stairs, a look of grim determination on her usually jovial face.

"There are just so many places they could be," Danny offered unhelpfully. "There're a lot of abandoned buildings around the town... unfinished hotels, for example. Also, dozens of remote farmsteads and ranches. Huge haciendas all over the city. There's even an abandoned bull ring a couple of miles north of here. If the guy is wealthy, he might even own one right here in town... perhaps on this very street."

Kenny nodded. "That's true. In some cases, one family or company owns an entire block, some containing multiple hotels, stores and restaurants." He shook his head. "Needles in a damn haystack."

"If that was the case, surely someone would've noticed the girls being taken there," countered Kane, "even if it was in the middle of the night or the early hours. No, I feel sure that if they're still in the area, it'll be somewhere outside of town."

"I agree," added Ridley. "Look, let's assume for now he's telling the truth and he is, or was, an archaeologist. That means he's pretty well educated. We can probably assume he's organised, and will not make any silly mistakes that could undo whatever disgusting plan he has. If he is who he says he is, then he's smart. Deranged, obviously, but smart. I hate him already."

"Okay," chirped in Stephy. "Got something. Back in 2004 there was an important archaeological find at Teotihuacan, just outside Mexico City. It was a huge haul of artefacts dating from the Aztec period, but rather than being attributed to one archaeologist, it's recorded as being discovered by 'a team' from Guanajuato University. Is that normal?"

Kane answered immediately. "No, it isn't normal. Of course there's usually a team of qualified archaeologists, with under-grad students working as assistants. But almost always the team is led by the head archaeologist, the person who had done their research and knew where to look. Hmm... I guess that adds a little credibility to his story. Kenny, you found anything?"

Kenny glanced up. "Maybe...?" He looked back at the screen. "It says here that in 2005, an unnamed archaeologist from the University of Guanajuato was removed from his position. It doesn't say why, exactly, and the source is just an anonymous blog. But the word *escándalo* is there... scandal, in English, and *imbécil*... that one's obvious." Kenny's lips curled into something like a smirk. "A scandalous idiot?"

Kane nodded, a hint of a smile raising his eyebrows, but it was devoid of all mirth. "So maybe there is something to his unlikely story," he said. "Well, well..."

The sudden heavy clopping of footfalls on the stairs got their attention, and they all flinched, but a couple of seconds later Vicki emerged, her cheeks flushed and a sheen of sweat shining on her forehead. "Got it."

She plonked into a chair and placed the road atlas on the table. Kane strode from his position sitting at the bar and found San Miguel in the large road atlas, flattening out the crumpled two-page spread with his palms. "Okay guys, let's have a look see, shall we... see if we can speculate where he's hidden those poor girls." A pained frown of concentration wrinkled his forehead as he muttered unintelligibly and his fingers traced invisible lines across the map.

Ridley leaned in and placed her hand over his and, smiling, she said, "You do love a treasure hunt."

Kane glanced up at Ridley and grinned. "Yes, I suppose I do."

She nodded, adding, "And those girls are lucky to have you searching for them."

Chapter Twenty-Four

Cañada de la Virgen

"It is not my fault you know," the man said in his native Spanish, his voice gentle. "Did you know that?" Quetzal stood a yard away from the clearly terrified little girl, whose tears slid from beneath the blindfold and down her puffy cheeks onto her filthy pink t-shirt. Quetzal didn't know her name. Names didn't matter to him. Not the girls' names, anyway.

When Quetzal finally revealed his own true identity, which he would soon enough, he'd be known to the world as Humberto Palomares, a disgraced thirty-eight-year-old professor from Guanajuato, currently missing without a trace. Disgraced, though he maintained his innocence. Nevertheless, Palomares was about to commit an atrocity, the gravity of which had not been seen in Mexico since forty-three teachers went missing presumed dead for daring to speak out against a corrupt government a few years ago.

The girl continued weeping, the darkness of the

chamber swallowing the sound of her sobs and, Quetzal suspected, rendering her more frightened than she could ever have imagined.

"It is not my fault," Quetzal said again. "Of course, it is not your fault either, and for that, I promise you I am truly sorry." He even believed he meant it. He stepped forward and stroked the girl's hair, which made her scream, a high-pitched sound that reverberated back off the ancient stone walls as if it were fifty frightened girls down in that chamber, not one.

In truth, there were eleven other girls just like her, all trapped in exactly the same horrifying predicament. Quetzal's minions had chosen these particular girls for their youth, their femininity and their innocence, as requested by the man paying for them. "I have to make a point," Quetzal muttered often to himself. "Now they will have to take me seriously."

None of the dozen girls would have understood what was going on when they were taken, and still wouldn't now, trussed up like animals and with no idea where they even were. Each of them would still believe they were the only one. They'd been taken alone and kept carefully apart from one another. Alone. Cold. Blindfolded… It was the stuff of nightmares.

Except this nightmare was real.

And now this little girl was being told it wasn't her fault. Quetzal couldn't help but pity her; she had likely never done anything wrong in her life. Nothing. Nada!

She wept silent tears into her blindfold. In a moment of weakness, Quetzal wondered what she was thinking. *But why, God? Is it because I took the five-peso coin from mama's purse? I only took it because my friend had no money for lunch at school last week. I am sorry, God. I am sorry, Mama.*

Soon, though, the little girl's pitiful whimpering grated on Quetzal's nerves. "Enough!" he barked. "You should feel sorry for me, girl, not for yourself. I am the one who has had everything taken from me, not you. It is true... if I do not get what I want, I will take your life. But you should feel lucky. It will be a great sacrifice, a worthy sacrifice. Your death will be honourable..."

Quetzal's voice trailed off as he walked away, leaving the petrified little girl alone, chained to a stone plinth and shivering in her over-sized and now tear-stained pink t-shirt, probably certain she was going to die now, perhaps for the sin of stealing five worthless pesos for her friend.

Chapter Twenty-Five

Quetzal had moved to another section of the underground complex. He took a deep breath and stepped towards another of the little girls he held captive. He removed her blindfold, and to his horror the tiny girl's eyes suddenly twitched behind their lids. She was coming around, and Quetzal knew that if he didn't act quickly, before she awoke fully, he may lose his nerve completely.

He *would* not let that happen.

Quetzal took another step closer. The huge dose of sedative he had given her was wearing off. He stood watching for a further minute, gently tapping an ancient Aztec weapon, a macuahuitl, against his open palm. Then, when he'd mentally prepared, he placed down the weapon —a cross between a club and a sword—and moved swiftly, stooping down and lifting the frail girl with ease into position on the chacmool. He laid her gently down on the cool stone, her neck exposed, her head lolling off the back of the chacmool's own grotesquely carved stone head. Quetzal then grabbed the front of Rosa's t-shirt and tore it open, exposing her skinny chest, her ribs protruding beneath her caramel-coloured skin.

The light from the torches in the chamber flickered, as if affected by a sudden gust of wind from along the tunnel. It momentarily took Quetzal's attention away from the little girl, but he shook his head and returned to the stricken subject. And then he froze.

Her eyes were open, and she stared at the monster standing over her with such undoubted, wide-eyed terror and confusion that he recoiled, stumbling. After a moment he composed himself and took a couple of steps back. From a few yards away, Quetzal looked at the girl, now unsure if he could carry out the act he'd been planning for so long.

His mind drifted; to the reasons he'd come up with this macabre plan in the first place. The indignation he'd felt when they'd fired him from the university. The resentment and shame he'd experienced when ridiculed about his claim he was a distant relative of revolutionary hero Emiliano Zapata. It was a fact; he was a descendent of that most famous of Mexican heroes, but no one believed him and it had always irked him to the point of madness.

There was also the string of failed relationships, the lack of friends, and the complete and total notion that he was a worthless entity in the world and that no one cared if he existed or not.

No more! Quetzal—in the real world, Humberto Palomares—had a point to prove. He *did* exist. He *had* a purpose. And he *would* prove that point right now, and with sickening brutality.

He stepped to where he had placed the weapon on the ground, the obsidian blade glistening beneath the flickering torchlight. Then he snatched the weighty weapon up and raised it above his head. With an untamed roar, he shouted,

"You will hear me, world, you will all hear me. And Hiram Kane…" He paused, staring at the terrified girl's wild eyes. "This is all your fault, Kane, and this girl's blood will be on your hands. You will listen to me after this, I promise you that."

Then the madman raised the weapon higher still and after a moment at its natural zenith, he swung.

With a grunt, Quetzal stopped his swing inches from the girl's throat, then stepped back from the chacmool and lowered the weighty weapon to his side.

It had been a trial run. Quetzal wanted to test two things. First, test that he was indeed capable of actually going through with it. He now believed he could. Second, he was recording the scene on video, and he wanted to make sure the equipment was set up correctly and fully operational before the time of the main event arrived.

The man in the Quetzalcoatl outfit then turned to the camera, which zoomed in on the magnificent giant headdress, resplendent with long, blue-grey plumage set into a solid gold crown-type fitment, and bedecked in an array of dazzling jewels. Then the camera focused on the area of the eyes, though Quetzal suspected the lens couldn't actually see his eyes beneath the mask. The mask was a vital part of the pageant, but he did wish the would-be viewers could witness what he believed were the wild, glaring eyes of a man who had, perhaps, finally crossed over the threshold into madness. His therapist had suggested he might need official psychiatric help, and the man Palomares couldn't disagree. Of course, he ignored the doctor… he had things to achieve and glory to reclaim.

Quetzal went to the video equipment, and after flicking a few buttons and running the recording back a couple of minutes, he smiled inwardly. Everything had recorded perfectly, both the video and audio playing back with crystal clarity. *Perfect indeed*, he thought, then stepped back into the cavern, his heavy footfalls echoing off the cold stone walls. Stones that had seen many lives and even more deaths. Most of them glorious. Others less so. What was to happen next was inevitable. A sacrifice. The death of an innocent. One more step towards his glory.

Quetzal stepped closer still. This would be his first sacrifice. Most sane humans would call it murder; *Perhaps with some justification*, he mused. But Quetzal was no longer fully sane. He had transitioned way beyond that clinical evaluation. *Am I truly insane? Hmm, borderline. Disturbed? Yes, I am disturbed*, he had to admit, *one hundred percent… but it is all their fault!*

And thus, Quetzal, the Feathered Serpent, was more than ready to kill.

The little girl's heart raced as she felt the presence of the creature hovering over her. Pure, unfettered fear now enclosed her in its icy grip, and the shame she felt when she peed down her leg was more than she could bear, though she couldn't scream; fear and pain had silenced her, like Death himself might have. Her body quivered and her fists tightened, but then her head lolled as her eyes rolled back into her skull, and her cheek crashed into the cold stone of the plinth, knocking her out cold. The sound of her bone cracking echoed like a fired pistol.

Death… Quetzal… stood over the stricken virgin. He didn't smile. This was hardly fun. But it was necessary. It wasn't something—killing this girl, this child—that he particularly wanted to do. Yet, he was more than willing. He still harboured hopes that it would all be over after killing this first child, though admittedly he cared less now about their lives. But if it was not over soon, if he did not receive what it was he'd requested, then Quetzal would willingly commit eleven more murders before the clock turned one-hundred and eighty degrees. That was just too bad. Just the way of things. They all seemed like nice girls. Nice kids...

Kids... All the better then, he thought without as much as a flicker of emotion. *Sacrificio dignos.*

Worthy sacrifices.

For a moment, Quetzal reminded himself there were two god figures he worshipped. One was Quetzalcoatl himself; the God of wind and wisdom, the figurative boundary between the earth and the sky.

The other was Hiram Kane. A man. A mortal. Yet, a mortal man who held total power and complete control over his own destiny.

Quetzal worshipped both figures, but there could only be one victorious among them this night. It would not be Hiram Kane.

Ha llegado el momento. *The time has come.*

This is what they've made me do, he thought. *And soon the whole world will know it. The whole world will witness my pain, and they will feel it through the pain of others. They will witness my valiant efforts and my worthy sacrifices. They will all watch this little girl die.*

Quetzal found himself on a path now, a twisting trail that over the course of months and now even years, was a journey that had reached an inevitable conclusion; many deaths. Likely his own, too. But that was okay.

The little girl's death... yes. Any second now...

He carefully lifted the heavy macuahuitl, its obsidian blades glimmering beneath the flaming torches.

The girl—still mercifully unconscious—was slumped across the stone plinth, known as a chacmool. The carved stone figure, laid-back but with its head in an upright position, was the platform upon which many pre-Columbian cultures made their sacrifices. Its shape enabled the victims to be laid out flat, with their chests and necks exposed for easy access. She was hanging from the chacmool now, the straps around her wrists holding her arms behind her, while her tiny body hung limp. One of her shoulders was dislocated during the fall, but she was spared that agony after passing out. He would sacrifice her, yes, but he didn't want to cause her unnecessary harm. Her head remained lolled to the left, her wide eyes unseeing, staring at Quetzal. *She's defying me, even though she doesn't know it.* Even Quetzal wasn't immune to the ridiculousness irony in that moment, and he almost smiled. Almost.

It was to be a transaction of sorts. A life for a prize. *Destiny? No. A right? No, not that either. So what is it?*

Quetzal took a seat on the cold stone step a few feet from the little girl's supine body. He didn't mean to delay, but he didn't want to look at those haunted eyes, either.

It was too late for him to back out now. He was fully committed. The video was recording, and in a matter of minutes the whole world would know that unless Hiram Kane stepped up to the impossible challenge Quetzal was about to set him, many innocent young girls would die.

"Vamos a hacerlo," muttered the madman. *Let's do it.*

Chapter Twenty-Six

Kenny's Place

The phone rang, startling those at the map table.

Kane looked up, alarm ringing in his mind to match the phone ringing on the table. "It's him."

He checked his watch. 6:00 pm. He gulped, then snatched up the phone.

"What do you—"

"Mister Kane... are you watching the television?"

"No. Why?"

"Please, turn on the television, a news station... there's something you might find... inspiring?" Kane did not like the tone of cool amusement in the lunatic's voice.

He had switched the phone to loudspeaker, and Kenny had already reacted, flicking on the large flat-screen hanging on the wall. It usually showed sports or music videos... not this time.

"Did you find a news station, Mister Kane?"

Kenny flicked a couple of buttons on the remote, locating a news outlet, then nodded to Kane.

"Yes, we have the news. Why?"

"You'll see," the madman said, then hung up.

Kane drew his gaze over to the screen, then slumped back in his chair. The images displayed were far worse than anything he could have expected or even imagined.

The insane bastard—Quetzal—had somehow gained control of the television networks again. The view was of a dark space, perhaps just a darkened room. It was still light outside in San Miguel, so if this was a live feed, and local, it was definitely filmed inside. The camera zoomed in a little, and slowly into focus came the most barbaric thing Kane had ever seen. Judging by the horrified gasps of those watching along with him, it was the same for them.

A little girl lay sprawled over some kind of rock, tied to it with what appeared in the gloom like some kind of leather straps. She seemed to be alone, although somewhere out of shot something moved, casting a billowy shadow to shift across the ground. The camera zoomed in a little further, and Kane could clearly see the girl was strapped to not just a rock, but some form of small carved platform he recognised immediately.

"Chacmool," Kane whispered.

"Pardon...? A what?" asked Vicki.

Kane glanced at Ridley, horror etched across her face; as an art historian, she would know exactly what it was. Worse still, what it likely meant. He then looked at Vicki. "It's a chacmool... a... a sacrificial platform."

Vicki's eyes widened in horror.

Surely he won't, Kane thought, and he could tell Ridley was thinking the same. With a shudder, he also suspected they already both knew the answer.

Kane looked back at the screen, even though it was the last thing he wanted to do. The darkened image wasn't clear enough to make out minor details, but Kane stared anyway in an attempt to answer an awful question searing its way into his mind:

Is that Rosa on the chacmool?

The girl's head was turned slightly away, making it difficult to identify her. Kane's chest burned at the sight of the helpless little girl, whoever she was.

Kane noticed that none of those gathered in the bar at that moment seemed to be able to look away from the large TV screen. Until now, the scene had been silent and almost still, the only movement that hint of a shadow. Then came a voice. It was him. The madman.

Quetzal!

"This is a message for all the world, but for several people in particular. I mean you, Mister Kane. And you, my former employers. So-called friends. My so-called family. Everyone. I want you all to know that what I do here today, I do so reluctantly. People have been betraying me my entire life. Thus, I am acting only out of necessity. What you are about to witness is simply to make you all accountable… especially you, Mister Kane. Most people are accountable for their own actions in life. But not today. You, Mister Kane, you will now be accountable for *my* actions. I suggest you watch carefully. I am sure by now you know that there are many young, innocent girls missing from their homes and families in San Miguel de Allende. Well, can you guess who has them? That's right. I do. All of them are somewhere I guarantee you will never find them. And know this; what is about to happen to this girl will also happen to each of the other girls, one every hour, unless I get what I want, until they are all dead!"

"Turn it off," cried Danny, "he's insane..."

"No," barked Kane, although he knew exactly how Danny felt. "We have to know where he is... maybe there's a clue..."

The shadow on the floor of the darkened space grew steadily larger, and then the screen went black, as if something had covered it. Then, slowly, the edges of the dark screen lightened gradually, as if something was moving away from it. After a few seconds, the ghastly silhouette of some kind of headdress became visible. Most of those watching inadvertently recoiled.

The monstrosity on the screen had to be a person wearing some kind of mask; the silhouetted shape was terrifying. The shadowy form moved to the right of the screen, just enough for the little girl on the chacmool to be visible again. She stirred, moaning in what was obvious fear, though she didn't appear to be injured or hurt; in the gloomy image, it was impossible to be sure.

"She must be out of her mind with fear," said Kenny quietly, his fists bawling up in obvious rage. Yet, just like everyone else on his terrace, he couldn't take his eyes from the macabre spectacle.

The man leaned over the girl, as if saying something, though he spoke too quietly for it to be picked up by the recording gear. Then he stepped back a little. Slowly, he raised his hands, and for the first time, those watching saw he was holding something in both hands. It was still silhouetted, though Kane knew in an instant what it was. The object the psycho held was an ancient Aztec weapon known as a macuahuitl, a kind of ornate sword. Designed for one purpose... ceremonial killing.

"No... N0!" he bellowed, and stood up so fast his chair

crashed to the floor behind him, making the others flinch in their seats.

Mariana sobbed as Vicki tried to shield the woman's eyes.

The rest watched, unable not to, as the monster swung the blade towards the little girl's neck with such force that her tiny head was separated from her slender neck with one fell swoop of the blade, as Kane, those with him, and surely millions of people across Mexico and beyond drew in involuntary breaths, and froze, paralysed by shock.

Quetzal stepped slowly to the side, exposing the scene clearly to any viewers. The girl's head was somehow still attached to her neck, but not by much... A few tendons seemed to be holding it against the bloodied stone head of the chacmool. The man stepped forward, once more obscuring the scene. The shadowy form stood in front of the girl for a few seconds, and when he stepped back, almost painfully slowly, Kane and anyone watching instinctively knew what they'd see. The girl's head was gone.

"Rosa!" Mariana screamed.

Now the angle suddenly changed; a second, new camera showed the view from a different position. From this perspective, the girl's head was now visible on the floor, resting at the feet of the shrouded killer.

"It's... not..." Kane struggled to speak, the horror of what he was seeing stealing his voice.

"That's not Rosa!" Ridley stated, one hand to her chest and the other over her mouth.

The little girl's face was clearly visible now in the pale, flickering light. Mariana lifted her tear-stained face and looked at the monitor, releasing another sob, this one a mixture of horror at what she saw, but understandable relief that the dead girl was not her daughter.

"Mio dios... mio dios!" she wailed, fingers clutching at her hair. *My God... My God!*

The killer looked up towards this new camera, but again, his face still wasn't visible beneath the mask. He stared at the camera, as if to gloat about his power and his recent, despicable actions. Then, with a few deft, swift and skilled movements, he used the lethal weapon to disembowel the girl, spilling her guts across what appeared to be a stone floor. Mercifully, Kane thought abstractedly, the girl was already dead.

Dead. A little girl is dead, killed on live television... Dead!

The dark figure turned once more to the camera and stepped forward, stopping so close that despite the darkness, his eyes were visible to those watching. After a long pause, in which the eyes remained unblinking, he finally spoke. "Mister Kane. It is now just after six pm. At seven pm, I will do the same again. That is, unless you get me what I want. One hour, or another girl dies."

Then the screen went blank, and the only sound in Kenny's bar, apart from Mariana's breathless sobbing, was that of the most deafening silence Kane had ever heard.

Chapter Twenty-Seven

Cañada de la Virgen

Humberto Palomares could not believe his luck. He had already felt confident of achieving his ultimate goal; proving once and for all to the world that he was *not* a nobody. But now, after the phone call he'd received out of the blue from Rafael, his former student and protégé... and lover... and then the broadcast, which had gone better than he could have hoped... Well, his confidence had multiplied tenfold.

Humberto had been a promising scholar. He came from an ordinary family; ordinary at least through the last few generations. He well knew that his ancestry was important, but for reasons unbeknown to him, his family never discussed that and went about their business as a middle-class, hardworking family in the city of Guanajuato, nestled in the state of the same name. It was never mentioned.

Humberto had always had a fascination with ancient cultures, and pursued with vigour a career in archaeology, ultimately enrolling at the University of Guanajuato. By the age of thirty he had become a professor of archaeology, and just a few years later, on a 2004 dig at the ancient Aztec city of mighty Teotiuhuacan, a few miles northeast of Mexico City, he had uncovered the find of a lifetime.

An archaeology team led by Professor Palomares discovered a tunnel beneath the Feathered Serpent pyramid at Teotihuacan. Lying untouched for centuries, the sealed-off passage contained hundreds of extraordinary treasures, that lay exactly as they had when placed there as ritual offerings to the gods, most notably Quetzalcoatl, the Feathered Serpent.

Among the myriad wondrous items Palomares unearthed were green, stone-carved crocodile teeth, mammalian eyes shaped from crystals, and stunning stone-carved sculptures of pouncing jaguars and other sacred animals. The most important discovery of all, however, was that of a beautiful ceremonial knife, used for ritual sacrifices in the fifteenth and sixteenth centuries, before the Spanish and their cruel Conquistadors put an end to not only that empire, but many others.

It wasn't just its beauty that made that particular knife so special, but its rarity. Only a handful of ceremonial knives had ever been found. Humberto's had been the finest of them all. Its handle, skilfully hewn from a single piece of rare Mexican cedar, was carved into the form of a crouching man bearing the regalia of an eagle warrior, who looked out from the open beak of the eagle headdress, and clasped the haft of the ceremonial weapon.

The team and his sponsors had lauded Professor Palomares for his staggering find, and it was set to be an auspicious start to a long and distinguished career.

That's what was meant to happen. Things soon changed for the worst.

During a speech at the presentation of the discovery, to a range of scholars and dignitaries at a tuxedo event in the capital, Humberto Palomares made the biggest mistake of his life. He decided to use that speech to enlighten his peers and colleagues, and the watching press, particularly the Mexican news outlets, that he, Humberto Palomares, was a direct descendent of Mexican revolutionary hero, Emiliano Zapata Salazar, more commonly known simply as Zapata.

He had of course mentioned it before, and the claim was usually met with amused nods of derision. Humberto knew it was true. It was a family legacy. But with no official documentation to back up his valid claim, no one ever believed him. The fact his immediate family ignored the link infuriated him. So it became his word against history, and history had won. Yet, he had considered that celebration speech as his chance to shine and tell the truth.

The speech had started well. Humberto had become a good public speaker, and had grown in confidence after his amazing discovery. But the moment he said, with new, inflated confidence, "… and my esteemed ancestor, a hero to millions of Mexicans, Emiliano Zapata Salazar, would be very proud of me," things had started to unravel.

At first there was muted laughter among the gathered crowd. Then followed a few cheers and mocking whistles. But then another secret was revealed, and at that time in Mexican scholarly circles, it was a dirty secret indeed. One of his rivals, an older archaeologist whom Humberto himself had studied under, was jealous of his protégé's sudden fame. He knew of Humberto's sexual persuasions, but until that moment had ignored them. However, his weak-minded jealousy… not to mention the free-flowing Champagne and tequila… got the better of him, and he hollered out something that would very soon ruin not only Humberto's life, but his promising career.

"I wonder if your boyfriend is as proud of you as the great Zapata?" he called out. The murmuring crowd fell silent.

The colour drained from Humberto's face. His shoulders, held high and proud just seconds before, slumped. His knees almost buckled, and tears welled in his eyes. In the front row of the audience, a young man suddenly stood up and looked around, as if in shock. Like the professor's on the stage, tears filled his eyes, and then he bolted out of the auditorium, inadvertently proving the revelation and driving the accusatory knife home.

Professor Humberto Palomares knew in that moment that they would destroy his career before it had truly got started. Despite it being post-millennium, Mexico still lingered in the dark ages regarding many social issues other nations had accepted decades before. Homosexuality was one such issue, and while many of his peers and colleagues knew of and cared nothing for his personal persuasions, a few above him that really mattered did.

Over the course of the next weeks and months, they shamed the professor from his position at the university. He was ignored both socially and professionally, and little by little they smeared his reputation and left his life in tatters.

Ultimately, he had quit his position in shame. He wasn't fired, but his job had become untenable. Humberto felt betrayed. Not only had he lost his career, his friends and his reputation, but also the one thing he cared about above all else… the credit for one of the greatest archaeological finds in Mexican history. That find was now accredited to the institution as a whole, and his name had been quietly erased from all the records. It was the ultimate betrayal.

And it was also the final straw. Humberto Palomares became a changed man. If that name meant nothing to anybody any longer, then it meant nothing to him. He would become someone else. Some*thing* else.

As he stood there now in his simple motel room just outside of San Miguel de Allende, ready to return to the secret location and begin the next phase of his masterplan, he was proud of who he had become.

He was no longer the timid, worthless and insignificant Humberto Palomares.

He was Quetzalcoatl. Quetzal.

The Feathered Serpent.

God of wind, air and learning.

And the world would learn something from Quetzal over the coming few hours and days.

Chapter Twenty-Eight

They all sat in stunned, horrified silence for many moments, their collective breaths held at the atrocity they'd just witnessed. Tears slipped down several cheeks. Danny suddenly hustled to the bathroom. Kane heard him throw up. Ridly rose and went to check on him.

Kane's breathing quickened, a series of strong exhales through his nose a clear sign of the complete and utter rage he felt. He paced about for a few seconds, without saying a word, fists resting against his head. Finally, he approached the atlas laid out on the table and leaned over it, his two unfurled palms now placed face down either side of the well-worn pages.

Ridley came back from the bathroom and stood beside him, placing one hand in the small of his back. "This isn't your fault," she whispered, "before you start thinking it is."

He turned to face her, his eyes stony and cold. "Yeah?" he snorted. "Really? Not my fault? Then why is he calling me out by name? Huh? Why me?"

"Because... he obviously thinks you're the only one who can help him? Because he needs you. That's a... I guess he means it as a compliment."

"Yeah? Well, I don't need compliments," Kane barked, and immediately regretted it. "I'm sorry. It's just... I—"

"I know... it's okay," soothed Ridley.

"Is Danny okay?"

Ridly nodded. "He'll be fine."

Kane inhaled, then exhaled and said, "I... I need to... I must put an end to this madness." Kane turned back to the map and found the others, except Danny, now crowded around the table beside and opposite him. Kane's fingers traced along roads he didn't know, around green spaces, and back and forth across Historico Centro, yet he saw nowhere obvious on the map the girls could be.

"What about the bullring?" offered Kenny. "A few festivals are held there during the year, and obviously a few bull fights, but most of the time it's deserted and unused."

"Where is it?" asked Kane.

Kenny leaned over the map and pointed it out; two blocks south and two blocks east of the main square on Recreo. "Most tourists actually miss it, as it's discretely tucked inside an entire city block. In fact, the main entrance appears to be nothing more than someone's large double doors to their hacienda or garden."

"Too public," stated Kane, appraising its location on the map right in town. "I just can't see how anyone could have transferred all those girls there on such a public road, not without raising any suspicion."

"You're probably right," agreed a nodding Kenny, whose own rage was obviously bubbling just beneath the surface.

"Where else?" asked Ridley. "Where else might they be? Vicki, Stephy... Danny... you guys know this town well... any thoughts?"

"Sorry," the returning Danny said, and coughed to try and hide what his brother didn't miss. "My knowledge is limited mostly to the bars." He didn't look up, and took his seat back at the bar, facing away from the group, his shame hidden.

"I agree, it can't really be in town, can it?" added Vicki, her arm around Mariana's shoulders. "Too many people, especially during the Alborada, even late at night. It must be outside Centro somewhere." She reached in and flicked over the pages of the atlas. The map now showed a much wider area, encompassing the lake to the west and the Botanical Gardens to the east. Kane and the others all looked at the surrounding areas, but after a minute, no one had suggested an obvious location in which to hide the girls away unhindered.

Then Kane stood back suddenly, and shook his head, furious at his own stupidity.

"The chacmool!" he stated, as if it was obvious. "The chacmool is that stone plinth on which the girl was... where he did what he did to the girl. They're found all over Mesoamerica, and across many cultures, including Aztec and Mayan. The question is, where's the nearest ancient site to San Miguel a chacmool might be found?"

"That's easy," said Stephy, the first words she'd spoken since before the horrors on the television. "Cañada de la Virgin."

Vicki nodded, as did Kenny. Kane and Ridley remained unmoved. Danny turned in his seat to face them. "Canãda de la Virgin?" he repeated.

Kane's Spanish was decent, but he had no idea what that meant. "What and where is that?"

"It's can-yada, with a Y," corrected Stephy. "It means Glen of the Virgin. It's an Aztec pyramid… just outside town."

Chapter Twenty-Nine

Kane shook his head again, ashamed he hadn't worked it out sooner himself. "Of course."

"Of course what?" Ridley's puzzled expression matched the others around her.

Kane explained, "A pyramid; built by the Aztecs. He has taken very young girls; the virgins. And that can only mean one thing... he intends to sacrifice them... all of them!"

There followed another collective silence as they all processed this latest bombshell. Then Kane asked, "How long does it take to drive there? To the pyramid, I mean?"

Vicki said, "About forty-five minutes from here, more or less."

Kane nodded, then shook his head. "We still don't know what he wants," he stated, about ready to explode with frustration. He glanced at his watch, horrified to see it was now almost seven. "There's nothing we can do to stop him—"

Just then the phone rang again, sounding extra jarring in the quiet bar.

Mariana cried out, as though she had been punched in

the face. Kane stared at the phone, letting it ring. A terrible rage consumed him, the horrific sight of that poor little girl being sacrificed while he stood helpless rendering him physically incapable of movement.

"Hiram?" Ridley said. "Darling?"

Ridley's voice jolted Kane out of his paralysis and he snatched up the phone.

"Here!"

"Mister Kane... I expected better. Then again, you've lost people before. Plenty of innocent people... the kids in Peru. The old man in Japan. Your brother..."

Kane raged, his face red and his knuckles clenched. "Dammit, what do you want? You have to stop this madness."

"Yes, I suppose it would help you to know what it is I want from you. So, now I will tell you. Like I said, I am... correction, I *was*, an archaeologist. A great archaeologist, if you'll forgive my arrogance. And yet my greatest discovery was taken from me. By now I'm sure you've worked out—"

"You didn't give me enough time."

"True, but take comfort from the fact that first girl was always going to die. I simply had to make sure I had your undivided attention. Now I think I have it. So, do I, Mister Kane? Are you listening now?"

Kane exhaled through gritted teeth. *I'm gonna kill that fu* — "Yes... yeah, I'm listening."

"Good. Then listen carefully. I was the archaeologist who located the greatest archaeological find in Mexico in recent decades, and yet, because of some people's jealousy they have denied me what I rightly deserve... the credit and fame such an amazing discovery warranted. But—"

"No!" Kane yelled, startling the others. "You're telling

me you murdered that poor girl because you feel let down by your peers?"

"Mister Kane, I suggest you get a hold of your emotions and listen carefully, or else I will be forced to sacrifice another of the girls."

Kane sucked in a deep breath and held it for a moment.

"Mister Kane?"

With an explosive gasp, Kane released the air from his lungs. "I'm... listening."

"Good. Now, included in that magnificent horde I located beneath Teotihuacan was one extra special artefact. A ceremonial knife, beautifully carved by highly skilled Aztec craftsmen sometime around the fifteenth or sixteenth century. It is an exquisite piece, and it was the proudest moment of my life to have located such a rare and beautiful artefact. The university was proud too. Proud of me. But I found it, and now I want it back. It is presently on display in the Museum of Antiquities at my university in Guanajuato... well, it *was* my university, until they forced me out. So, Mister Kane... I want you to return my knife. And until I receive it... well, I think you know what will continue to happen." There was a moment of silence on the line, then, "It is almost seven; that will be continuing now."

"No, wait... Guanajuato is, what, ninety minutes' drive from here? There's just no way I can—"

"That is your concern, Mister Kane, not mine. I suggest you work something out. Adios."

"Just give me more time, please," Kane shouted.

More silence on the line for a few seconds, then, "Mister Kane, I happen to believe you are a man of your word. Believe it or not, I am a man of my word too." Another pause, during which Kane heard a deep breath. "Two hours. A minute late, and then the third girl dies..."

"Wait... third girl? I thought you said—"

"You must understand I have to keep you on your toes... it is already too late for the second girl."

The phone went dead, and Kane dropped to his knees, his head on the map table as frustration threatened to get the better of him.

"Are you okay? What're we going to do?" asked Ridley, just as the television flicked from the news, and to images of what they now believed was beneath the ancient Aztec pyramid just outside San Miguel.

Once again the scene was of a darkened chamber, the stone carved walls and floor now obvious to Kane, who had risen to his haunches. Another girl was strapped to yet another chacmool, and the only obvious difference this time was that the girl was not wearing a pink dress like the first, but what appeared to be a denim skirt and a green blouse, though it wasn't certain because of the shrouding darkness.

Kenny took charge and flicked off the TV. "I've seen enough. We know where it is now, and we know what will happen. Watching that is a waste of time we don't have."

"You're right," said Kane quietly, and he rose to his feet and stepped to the front of the group.

"Now we know where he is and what he wants. Does anyone here have friends or contacts in Guanajuato?"

Kenny said, "Me, yes. My girlfriend Sandra has a brother, Pancho. He knows the Chief of Police of Guanajuato City. Let me make a couple of calls." Kenny grabbed his phone and stepped out of the bar.

"Okay, finally some good news. Vicki, if Kenny can make contact with the Chief and can arrange access to the knife in the museum, would you be prepared to drive to Guanajuato to collect it?"

"Without hesitation," she said. "Yes, of course."

"Danny, Stephy, would you both go with her?"

"Yes," replied Stephy in an instant.

"I'll go too," Danny confirmed. "But what will you do?"

Kane turned to Ridley. He looked into her eyes and saw she had already worked out what the pair of them were going to do. Kane turned back to the others, determination creasing his forehead into deep lines. "We're going to the pyramid."

Vicki turned to Rosa's mother. "Mariana? We need you to stay here. I have a friend who will come and look after you."

Mariana nodded. Kane knew what she was thinking: *would the next girl sacrificed be Rosa?*

"Mariana," Kane said softly, "I will return Rosa to you, I promise you that."

Mariana nodded, tears falling freely. "Gracias... thank you," she said quietly, though Kane saw in her eyes that she knew he could not keep that promise. For all they knew, Rosa was already dead at the hands of that monster.

Kenny stepped back into the bar, a grim smile forced onto his face. "Pancho did well. I called him at work, and he immediately called the Chief. He told me the Chief says he'll meet us at the museum as soon as we get there. Vicki, if you leave now I think eighty minutes should be enough. He's expecting you."

Kane put his hands on Vicki's shoulders. "Vicki, don't kill yourself rushing there, but I don't need to tell you... time is against us," he said to the feisty Texan.

She nodded. "Don't worry. I know the roads well and there'll be little traffic at this time. And when we've got the artefact? Then what?"

"Listen, we don't know for sure he's at the pyramid, not a hundred percent, though it looks that way. As soon as you've secured the knife, call me and we'll tell you what we know. Do you know the way to the pyramid from Guanajuato?"

"Yeah. Luckily it's the west side of town, so the drive back from Guanajuato will be shorter... maybe fifty minutes."

"Good, assume to meet us there, but like I said, call me when you have the knife." Kane turned to Kenny. "Look, I'd understand if you said no, but can I please borrow your car?"

Kenny looked at Kane as if he was mad. "No, you may not borrow it. I'm driving, and don't try and talk me out of it. I'm coming, and we leave now."

Kane nodded. *Good man.* "Right then. Let's go."

Danny grabbed Kane's arm and turned him around so he was facing him. "I don't suppose I can talk you out of this can I?" he asked.

Kane stared at his brother and a grin twitched the corners of his mouth. "No. No, definitely not."

An almost identical wry grin crept onto Danny's face, matching what Kane knew had somehow become a kind of Hiram Kane trademark, or so Ridley often told him. "Good. I'd have been disappointed if you'd said yes. But be careful. Please?"

"I will if you will," replied Kane, and the reunited brothers pulled into a tight hug.

Less than two minutes later, Vicki, Stephy—her show that night forgotten—and Danny were racing along the highway to Guanajuato, while Kenny, Ridley and Kane were speeding through San Miguel's lively downtown streets, heading west out of the city towards the circa-fifth century Aztec pyramid, and to where Kane suspected they faced certain danger at the hands of a deranged madman.

Chapter Thirty

Vicki led Stephy and Danny down the stairs and out onto Hidalgo in a hurry, her short legs covering the ground at a surprising rate. A minute later, she'd hustled them into her little silver car parked at a lot a half-block away, and after barking at them to put on their seat belts with all the authority of a high school headmistress, she accelerated out of the lot, rear wheels screeching on the slick cobbled street, and sped back up the gentle slope of Hidalgo. Next she flew around the corner that separated the main square from what she considered her personal wine shop, La Europea, and flew down Canal, before finally hitting the first main road, the Libramiento, and racing off towards Guanajuato, leaving a collection of both bemused and angry pedestrians in her wake, unaccustomed to seeing a white-haired older gringa lady driving with such skill and tenacity.

Out the corner of her eye, Vicki watched as Stephy shared a somewhat relieved glance with Danny in the rearview mirror, and Vicki smiled inwardly. *Kids these days... don't know nuthin' 'bout drivin'.*

Stephy, who sat in the front seat, asked, "Do you actually know the way to the museum, Vicki? If not, I can pull it up on Google maps…"

"Sure I know where it is, Stephy darlin'. In fact, I was in Guanajuato at the museum a few weeks ago, and I think I even remember seeing the knife that crazy man is talking about. Beautiful object indeed if I'm thinking of the right one. Now, if you don't mind, I'm going to focus on the road…"

Stephy got the hint and fell silent; Vicki sensed she was relieved to hear it.

Sitting beside Vicki, hands clutched tightly to the sides of his seat, Danny's only thoughts were on his brother. He knew Hiram was brave, sometimes even too brave for his own good. He'd followed his elder sibling's life and career from afar, ever since he had left all those years ago, and Danny knew almost everything about all the adventures and dangers he'd faced. But he also knew Hiram was both smart and tough, and that he would do everything he could to save those poor little girls.

Danny closed his eyes and saved his energy. Somehow, Danny Kane knew that there would be a role for him later this night. What it was he couldn't possibly know. But if found himself in a position to help either Hiram or the girls, he had to be ready.

A half mile behind them, Kenny Peters eased his car along the highway to the turn off towards the pyramid. He had visited the archaeological site a couple of times before, the last of which was the time he had taken his visiting nieces out there. They were on school holidays from Windsor, Ontario, and had flown down to visit their favourite uncle Kenny in Mexico. It was a scorching hot day, Kenny recalled, but he'd loved seeing the excitement in his nieces' eyes when they'd first seen the remote pyramid. He thought of his nieces now, of how frightened they'd be if they were the ones kidnapped, snatched from their homes and their families by strangers, and kept hidden in some dark cave or chamber for days on end. Who knows if the bastard had beaten them already, or even fed or given them water, and Kenny's heart ached for those girls the psycho had taken. He hadn't realised he was clutching his steering wheel so tightly, and eased his grip, letting the blood flow back into his strong hands.

He turned his attention to the pyramid. Kenny considered himself a hobbyist archaeologist. He had never studied those cultures officially, but he had read plenty of books about most of the ancient cultures across the Central American region and in Mexico. Yet, he hadn't paid much attention to the actual structure at Canãda de la Virgin. Kenny figured he would be back there more than once over the coming years, and the last time he had been more focused on keeping an eye on his young nieces, making sure their curiosity and adventurous natures didn't see them come a cropper on the steep sides of the pyramid.

Kenny thought back on his visits, and didn't recall seeing any kind of official entrance into the actual pyramid itself. Based on that, he wasn't convinced the girls could really be hidden beneath it. *Ha, what do I know?* He was an amateur at best, especially considering who sat alongside him in his car. Hiram Kane, a leading explorer and somewhat of a legend as the very man who had rediscovered

Vilcabamba. If anyone could find those girls in time, it was surely Kane.

Kenny focused his gaze on the road. It was only about a thirty-minute drive out to the archaeological site, and he knew the roads well. For all they knew, the madman might have people watching them, following them from town and ready to alert their leader of anyone that came to the pyramid. Of course, this Quetzal bastard would be expecting them, having purposely and—very publicly—called Kane out in person. But Kenny knew of an alternative route, a way that was off-road and unfit for normal cars. It would add at least an extra fifteen minutes to their journey, but when he had proposed it to Kane, the Englishman had agreed it was a good idea.

"He knows we're coming," Kane had said, "but if we can approach without him knowing exactly when, we might just gain an important advantage."

So when they reached the junction along the now dark and empty highway, when he should have turned left, Kenny chose right, and just a hundred yards along, he pulled his car over to a gravel patch on the side of the road.

"This is the way my friend Beth takes when she brings tourists out on her horse trekking excursions. It's a private track, but under the circumstances I don't think Beth will mind. Hiram, if you just hop out and open the gate, I'll pull the car in and take it as far as I can. The rest of the way we'll have to go on foot."

Kane jumped out, and thirty seconds later, with the gate closed behind them and with his main beam off, Kenny eased the car along the dirt trail into what was now total darkness; the only light was the ambient glow of an almost full moon from behind thick, swirling clouds.

About a mile later Kenny pulled the car to a stop, and

they jumped out. "It's that way," he said, and pointed straight ahead towards a large, shadowy clump of trees.

"We'll have to take your word for it," teased Ridley, adding a wink.

Kenny grinned, then took from his car boot a couple of torches. Seconds later, the three of them set off towards the trees. Kenny assured them it wasn't far to walk, but to be careful of the uneven ground.

Hustling at a steady but purposeful pace, it was just as Kenny had suggested, and only a little over ten minutes later they saw a dark mass loom out of the night ahead of them, its solid silhouetted lines standing it out from the soft lines of the surrounding countryside.

"There it is," whispered Kane.

Kane was an expedition leader. He had spent most of his adult life leading people from all over the world on trekking expeditions to far-flung pyramids and temples, mountains, and even formerly lost cities. Unless he was discovering new ones, that was. It's what he loved to do, and he could even argue it's what he was born to do. His great grandfather was assistant to legendary Andean explorer Hiram Bingham, the man who rediscovered Machu Picchu in Peru in 1911. The Kane family had gone on to become leading names in the exploration world, and Kane was now its most famous member, a household name after he discovered Vilcabamba, deep in the Peruvian Andes after several near misses over the previous years.

Despite the horrors that were apparently happening beneath this remote pyramid, and despite the obvious danger the girls were in, and the apparent atrocities already acted out on at least two of them, Kane couldn't help but feel that familiar knot of excitement in his guts. This was the very definition of adventure.

However, this time there was a more sinister reason for success. For all he knew, the lives of at least ten more innocent young girls were on the line.

He could not let them die.

He *would* not let them die.

Chapter Thirty-One

Vicki skidded her compact car to a stop at the main entrance of the museum after negotiating the twisting labyrinth of tunnels the city was famous for. Once the home of the world's largest silver mines, those ancient excavations now threaded for miles beneath the city as the main roads across town.

Standing at the gates to the Archaeological Museum of Guanajuato was a huge man, and though dressed in civilian clothes, he exuded authority.

"I bet a hundred pesos that's the Chief," said Danny, and they all chuckled.

"I bet you're right," added Vicki. They climbed out of the car, and the Chief approached. He threw his cigarette onto the street.

"Señora Beekee?" he asked, but it wasn't a question. Kenny had told him via Pancho whom to expect.

"Si, Señora Beekee," Señora Vicki replied. "Mucho gusto." *Nice to meet you.* Over her years living in Mexico Vicki had given up trying to correct the pronunciation of her name; the Spanish speaking Mexicans were somehow unable to pronounce Vs, instead changing it to a B. Thus, she was now known to most people, including her friends, as Miss Beekee, or Señora Beekee, much to her annoyance. She dealt with it as she dealt with a persistent mosquito, however, and mentally swatted it away.

"Follow me," said the gruff Chief they now knew was called Chief Jose Guerrera Reyes. Vicki's Spanish was good. His name meant Jose Warrior King. It seemed an appropriate name.

He led them swiftly through the gates into the museum's courtyard and a moment later they were passing through the open doors, where a studious looking older man with a scraggly beard and small round spectacles greeted them.

He spoke immediately. "I have to warn you," he said in perfect, lightly accented English, "you should be very careful with this… this man."

"Why do you say that?" Vicki said.

"Chief Reyes has told me everything you know, and the item you are after." The professor took his glasses off and wiped the lenses with his handkerchief. "I know exactly who your mystery man is."

"Well?" Vicki placed her hands on her hips. "Fancy sharing that information with us anytime soon?"

"Humberto Palomares was once a promising scholar; he let his ego get in the way of his research."

"Great," Vicki snapped. "Now that we have a potted biography of this crazed, child-sacrificing murderer, maybe you could hand over the dagger."

"You see, he left this institution in, shall we say, rather odd circumstances," the professor continued, as though he hadn't heard anything Vicki had said. "And I have to say,

I'm very reluctant to let the artefact go. I'm afraid we will never—"

"If it's okay with you," Vicki replied tersely, cutting him off in her most matronly voice, "the lives of many young girls are on the line, and if we don't get this artefact back to San Miguel quickly…"

The professor looked down at the little lady, a trace of amusement in his eyes. "I'm afraid I cannot allow you to take the artefact with you."

"Are you serious?" Vicki yelled. "I thought Chief Reyes had explained everything to you?"

"Oh, he did, and I am perfectly aware of the seriousness of the situation," the professor said. "But I am afraid you don't understand the responsibility I have for guarding the precious artefacts residing here under my care."

"Professor," Chief Reyes said, "think of the girls this madman has kidnapped."

"Yes, yes, I feel terrible for them, obviously. Any decent person would." The professor removed his glasses and polished the still clean lenses again. "But I simply cannot let this precious artefact be handed over to a madman like Palomares. Who knows what he might do with it."

"Chief Reyes," Vicki said, "don't you, as an officer of the law, have the power to requisition this item, considering the circumstances?"

Chief Reyes stood up a little straighter. "I certainly do, Señora Beekee. Professor, I command you to hand over the artefact right now."

The professor also stood up a little straighter, although he was much smaller than Reyes. "No, I will not."

"In which case I have no choice but to…"

A massive, hulking man stepped out of the gloom from behind the professor. His shirt was stretched taut across his chest, and his shoulders rippled powerfully as he moved. He glowered from beneath heavy eyebrows.

"As you can see, I am prepared to defend myself and the artefact," the professor said. "Please do not try to take the object by force, Chief Reyes. I will have no choice, nor hesitation, in taking you to court for theft."

"Are you serious?" Vicki turned to Reyes. "Can't you just shoot him?"

"Señora Beekee, I cannot just go around shooting people," Reyes said with a shrug.

Vicki placed her hands on her hips and stared up at the chief, her mouth hanging open in mock surprise. "Chief Reyes, I do believe I am standing in front of the only honest cop in the whole of Mexico."

Reyes shifted his feet and looked at the floor. When he looked back up there was the hint of a smile on his face, and a twinkle of mischief in his eyes.

"Mateo?" Reyes said. "Is that you?"

A puzzled expression crossed the big man's face.

"Aren't you the son of Sofia Rodriguez?"

Mateo nodded. Vicki was starting to think there wasn't much going on up there between his ears.

"Does your mother know where you are tonight?" Reyes snapped.

Mateo lowered his head and shook it.

"And what do you think she will say when I tell her that I have caught you obstructing police business, and preventing us from saving the lives of those innocent girls?"

Mateo said nothing.

Reyes sighed heavily and, Vicki thought, rather over-dramatically.

"That poor woman, after everything she has had to

endure all these years and now she is about to find out her son is a criminal. The shame will almost certainly kill her, and my heart breaks at the thought of delivering the news." Reyes paused, and again it seemed for dramatic effect. "But I have my duty as an officer of the law, so what else can I do?"

Mateo's chest hitched, and a sob escaped from his mouth. "Please don't tell her!"

"I won't," Reyes said, "if you promise me you will help us get hold of that artefact right now."

Mateo lifted his head and nodded. He turned on the professor and planted a meaty hand on each of the smaller man's shoulders.

"What? No, stop it! You're working for me, not these idiots."

Vicki smiled. "I think it's time you handed over the artefact."

"But, you don't understand, I—"

"Now!" demanded the fiery Texan, cutting him off yet again, this time with definitive finality.

With one last disappointed look at Mateo, the professor shook his head, and said, "Follow me."

They followed the professor through a maze of corridors and up flights of stairs until they arrived at his office. Mounds of books and papers spilled from the professor's desk, and the walls were lined with stuffed bookcases.

Vicki shook her head at the sight. *How can anyone work in these conditions?*

The professor pulled open a drawer in a filing cabinet and lifted out an object wrapped in a grey shroud. He held on to it for a long moment, seemingly unable to actually hand it over to them.

"Professor, please…" Vicki said.

With a curt nod, the professor passed the object to Vicki. Inhaling, Vicki unwrapped the cloth.

There it was; the Teotihuacan ceremonial knife.

The key to saving Rosa's life, and as many of the other girls as was possible.

"Let's get out of here," Danny said.

Vicki nodded. She wrapped the dagger up again and then stalked out of the professor's office, a look of grim determination on her face.

In the corridor she suddenly stopped, and Stephy and Danny collided into her back.

"What's wrong?" Stephy said.

Vicki turned back to the others, a sheepish look on her face.

"Um, Professor? Would you mind showing us the way out please?"

A little over five minutes later, once the professor had led them back through the maze of corridors and flights of stairs, Vicki was once more tearing through the tunnels of Guanajuato, foot to the floor and clutching the wheel almost as tightly as Stephy now clutched the ancient Aztec ceremonial knife. They didn't speak, focusing instead on the road and the task at hand, each of them hoping the knife would be enough to save the lives of many innocent young girls.

Ahead of Vicki, the Chief's car led the way out of the last tunnel and onto the highway back towards San Miguel. Jose Guerrero Reyes was fifty-two years old and had served with the Guanajuato Police Department with distinction for almost thirty years. Unlike many of his peers, he had never once been tempted by the rife corruption that happened all around him, and on more than one occasion he had risked his career, maybe even his life, in reporting those officers who had. He was proud of his record, and although it had slowed down his path to the rank of Chief, he did not regret a single thing.

The current mayor, who took office a little over five years ago, had promised a crackdown on corruption, and in Reyes he had found the perfect man for the job. Corruption within the force was down almost eighty percent, and not only that, more and more local businesses were being left alone by the police, more used to paying for protection that receiving it by default.

Chief Reyes was approaching retirement age, and he had slowly been winding down his activities in recent months. But as soon as Pancho had called him, he knew he had to act. They had all heard of the terrible incident of the missing girls, but until now no one knew it was a perpetrator from Guanajuato who had, and still was, committing the awful act. It made Chief Reyes mad, and he was determined to do whatever he could to help. His gruff nature wasn't normal. In fact, he was usually a softly spoken man. But the call from Pancho had lit a fire in his belly, and he knew that he would do all in his power to stop the man the professor had identified as Humberto Palomares.

Chapter Thirty-Two

Kane, Ridley and Kenny approached the looming mass in silence. It stood out against the dark sky, big and brooding, as if containing some innate malevolent force. Kane was an expert when it came to ancient cultures, and though his specialty was the Incas of South America, he was well read on Meso-American cultures too, including the Aztecs. Compared to some pyramids he had seen, including the more well-known ones in the Yucatan and further south in Guatemala, most notably the huge pyramid at Chichen Itza and those in Tikal, the one before them was comparatively small.

Standing about thirty feet high, and with a base footprint of approximately only ten-thousand square feet, this was one of the smaller intact pyramids in all of Mexico. But that didn't in any way diminish its formidable presence. So much history must be buried beneath and among its ancient stones, Kane knew, and no doubt thousands and thousands of worshippers and travellers over the centuries had stood in awe at its innate power, which of course was the point.

Yet as Kane crept slowly and quietly towards it, he hoped they could do something to prevent a new, barbaric history being created. A history more abhorrent even than any that had gone before it. A history that would result in the slaughter of a dozen innocent children.

"Let's stop here a moment," he whispered, and drew Ridley and Kenny to a halt beside him. "Listen, we have no idea what we're going to face if we can even find our way inside. He has to know we're coming, right, so there must be a way to access the inner sanctum of the pyramid. If memory serves, there should be one main entrance, though we have to assume it's not easily accessible to the public. But if this madman, whoever the hell he is, has gained access, then we certainly can too. It's likely hidden and will be almost impossible to locate in the dark, so we'll have to use our torches. That'll make us easier to spot if he or his people are watching."

"We have no choice!" Ridley stated. "We have to get in there, and soon." Ridley couldn't keep the anger and impatience from her voice, but Kane knew she was right. There was nothing for it. They would just have to take their chances. Besides, the madman had demanded they come, and bring with them the artefact he so desired. There was obviously a way inside. Kane hoped it wouldn't take them long to find it.

Making their final approach from the north of the structure, technically the right side, they split into two, Kane himself taking what would be the front of the pyramid complex, and Ridley and Kenny heading towards the rear. Kane was certain he'd have more luck at the front, and if there was danger awaiting them, he wanted to be the one to face it first.

"Okay, let's go," ushered Ridley to Kenny, and they

crept forward, careful to keep low and to use their torches as sparingly as possible. Kenny followed, his nerves evident to Kane as they disappeared out of view, though Kane sensed determination was Kenny's more dominant emotion, especially after witnessing the reaction when he'd mentioned his beloved nieces earlier.

Kane waited a few seconds for the darkness to swallow them, and then trotted with caution in the other direction, edging around the front of the complex. Despite the near total dark, Kane's eyesight was perfect and he could easily make out a well-maintained stone path, laid by local government to accommodate growing numbers of tourists over the last decade since they had opened the site to the public. He followed that path now, hoping he found whatever entrance there might be soon. He turned left around the final corner and half jogged, half walked the thirty yards to the centre of the front edge of the structure and paused, looking around him. If he wasn't fairly certain of the nefarious activities happening somewhere below ground at this site, he would never have believed it. There was nothing to indicate anyone was here at all, let alone a mad archaeologist and a dozen young girls, and whoever else he had working for him. The tightening knot in his gut convinced him they were in the right place.

There is definitely no entrance here, Kane mused. Must be on the periphery of the complex. He suspected that in just a few seconds Ridley and Kenny would appear, and less than a minute later he was proven right. "Nothing?" he whispered. Ridley offered a nod in response. "Right, follow me."

Kane led them away from what was the main front of the pyramid, over to where a finely carved wall acted as an outer defensive barrier. Kane flashed his light on the wall, briefly admiring the intricate carvings, until something caught his eye. He recognised the figure he saw, and his adrenaline surged. *Quetzalcoatl? Is that what this is?*

Ridley sensed Kane had tensed a little. "What is it?"

"This figure here, it's Quetzalcoatl, commonly referred to as the Feathered Serpent. Quetzalcoatl was the god of wind and wisdom, and although considered to be one of the creators of humanity, he was also believed to be a portent of doom and of terrible events, some kind of link between Earth and heaven."

"And what do you think this means for those girls?" asked Kenny, concern lacing his voice.

"I think it means we need to get inside this pyramid right now," Kane hissed, more determined than ever.

Chapter Thirty-Three

Quetzal watched on calmly and with no little amusement as Kane and his two friends at last approached the entrance. He had multiple cameras installed discreetly throughout the complex, both inside and out; although no one would ever see them, Quetzal saw everything. He knew very well that Kane would come for him and the girls as soon as he worked out where he was. That was all part of Quetzal's plan; so far, it was going as he had hoped.

It wouldn't be long before they located the entrance, and they were close already. A couple more minutes... He was impatient for them to arrive, but he had waited long enough, and a few more minutes wouldn't make the slightest difference to the ultimate outcome. That was assured. Whatever transpired between now and then, his victory was inevitable. But with just a little luck too, he would also get to fulfil all of his true desires.

As he watched them approach the entrance, Quetzal realised he was more excited than he'd expected about witnessing their reaction when they discovered the first victim. It would be a huge shock for them, even though they'd almost certainly seen it live on television. Quetzal still feel a little uncomfortable about that 'incident', but it was crucial to have grabbed Kane's complete attention. He'd been proven right, of course; right now Kane was seconds away from entering his lair. That was what it was now, his lair... and deep within that lair, a wild animal awaited.

In truth, something had changed. When he'd first conjured up this gruesome plan, he had genuinely only wanted to regain his prized possession, the ceremonial knife, snatched away from him because of his... his *perceived* differences. Yet, now, over the last few hours, he'd felt a shift in his psyche, some altering of what he actually wanted to achieve. Now he had committed those heinous crimes, there really was no turning back. There could be no possible outcome in which he would regain his reputation, or in which he would get back the credit he had achieved when he'd found that archaeological discovery of a lifetime.

He now had to admit that the endgame had changed. He no longer cared for the knife, although it remained a source of pride for Professor Humberto Palomares.

But he was no longer that meek professor of archaeology. Not even close. Because of the actions of others, that man was dead. In his place was a God. Quetzal had emerged, the living, breathing representation of Quetzalcoatl, God of wind and wisdom, and portent of doom. *They turned me into this,* he thought, *and I shall have my revenge.*

And that revenge was to be acted out upon more than one entity. Of course, he would bring shame upon his former employers, the University of Guanajuato. They had ruined his reputation and stolen his glory. *When the world finds out what really happened, all will know that I was the true genius behind that world-famous discovery.*

Choosing young girls as his sacrificial victims wasn't random. As a child, girls had ridiculed Humberto, even bullied him. His two sisters had despised him. His mother barely ever gave him a moment's affection. He assumed that's why he'd preferred boys as a child, and why the other boys teased him, calling him a sissy. *At least Rafael loves me.*

First his mother and sisters had shunned him. The girls in school did the same. Later, young women at the university had never even known he existed. Finally, his female peers mocked and ridiculed him behind his back. They had mentally abused him, even if they believed he hadn't known it. Humberto Palomares *had* known it. He'd known all of it.

Now Quetzal would make these young girls pay for the sins of their forebears, whether innocent or not.

And there was Hiram Kane. For many years, Humberto had admired Kane from afar. Their careers had taken similar paths; both men had made the archaeological discoveries of a lifetime, yet only one could revel in that glory. It wasn't Professor Palomares. He had been as shunned and shamed by the archaeological community, and had his career totally destroyed. On the other hand, Kane enjoyed a worldwide reputation for his discovery. While warranted, Humberto despised him for it.

It was Kane he hated most, in fact, despite Kane never having done anything to him personally. That was just too bad. It was just the way things were.

Of all the revenges he had planned, that's the one he anticipated the most. The girls? He didn't care so much about the girls; they were merely pawns, a platform for the second most important revenge; against his institution, and the archaeological community as a whole. They would truly be satisfying revenges. The girls would be an added bonus.

But of Kane?

He wanted to watch Hiram Kane suffer.

If Humberto had learned anything throughout his own years of suffering, it was that no matter what a person did to fight it, those who had the power would always win. He was kind to girls in school, yet they favoured almost every boy over him. He was undoubtedly the brightest academic star at university, yet other, lesser students progressed faster. By force of will he had become a professor, the youngest ever at his institution, yet he had never received the support he desired or the plaudits he deserved. And the ultimate betrayal? His employers had used their power to take everything from him... his discovery, his career, and worse, his dignity.

That was all about to change.

Kane had the world at his feet and a beautiful woman to share it with. Now Humberto—*Quetzal*—had power, and he would use it to bring Hiram Kane to his knees, and make sure Kane watched on as he reduced his love, Alexandria Ridley, to dust.

Chapter Thirty-Four

On a hunch, Kane jogged to the end of the stunning carved wall and turned sharply, then traced his steps back along the opposite side. And there it was; as he suspected, it was almost invisible to any casual passerby. Set into the ground was a wide grate, partially hidden by more large stone blocks. It could just have been an oversized drain cover; Kane knew at once it was a secret access to beneath the complex.

Ridley and Kenny slowed to a stop beside him, and Kenny whistled softly in surprise. "Guess this is our way in," he whispered, and took a deep breath.

Kane looked at him. "You okay?"

Kenny glanced between Kane and the grate, their entrance into the pyramid. "Sure. I'm fine. Why the hell wouldn't I be? We're about to crawl beneath an ancient pyramid, hunting a crazed murderer who enjoys beheading little girls on live TV. What on earth could be wrong?"

"You seem on edge, that's all."

"You think? Really?" Kenny huffed, then sighed and

wiped a hand over his face. "Hey, I'm sorry, small spaces freak me out a little sometimes, and given the circumstances..."

"You want to stay up here while me and Alex head inside?"

"Absolutely not. I'll be fine."

Kane nodded. He'd known the answer before he asked the question, but needed to be certain.

"Are you sure this is the way in?" Ridley didn't look convinced.

"This must be it," confirmed Kane. "It's a remote location with few tourists, and I doubt anyone ventures this side of the boundary wall, right? So it *is* the perfect place to hide those girls after all. It's not a large pyramid complex... one of the smallest I've ever seen, though I guarantee it's vast below ground."

"Guess there's only one way to find out," added Ridley, as calm as if she were a tourist herself. "Shall we?"

Kane nodded. Ridley was afraid of nothing, except her own demons. She'd had her troubles in the past, but had long ago put them behind her. Kane was glad she was there. "Yes, we shall."

He dropped to his knees and ran his fingers along the edge of the grate, not surprised to find it'd been opened recently, perhaps even that evening. His senses alert, Kane looked around, almost expecting to be confronted with a weapon of some kind. No one was there, and he exhaled. *A little fear is good for focus,* he mused. Placing his feet apart, he motioned for Kenny to grab the other side of the grate, and after a three count, they first eased it up, and then to the side.

"Listen, Kenny. I appreciate what you've done for us so

far," Kane said, looking pointedly at the Canadian, "but if you'd rather not head down there, then—"

"Don't even think about it," Kenny stated. "As I said, I have nieces. I can't even imagine what those little girls down there are going through right now. I don't want to imagine it. I'm coming in there with you, and that's the end of it." He held Kane's gaze, unmoved.

After a few seconds's pause, Kane understood Kenny could not be swayed, and sighed. "Okay then… I'll go first. Kenny, you tuck in behind me. Alex, follow last, okay?"

Ridley nodded and gave Kane a confident, reassuring smile, and his heart swelled with pride. He wanted to tell her, but frightened little girls were in desperate need of rescuing from a deranged madman. Instead, he said, "Let's go."

Kane shone his torch down into the darkness and saw a narrow flight of stone steps leading beneath the complex. Without warning he was again struck by an overwhelming sense of déjà vu. He was back in Bali, fighting to rescue a little girl from a human trafficker. That time he saved the girl… *This time…?*

He shook his head, and hustled down the steps, then waited for Kenny and Ridley to join him. Ridley closed the grate behind her, and twenty seconds later they stood together in the damp darkness, the sudden cool air in stark contrast to the warm air above ground.

Kane faced a choice; left or right. He didn't know where the tradition came from, but in such situations he always chose left, and did again. "This way," he said, and as quietly as possible he led them along the narrow tunnel, senses on edge and ready to face whatever trouble might come their way.

A hundred yards ahead of them, Quetzal smiled. He had been following Kane's progress on the live video feed. His plan was working seamlessly so far, as he knew it would. Hiram Kane could always be relied upon to do the right thing, and Quetzal knew as soon as he'd called him out publicly the man would come running.

He thought back to the phone call from his protégé, and still marvelled at the amazing stroke of luck that had brought Kane into his plans. Never in his wildest dreams did he think he'd be handed such an opportunity, but there it was. He wondered if at last his luck might be changing. Not that it mattered. Luck or not, Quetzal was certain of one thing... either, he'd have his revenge, then get caught, arrested, and spend the rest of his life in prison. *Or, more likely,* he thought, *I'll be dead.* Either way was fine with him. He would have his revenge, and one way or another, he would have his fame.

Quetzal smiled and watched on as Kane led his followers deeper into the tunnel complex. His skin shivered in anticipation. In just a couple more minutes, they would encounter a nice little surprise, the first of several as they hunted him down. He had left little Rosa there to greet them. Of course, without a head she couldn't greet them with words. This way was much better. *So much better...* Quetzal smiled again.

Chapter Thirty-Five

The temperature continued dropping as Kane surged onwards, the tunnel narrowing and their torches nearly impotent against the stygian darkness. They almost slammed into what appeared to be a dead end, until Kane felt a subtle, cool draft from somewhere ahead. They edged closer to the solid stone mass before them, and almost by touch alone, Kane discovered a near-invisible archway around the dark edges of the sheer stone wall.

Kenny gasped. "How'd you... how could you know?"

Kane turned, and despite it all, he grinned. "Didn't you watch Indiana Jones up in Canada?"

Ridley snorted, Kenny shook his head and Kane's smile faded as he turned the torch back to the archway and crept through it, half expecting some kind of macabre discovery. Instead he'd led them into a larger chamber, where they were suddenly bathed in the light of a dozen flaming torches. They looked at each other, eyes widening in surprise. But when their gazes faced forward again, their

The Feathered Serpent

eyes growing accustomed to the new light, as one they recoiled in absolute horror.

There, trussed by straps to a reclined stone altar, and as naked as the day she was born, was the ripped open and ruined body of a tiny young girl. She had been sliced from sternum to groin, her guts spilling from what was essentially just a carcass, and her ripped out heart had been discarded without ceremony onto the stone floor. That wasn't the worst part. The girl was absent her head. Although Kane had seen it happen on television, he had foolishly hoped it was just an illusion, some intricate trick to lure him to his deaths. But he was wrong.

They were all so very, very wrong.

Ridley fell to her haunches, her breaths coming in ragged gulps as she fought to retain control.

Kenny immediately turned and hustled a few steps away before puking.

Only Kane remained with the girl. He dropped to his knees beside her. This had been a brutal slaughter of a young child, barely ten-years-old. Yet, Kane found he wasn't as shocked as he should have been. Over the last few years he had experienced first-hand just how depraved humans could be, how callous, and how vicious. He had even witnessed a man decapitated by a sword from just three feet away. But a child? This was a whole other level of sick, barbaric depravity.

Kane had to keep control of his emotions. He had been warned. He knew there would be others like this. And he knew it was down to him to prevent more senseless murders.

Kane reached out his hand and closed the girl's unseeing eyes. He then took a deep breath, and gently lifted her head, shrouding it within her discarded t-shirt.

He stood and faced the others. Kenny sucked in as

much air as he could, the sound loud in the cavern. This was not what he signed up for, but Kenny was tough, and given a moment or two, Kane was sure he would pull himself together.

"Buckle up, Peters," Kenny muttered, then shook his head and returned to Kane's side.

Ridley stood too. Her shock was replaced by an expression of fierce determination. With a fired up Ridley by his side, everything was better, and Kane inhaled.

He fixed his gaze on first Kenny, then Ridley. Exhaling, he turned. "Let's go," he hissed. "Let's find us a monster."

They surged on, more intensity in their strides as they stalked through the deep stone tunnels.

They still had no idea what was going to happen, or whether the killer was even still there beneath the pyramid. Kane believed he was; he could almost sense the malignancy in the air. He was sick to his stomach. More children killed, and for what purpose? To make a point? To gain back some credit? *Boost your fucking ego?* It was absurd. There were better, saner ways to get a message across than killing innocent people. Yet he'd seen it before. Often. Way too often, way too many people beyond conscientiousness, beyond normal human rationale. There was a specific word for that diagnosis; psychopathic.

No matter what had happened to this man in his life, no sane person could plan this and claim they were sane. No, this was the work of a lunatic, which made him incredibly dangerous. They would have to be careful.

Suddenly they came across the next victim, and froze in their tracks.

This time the girl appeared a little older. She had been

killed in the same manner. Kane hoped the decapitation had happened before the disembowelment; at least the pain might have been minimal. It was the best Kane could hope for these girls.

Kane felt as if he were following a macabre trail of human breadcrumbs. A truly gruesome, abhorrent thought. He ushered them on; there was no time to dwell on the dead when the living were waiting to die.

Chapter Thirty-Six

The convoy of vehicles led by Chief Reyes was soon within a few miles of the pyramid site of Canãda de la Virgin. They had agreed to rendezvous at a safe distance from the archaeological site, then pause to formulate their plan. The important thing was to somehow let the psychopath know they had secured the artefact he'd demanded. At this stage they had no idea how to go about that. Kane had instructed Vicki Allen to call him as soon as they were there, so that's what she did now.

She called his mobile and waited for an answer, but after letting it ring for a full minute she ended the call. "No response," she informed the others. "What do we do?"

"We have to wait," said Danny. "I'm sure there's a good reason he hasn't answered," he added, though a knot of apprehension tightened in his gut. Of course he knew his brother was more than capable of looking after himself, and that he'd had to prove it far too often in recent years. Nonetheless, *if anything bad happens to him now...*

Danny didn't want to ride that negative train of thought and repeated his stance. "Let's give him more time."

The Chief agreed. "We do not know what is down there at this time. Although I hate to sit around, probably wasting time, we must wait for confirmation from your friend about what to do."

Danny fidgeted as they waited a further ten minutes, before his anxiety got the better of him. "We have to get down there, now. We can't wait any longer. What if they're already inside the pyramid and can't get a phone signal? It might be as simple as that."

"I agree," said Stephy. "Let us at least get closer to the pyramid. That way we can react as soon as we hear something from them."

The Chief remained silent for a moment, then turned to his second in command, a man named Juan Solis. Solis gave the hint of a nod, which was good enough for Chief Reyes. "Okay, let us drive to the archaeological park's main entrance. We will wait there. No one goes in without my authority. Understand?"

A few nods greeted his words, and seconds later they were driving again, covering the last mile in a few minutes. They pulled up at the main entrance, a rather innocuous looking wire fence with a small sign indicating where they were; a bigger one warned them to keep out.

They stepped out of their respective cars. Danny enjoyed the warm yet fresh air rather than being cooped up in the vehicle. He watched as Vicki set about calling Kane every couple of minutes. There was nothing else to do. That was her responsibility, and she confirmed to Danny she would call and call until she reached him.

Danny thanked her and took a few strides away from

the group. He was just about to turn and head farther out of sight when the Chief called out to him.

"Hey! ¿A dónde vas? Sorry… where are you going?"

"Erm, the baño," Danny replied with a sheepish grin. "I need the loo."

The Chief nodded and lit another cigarette.

Hiding his relief behind a fake cough, Danny turned and made off towards a clutch of ancient mesquite trees, where he lingered for a few moments to see if anyone followed. When he was certain they hadn't, he headed off again, veering directly away from the cluster of people and their cars. He soon found his way to the corner of the fenced area of the complex. He took a few deep breaths. The last time Danny had entered somewhere he shouldn't have was when he was twelve. He was with his brother that time. He hadn't meant to disappear the way he did. It just kind of happened. At first it was a game, a way of showing Hiram that he wasn't always the best or the smartest. Not that his brother felt that way. Danny knew he didn't, knew Hiram had loved his little brother and always did everything he could to make him feel equal. Still, that's not how Danny had felt. Not at all.

When the brothers had skipped school that day and broken into the Old Rectory, Danny had planned on playing a little trick on his brother. He had hidden out for half an hour, and revelled in the fact he could hear Hiram getting more and more anxious and stressed that he couldn't find Danny. Finally, after an hour of searching, his brother seemed to have given up and left Danny there all alone.

That moment is when he decided he would leave. He thought he might stay away a day or two, maybe a week. But as the days ticked by, and he realised he could easily remain 'missing', days became a week, then weeks, which soon turned into months. A year later, when news stories about his disappearance had dried up, and it appeared as if his family had forgotten him altogether, Danny decided he would never go back. He made his way to London, and forged a new life living on the streets, or sharing abandoned warehouses with other homeless kids. At first he'd thrived on those streets, but a few years later, when he was sixteen, it was time for a change.

He acquired some forged documents from a street friend, and changed his identity. He died his mousy brown hair black, and doubted his family would ever recognise him anyway. He started working in various restaurants around London, and finally, by the time he was nineteen and had saved enough money, Danny set out on his travels. After a few years working his way across Europe, he made his way to Australia, where he spent several more years working at a pub in Coogee Beach, Sydney. Then he moved onto New Zealand, where he worked for a while at the Mad Dogs and Englishmen pub in Auckland among other places around the country.

Over those years though, Danny felt a growing remorse about what he had done, letting his family believe someone had kidnapped him, or worse. The shame and guilt grew and grew until Danny turned to drinking to numb the ever-growing burden of guilt. Eventually he decided to take his issues and his few belongings and head for a new start amid the anonymity of central Mexico, where he could live for cheap and drown his sorrows at the bottom of a glass for the next however many years he had left.

That's how he had come to San Miguel, and ultimately, how his family had found him. He would never forget the kindness shown to him by Kenny Peters and he would always be grateful to him for contacting his family. Equally,

Danny would never forgive himself for the suffering he had caused his family, not least his brother.

That's why he was leaving the others behind him now. He had to do something. *There must be another way into the pyramid,* he thought, and within seconds he had scrambled over the flimsy fence and was hurrying along, staying low to the ground, towards the ancient structure, hell bent on helping those poor girls and, of course, his beloved brother Hiram.

Chapter Thirty-Seven

Kane, Kenny and Ridley pushed on, their hearts sick with horror but their anger steadily growing. After another minute of negotiating the twisting, narrow stone corridors they emerged into a slightly larger chamber, when from out of nowhere the madman's echoing voice brought them to a halt.

"I must say, I did not expect you to bring your lovely woman with you, Mister Kane. But I am glad you did. It should make things easy for me. And who knows, perhaps for you, too? I know you are a man of honour. The world knows it. You have made many sacrifices. But please, Mister Kane, look at the lovely Alexandria now, if you would."

The three of them stood and stared at one another in stunned silence. "He's watching us," muttered Kane, and scanned the walls and ceilings for hidden cameras. He saw none, but knew they were there somewhere.

"Mister Kane, I am many things; patient is not one of them. It is in both of our interests, not to mention the girls I have with me, for you to do exactly as I say. So I ask again, take a look at Miss Ridley. Take a good look, because you will have to make a big decision later, and I want you to be sure of your answer."

"Enough of these damn games, you psycho, I—"

"Stop!" The man's voice reverberated so loudly in the enclosed stone tunnel it shut Kane up immediately. "What did I tell you? The girls?"

Kane did as he was told and locked eyes on his love. "What do you want?" he hissed at the unseen, unhinged bastard taunting him.

"Very good. What I want is what I have already told you... I want my knife returned to me. That is not so much to ask, is it? So, here is what you have to do. Your friend... I am sorry, I do not know his name... you will send him back to the entrance to collect the knife. I know it is there. I have contacts everywhere, Mister Kane, and I also have cameras watching everywhere too. Your friends have arrived and they have the knife with them. So, send your friend back to collect the knife and he will return, alone, with my beloved possession. He will meet you, with me, in the main chamber. Send him now. Go on, do it... the girls are waiting."

Kenny glanced at Kane. Kane nodded, and with more bravery than he obviously felt, Kenny nodded in return. Kenny then looked over at Ridley, silently mouthed the words *Be careful,* and turned and retraced his steps back towards the entrance to the tunnels, as quick as he dared move in the darkness and across the uneven ground.

Kane inhaled, barely able to control his burgeoning rage. "What about us?" he asked.

"Here is what you must do. The two of you will continue on. Soon you will come to the main chamber, where I will await you both. I have to say, I await you with great excitement. Then we will play a game. Can you guess what the game is? I assure you it will be fun... perhaps not for you, and definitely not for those poor girls... but very fun for me. I call the game 'sacrifice'. And so I ask you, Mister Kane... are you ready to make the ultimate sacrifice?"

A terrible, haunted laugh, the horrifying cackle of a demented maniac, reverberated off the walls from invisible speakers.

And, in that moment, Kane knew that whatever he did, all the little girls would die.

Chapter Thirty-Eight

Danny assumed there wouldn't be an obvious sign-posted entrance into the pyramid, and if there was a way in at all it would be somewhere away from the main structure. With that in mind, he headed towards what appeared to be some kind of perimeter wall. Seeing nothing obvious there in the darkness, he edged even further away, back towards the fence he'd scaled but on the inside, and was working his way along the fence when he stumbled and fell, slamming hard into the ground. Luckily he wasn't injured, but as he muttered about his clumsiness, he found himself face to face with some kind of drain cover. *Could it be a way in?* He didn't waste another minute finding out, and using all his strength he hauled the grate aside, and gazed into the opening to a dark tunnel. It did not look at all appealing. "I have to try," he told himself, summoning his cajones, and scrambled into the hole.

Stephy had a question for Danny, but when she looked for him, he was gone. "Have you seen Danny?" she asked Vicki, who said she hadn't.

"Sorry... I was busy trying to call Hiram, sadly with zero success thus far. I... I should've paid more attention—"

Vicki was cut off when suddenly, from out of the darkness came a running Kenny, approaching the cluster of vehicles. So sudden and noisily had he appeared, that the police, including the Chief, raised their weapons and shouted at him in Spanish.

"Detener!" they bellowed. "Detener!" *Stop! Stop!*

But Kenny didn't stop, and carried on approaching the group. The younger officers, eager to take down the unknown intruder, flicked off their gun's safeties, but luckily the older Chief recognised the Canadian and barked orders to his men.

"Baja tus armas!" he shouted. *Lower your guns.*

Kenny approached Chief Reyes, and the pair briefly shook hands, before Kenny leaned over, out of breath from his hasty return from the depths of the pyramid. "Es bueno verte de nuevo," Kenny said, his breaths ragged. *It is good to see you again.*

"Igualamente," replied the Chief. *Same to you.* The Chief smiled, but it faded quickly. "Are you okay?"

Kenny nodded. "Si, I'm okay. Do you have the knife?"

"I have it," Vicki said as she came over and handed Kenny the ancient weapon, still wrapped inside its aged cloth. "I tried calling but got no response. Have you been inside?"

Kenny looked at her, his bottom lip trembling slightly. "Yeah. I... I have been inside. I... We saw the... the girls... two dead girls... their heads..." Kenny's voice trailed off as he recalled the horrors he'd seen beneath the pyramid.

Vicki shook her head and grabbed Kenny into a tight hug. "Is Hiram inside still? And Alex?"

"Yeah, they're in there. I have to go back with this... thing... I have to go now." Kenny looked at the Chief. "Señor Reyes, it is *very* important you and your men don't follow. The man inside is very, very dangerous, and he said that unless I come alone, he will kill all the girls. Do you understand? Please, do not follow."

Chief Reyes stared at Kenny for a long moment. "You know that is not possible. It not only goes against all my training as a policeman, but also against my basic instincts as a human being, not to mention a father."

"I know, I know, but—"

"But nothing." The Chief sighed. "Imagine if your wife or girlfriend or child was in there. Would I hesitate to plunge into danger to save her? Would you?"

"Of course not," Kenny said, clutching the ceremonial dagger to his chest. "And I understand. But Chief... Señor Reyes... this man, he will murder more of those innocent girls unless his demands are followed to the letter."

The Chief sighed again, even deeper, and closed his eyes. "This goes against everything I believe in." He opened his eyes, then reached out and gripped Kenny's shoulder. "But if Pancho respects and trusts you, then I will trust you. If you say we should wait, we will wait."

"Thank you."

"But only for thirty minutes. If you have not returned in half an hour we will come. And we will not come quietly."

Kenny knew enough to know what that meant. Yet, if agreeing to that meant they wouldn't follow immediately, then his only choice was to accept. He nodded and took the Chief's hand again. "Okay, Señor Reyes. Fair enough. Right, I have to go."

And clutching the artefact as if a dozen lives depended on it, which for all he knew, they did, Kenny turned and raced off into the darkness, hoping beyond all hope he wasn't too late.

Chapter Thirty-Nine

Kane surged on, Ridley on his tail, and after just a couple of minutes they entered what appeared to be a massive central chamber. What they saw stunned them into silence.

The space was vast... unbelievably vast... and Kane knew they must have descended much deeper beneath ground than he'd initially thought. Around the stone-hewn chamber walls were dozens of flaming torches, the oil giving off noxious fumes that assaulted his senses. The high ceiling, perhaps eighty-feet above their heads, was laced with stalactites that hung threateningly, as if part of some macabre ancient booby trap waiting to impale them. It was like something out of a Hollywood action movie. Kane had been labelled a wannabe Indian Jones before. That didn't seem funny now. Not funny at all. But that wasn't the most amazing thing. In the centre of the enormous chamber was a second pyramid, smaller, though identical it seemed to the one towering over it above ground. This one was maybe fifty-feet high, and at its summit was a large chacmool;

otherwise known as a stone-carved plinth, designed for one purpose... death.

Then Kane spotted something that made his blood run cold. All around the base of the inner pyramid were a series of more stone plinths, each with a young girl strapped to it.

"Mister Kane," came that cold, demented voice again, "I am glad you made it. Now you will both do as I say. I am sure you understand what will happen if you do not. Are you ready to play my game, and do your duty?"

Ridley turned to Kane. She had a look in her eyes Kane didn't want to see but knew he would. There was no fear there. Not a trace. Instead, where fear should have been, and would have been in most people, was determination. Determination, and a steadfast desire to do whatever it took to save these girls. Kane was desperate for Ridley to run, desperate for her to escape this madness and get as far away from there as she could. Instead he nodded and offered the hint of a smile, and hoped he displayed the same confidence she showed.

But Kane was not confident. Not confident at all. In the past, when these kinds of things had happened, all too often, Kane had felt he could overcome any situation, face everything head on and make things right. Almost always, he had. Yet lately, whenever he was involved, people had a tendency to die. Recent events had rocked his confidence. Most recently in Bali, where a good friend had died and his niece had come close to perishing. Kane hadn't realised how deep that loss of confidence in himself had become. He had never been afraid of anything or anyone in his whole life. Never. Until now.

He glanced back at Ridley, who seemed to sense his feelings. She gripped his arms, willing him to hold her gaze. "We can do this," she said, her tone calm and authoritative.

"Not only can we, but we have to. Look at those girls, Hiram. Look at them."

Kane glanced at the girls strapped across the hard stone chacmools. He saw some of them looking at him, pleading with their eyes to emancipate them from this nightmare. They were young, between perhaps just six and thirteen. Young girls. Virgins. And that psycho was fully intending to kill them all. Kane was sure of it, despite anything they did.

Something switched in his mind then, seeing those terrified children, some unbidden wave of consciousness. In Ridley's hands, Kane's fists clenched. His muscles twitched as he removed them, and he stood a little taller now, his shoulders wider. He looked back at her.

"Thank you," he whispered. "Let's do this." He stepped out of Ridley's clutches and looked all around the torch-lit chamber. He took a deep breath, then called out to the madman. "Why don't you show yourself? Are you afraid?"

The unseen monster laughed. "Afraid of what, Mister Kane? Do you think you have any power here? Look around you. There is nothing you can do to stop me. Everything is in place. You are just my puppets, here to do whatever bidding I ask of you. I suggest you comply…" He let the threat hang in the air for long seconds, before adding, "Are you ready to play *Sacrifice*, Mister Kane?"

Kane paused, then declared, "I will do whatever it takes to save these innocent children. Then I will end this madness and take you down. That is what I'm ready for."

"Brave words, Mister Kane, if not rather foolish. Let me ask you again; are you ready?"

Kane took a few more deep breaths, certain the madman was watching them, whether unseen within the chamber or from afar via some hidden camera feed. "Yes. I'm ready. What shall I do?"

"It is a simple task. Do you see that pit over there, to your right?"

Kane glanced right and saw what Quetzal had referred to. "Yes, I see it. So what?"

"Simple... jump into it."

"What? I can't jump into th—"

"Do it!"

Kane looked once more at Ridley, and before he could say anything, she whispered, "It'll be okay... Go ahead. We'll be fine."

Kane nodded, reluctant, knowing he would lose any position of strength he might have had, but equally knowing the consequences if he didn't. He took a dozen steps to his right and glanced down into the pit. There was a single flaming torch illuminating the stone-hewn pit, that appeared to be around fifteen-feet deep. He instantly saw that if he jumped down there, and even if he didn't break an ankle when he landed on the unforgiving stone floor, he could never climb back out again. It would be impossible.

Is this to be my sacrifice? he wondered. *If I go down there will he let the girls live? Is this his sick game?* He couldn't know, but he would have to trust in Ridley to do the rest.

With a last glance back at Ridley, who nodded, her jaw set firm, Kane jumped down into the pit, into the unknown, wondering if it was the last thing he would ever do, and if it was the biggest mistake of his life.

He landed well, easing into a forward roll to break the hard fall. Unscathed, he stood and looked helplessly back towards the ceiling far above, certain he had indeed made a terrible, terrible mistake.

"Now it is your turn, Miss Ridley," came the voice of the clearly unhinged monster. "Please, climb to the top of the pyramid. Do it now."

Ridley took a few deep breaths, slowing her racing heart, then cautiously made her way to the base of the pyramid. As she moved, she glanced across to the nearest girl, perhaps ten feet away. The girl's eyes were wide with fear, and tears streaked down her puffy cheeks. Ridley didn't know how long the girls had been strapped to the stone plinths, but they all looked withered, hungry and thirsty. Their ragged clothes were filthy, though it was not their appearance that troubled her most. It was their collective silence.

They must be beyond terrified, she thought, and another glance at the nearest girl confirmed that. Then a wave of shock rushed through her, followed by a glimmer of hope.

Ridley recognised the girl. *It's Rosa!*

Ridley swallowed, trying to keep control and not let her emotions get the better of her. She couldn't let that madman know what was going through her mind.

Yet, she had to try to give Rosa some kind of hope, something to cling onto in these, her darkest moments. So Ridley smiled. It was a subtle smile, one she hoped wouldn't be seen by the crazed monster holding all the aces. She hoped Rosa could see it and that in that smile she would find something akin to hope. Then, to Ridley's amazement, Rosa smiled back.

Good. She understands we're here to help. I cannot let them down.
I will not let them down.

Ridley climbed the first step up the pyramid, a step so tall she almost had to scramble up it. Then she took another.

Then a third...

Chapter Forty

Kenny hustled his way along the dark passage, only too aware now of the evils that awaited him and the desperate need for haste. He surged on, sweating, and tiring, but his natural athleticism powered him forward, despite two decades of heavy drinking and semi-debauchery since arriving in Mexico.

Kenny was an all-Canadian child sports prodigy, excelling in ice hockey and football of the north American variety, a prized quarterback in his day. He'd even had an unlikely flirt with success as a breakdancing boyband pop star. Now he settled for being the best barman in town, if he did say so himself.

On he pushed, as fast as the darkness would allow, his mind racing. Kenny had only known Hiram Kane a few days, yet something about the man inspired great confidence in Kenny. He also suspected that the Mexican authorities were, against his vociferous appeals, likely following close behind him. Quetzal had told him to come alone with the artefact, and he had tried.

But Chief Reyes had seemed twitchy. He was sure the Chief wouldn't wait the thirty minutes he'd promised. Far from it. Kenny only hoped that the innate Mexican machismo would not get him or anyone else killed.

Kenny negotiated the secret archway they had discovered earlier, and averted his eyes as he passed the stricken head- and heart-less body of the little girl. Despite not looking this time, nausea threatened to overcome him, but he surged on, determined to do everything in his power to prevent another senseless sacrifice, all the while knowing a dozen heavily armed police probably trailed in his wake.

He forced his mind to focus on the dimly lit passage ahead, hoping with his whole heart he would make it in time. If not... well, he didn't need to imagine what might happen then!

Panting in deep, rasping breaths, Kenny finally reached the point he had with Kane and Ridley earlier, when they had stopped and been addressed by the madman. He paused, and placed down the artefact, then bent over, resting his hand on his knees and trying to catch his breath, sweat dripping from beneath his trademark 'Kenny's Place' cap. *Nothing like a little passive advertising, eh?* was one of his go-to phrases.

Kenny stood up straight again, listening, waiting for some instruction from the psycho. None came. *How long do I wait?* he thought. He felt sure he was being watched by a hidden camera. *Ten minutes? Five?* Kenny did not want to be seen in that chamber if the police turned up. That surely wouldn't end well. Not well at all. He had to at least appear to Quetzal as if he believed he was alone, however futile that seemed.

One minute, he thought. *Then I'll go.*

A long, agonising minute passed. Kenny was afraid,

both of wasting time, and the imminent arrival of the uniformed police. So, with no instructions forthcoming, and with no better idea than to forge on into the unknown darkness, that's exactly what he did.

After a deep breath to still his frayed nerves, Kenny resumed his headlong race beneath a forgotten, ancient pyramid in the heart of the central desert, doubtful he'd ever feel the beloved Mexican sun on his face again.

Chapter Forty-One

Danny suddenly froze.

His mind had been fully focused on his steps along the dingy passageway, but now an image so powerful flashed into his mind it stopped him in his tracks. The view he saw was of the Old Rectory, the place where, until a couple of days ago, he had last been seen by his brother. He had entered the dilapidated old building a few minutes before Hiram and had found an excellent hiding space upstairs. He'd scrambled onto an ancient piano, and reached up, hauling himself into the rafters of what he believed to be a study, though it was so dark he couldn't be sure. He had watched on as Kane came into the room looking for him, and had somehow managed to remain silent, though he wanted to shout out and make his brother jump. He nearly sneezed too, the dust almost proving too much. But he stayed silent, and Hiram left the room, calling out for Danny, distress evident in his frantic cries.

Danny had considered ending his game then, but he decided to sit it out a while longer, enjoying the rare feeling of control he had over his brother. Ten minutes later, Hiram returned again, desperately searching behind curtains and in cupboards, and he even tried to pull the planks of wood away from the windows to let in more light. But his energy was waning and he no longer had enough strength. His brother stood there below him in that room, hands on his head, his anguish obvious. He cried out again, and then again, and his lip trembled with concern.

Just a few feet above his head, Danny watched on.

And it was his brother's face he saw now. It wore a look of both guilt and fear; guilt because he had cajoled Danny into going there with him in the first place, and fear, because despite having searched every room in the entire building twice now, there was simply no trace of his little brother, and he had naturally started to fear the worst. Danny was missing, and Hiram knew it was all his fault.

It was then, Danny now knew for sure, that Hiram ran from the abandoned mansion and rushed to raise the alarm that his brother was missing. Danny didn't know that at the time. He thought Hiram had given up. Too easily, he had just given up. Danny had climbed down from the rafters and made his way swiftly outside, the sudden blast of daylight causing him to squint his eyes against the glare. He thought of racing after Hiram, telling him it was a joke, and asking why he had stopped looking. He also considered racing home, trying to beat his brother back. That would have been fun.

But he didn't. He somehow couldn't. Instead, he edged away from the building and scoped out a tree into which he could easily climb and hide. If Hiram *did* come back, and if he brought his family with him and even the police, now Danny didn't want to be found. In just a few seconds he had found the perfect tree, and hauling his backpack with him, with his coat and a bottle of water inside, as well as an uneaten sandwich from lunch, he climbed that tree and settled in to wait.

Less than half an hour later Hiram did return, and he did bring the police. Before long more than a dozen officers, as well as Hiram, their father and a variety of other family members, were tearing through that old house in a desperate search for Danny. Hiram told him that the police had ripped off doors and cleared away all the boards from the windows. They tore down curtains and flipped over beds. They searched all the outhouses and even down in the multiple cellars. A handful of officers searched all throughout the grounds of the Old Rectory; Danny recalled one even passing directly beneath the tree he was hiding in.

Yet, despite looking everywhere throughout the house and around the sprawling grounds, not a single person looked up into the trees. Not a single one. Danny remained there until the following morning, when, just before dawn, he climbed down from his perch, and stole off into the darkness. After a few days of walking southwest, travelling only after darkness had fallen and sticking to minor roads and country lanes, he found himself in the east end of London, tired, penniless… and free.

Danny had regretted that decision every minute of every day of his life ever since.

In their reunion at Kenny's Place, Hiram told Danny he had never given up on him, never once stopped looking for his brother. Every day he returned to the Old Rectory, scouring every room, even though the police had closed the building off as a crime scene. He would be stopped at the police cordon, but Hiram explained that when they saw him, saw the look in his eyes, the haunted expression of someone who had lost everything—and knowing there was no danger inside—they would let him through, sometimes even accompanying him, despite knowing there was nothing or no one to be found inside those decaying old walls.

No, Danny knew Hiram had never given up on him.

So, now, and with his own guilt powering him on, and a burning desire to make up for three decades of wrongdoing, Danny Kane surged on deeper into the dark tunnels, desperate to do his part, and desperate to help his brother rescue those girls from the clutches of a murderous madman.

Chapter Forty-Two

Ridley clambered up another couple of the giant stone steps, deliberately ascending slowly in order to allow time to compose herself and become familiar with the bizarre surroundings. She would comply with the madman's demands, at least for now. But as soon as a moment presented itself to take him down, she would be ready.

She scaled another step. Now Ridley was about halfway to the platform at the summit of the pyramid, she paused and looked around. Despite the harrowing situation, Ridley could not help but be amazed by the structure. Like Kane, Ridley had always been in awe of the wondrous things humans were capable of creating. Just to have the imagination to envisage such a place was mind-blowing, but then possessing the creative genius and engineering abilities to bring those ideas to life was a constant source of wonder for them both. Her mind flicked back to their recent visit to Peru. That trip had ended up with a terrible tragedy, and was a journey that had changed many lives forever, and ended several. Yet it had started out with the usual wonder and excitement most of her ventures did. The architecture they'd witnessed in Cuzco... the megalithic structures of the Incas... the magnificence of the towering Andes mountains...

Jesus, why do power-hungry men always have to fuck everything up....?

Ridley took another couple of long, deep breaths and returned her focus to the stone beneath her feet. She then looked up to the top of the structure. Still the madman had not revealed himself. *Where is he? Is he even here? Are we all being set up remotely?*

She didn't really believe that. From what she could tell, there was a lot of ego involved in all of this. Ridley was sure he was here in person, almost certainly watching her right now from the shadows, or at least on a screen nearby. He was the architect of this terrible drama, the puppetmaster, and they the pawns, and Ridley knew he would want to witness it all with his own eyes. Yes, she was sure of it. He would reveal himself soon. When he did, Ridley would make him suffer.

Then suddenly she heard pounding footsteps below, and she turned and saw Kenny skidding to a stop after emerging from the same tunnel she and Kane had entered the chamber from. He had made it, and in his hands he clutched what Ridley assumed to be the artefact the madman had demanded they bring him.

Well done, Vicki, she thought, *and well done Kenny. But now what?*

Chapter Forty-Three

Kenny juddered to a halt as he at last emerged into what he guessed was the main central chamber beneath the vast pyramid. His eyes flitted between what must have been dozens of flaming torches that cast a wildly flickering show of shadow and light across the cavernous space. The ethereal ambiance was beautiful, almost magical... that was, had it not been for the majestic yet truly horrifying sight at the centre of that chamber.

Rising from the stone floor was a stepped pyramid within a pyramid, this one a miniature replica of El Castillo, the Temple of Kukulkan at Chichen Itza he'd once visited.

The intricately carved steps rose towards the stone ceiling, at least fifty-feet high, and was a spectacular work of ancient architecture, hewn by men from the sheer bedrock beneath.

As beautiful and impressive as it was, Kenny's moment of awe didn't last long. Glancing around, Kenny's wonderment soon turned to horror. First he spotted Ridley. They shared fleeting glances, then Kenny continued scanning left.

What he saw turned his stomach. One after another, his gaze fell upon a series of young girls, almost mirror images of the sacrificial victims they'd found slaughtered back in the tunnels.

He counted ten girls in this chamber... he couldn't tell if they were alive or not, as they were all motionless. At least they still had their heads. *For now...*

Next he spotted some kind of pit. He looked back at Ridley, whose gaze was on him. *Hiram?* he mouthed, motioning towards the pit with his head, asking silently if Kane was in there.

Ridley seemed to understand and nodded, her face grave.

Well, shit! Kenny nodded back, then his gaze drifted to the top of the internal pyramid. Stood tall in the centre of the flat summit was Quetzal, his silhouetted figure holding still, but somehow appearing to dance wildly beneath the crazed flicker of the torch lights.

"Come to the top," came an echoing voice, though the voice didn't come directly from the figure atop the pyramid; rather, it was being piped in from some hidden sound system. The voice was calm yet commanding, and Kenny sensed he had no option but to obey the order.

Kenny kept his eyes on the figure at the top of the pyramid. There he was. The madman. The architect of this horrendous spectacle. The murderer of two little girls. It was all he could do to stop himself tearing up those steps and attacking the man where he stood. Yet despite his innate instincts demanding he go now and kill him where he stood, Kenny knew it was a bad idea. The madman was too confident, too sure of himself not to have everything planned out, and one false move, Kenny suspected, could sign all their death warrants. So he waited a moment, letting his emotions, and the need to take action, play itself out. It was the hardest waiting he had ever done, but he had to get control of himself.

Still, Kenny feared the worst. Waiting was all he could do just to give the desperate girls strapped to their stone plinths a fighting chance to survive… if they weren't already dead.

And if he himself was to die at the hands of the lunatic above, Kenny would at least die knowing he had done what he could to help, and that he was the man to help finally reunite the long-lost Kane brothers. In death, Kenny would always be proud of that decision he'd made just a couple of weeks previous.

He approached the stone-carved steps, the artefact clutched tightly in his left hand as he used his right to steady himself, then he clambered up the first of the twenty or thirty high, steep steps.

"That is good… keep climbing," boomed the tinny voice. Kenny thought he was close enough now it might have been Quetzal's actual voice he could hear, although muffled beneath the grotesque mask and feathered headdress.

"Keep coming."

Kenny did. He climbed one step after another, an ever-growing sense of doom with every negotiated step threatening to unhinge him.

"Good. Yessss… Bring it to me."

Quetzal's eyes glared, lids open to their extremes, focused only on one thing… the item clutched in the man's hand. Quetzal didn't know the bringer's name. He did not care.

The Feathered Serpent

Names were just that. Names. Mere words, with little or no meaning to those labelled by them.

That was, except him. Quetzal. Quetzalcoatl. Of course, it wasn't his given name. He hadn't gone by a given name for a long time, at least in his own mind. Humberto Palomares. The name was dead. As was the persona.

The irony was that by blood he belonged to a long lineage of important and culturally historical people that, had anyone ever believed him, and had he ever been able to prove it, none of this would ever had to have happened. Zapata. Such a simple, nice word, yet an evocative name. The fact that the word was now as synonymous with simple Mexican shoes as it was to the hero of the revolution only rubbed salt into Quetzal's deep emotional wounds.

So he had assumed the moniker of Quetzal. God of wind and wisdom. Bringer of doom. Deliverer of chaos. And now... sacrificer of virgins.

First was the small matter of the ceremonial knife, and his duty of dispatching the delivery boy.

Kenny paused on the penultimate stone level, more than reluctant to take the final step. He stood there and looked about the platform. It measured roughly ten feet by ten feet. At its centre sat another of those grotesquely carved stone plinths, identical almost to the one on which the poor girl had lost both her head and her heart.

"Son of a—" Kenny began, but was cut off by that voice again, this time in person. And from less than two yards away. He glanced quickly to his right, and recoiled so sharply he almost lost a fight with gravity and plummeted down those steps. At just five-feet-nine, Kenny's low centre of gravity, that had served him well on the ice rinks of

Ontario in his youth, stayed his fall. Recovered, he now looked right into the face of a monster.

From behind the elaborate mask of Quetzal, the madman looked down at Kenny. "Perfect," Kenny heard the creature say. "Please... one more step." Then he added, "Miss Ridley, please wait there."

Despite every last instinct in Kenny's mind and in his body now pleading with him *not* to attack, nut to turn and flee and run all the way back to Windsor, almost automatically he took that last step, almost certain now that this platform was soon to be the scene of his brutal, grisly death.

Chapter Forty-Four

"Hand it over!" Quetzal demanded, though even to his own ears his voice remained impossibly calm. Somehow unnatural. He felt as if he was now in a kind of zone, a trance, as if some inner voice was guiding both his words and his actions. Whatever it was, whatever doubts and indecisions he might have felt previously up until this point, they had long since passed. He no longer had a single such doubt about what he had to do, and even less about his ability to do it.

Kenny took a tentative step forward. Quetzal matched it, and the pair were now only a yard apart. Quetzal towered over him, the tall, feathered headdress only enhancing the difference in size. If Kenny hadn't known a mere mortal hid behind that costume, and if he believed in monsters, then he would have believed a real monster stood there before him.

Quetzal reached both hands forward. "Please?"

Kenny flinched. He knew what he held in his hand was a priceless artefact from an ancient time… a deadly weapon with a unique and specific purpose. For a fraction of a second Kenny considered wielding that weapon against the human monster before him. But just then, Quetzal reached behind his back and pulled out a huge sword, and before Kenny could react he had thrust its tip at Kenny's windpipe.

Kenny opened his eyes. He had seen the flash of the blade, dazzling beneath the torchlights, arcing towards his head, and had instinctively closed his eyes. Now he'd opened them, for a fleeting moment he wondered if he was dead. He felt no pain, and the scene hadn't changed. Then he felt the tip of the blade jabbing into his throat, and although he wasn't in fact dead, he knew for sure he soon would be.

"What, did you think I was going to kill you? So soon?"

Kenny didn't speak. He couldn't; the pressure of the blade on his trachea prevented him from moving any part of his body, let alone his mouth. And what could he have said, anyway? Please don't kill me? He had seen exactly what this man was capable of, and knew without doubt he could kill him if he so chose to. Kenny didn't want to die. He had a lot of good years left ahead of him, and he wanted so much to see his nieces grow up into the kind and beautiful young women he knew they would be. And of course there were the terrified girls all around them now. He didn't want to die; more than that, he had to help save these girls.

He remained perfectly still, waiting for a moment of distraction, something that might give him even the slightest of opportunities to take out this jumped up, sicko prick before him.

"I have to thank you, Mister…?"

Kenny remained silent.

"Come now, what is your name? Tell me, quick, and then I can thank you properly." And with that, Quetzal laughed.

"Kenny Peters. And what about you? Seems unfair that I tell you my name, but I still don't know yours."

The madman's laughter died. "My name is Quetzal, and you shall cower before my might."

Kenny steeled his will and rolled his eyes. "Oh man, and here I was thinking your name was Humberto Palomares. A professor, no less. I guess Quetzal is a little catchier, though I doubt you'll ever be taken seriously again in academic circles—or any other circles, come to that—with a stupid fucking name like that."

"Enough!" Quetzal roared.

Kenny winced, wondering if he had gone too far in goading the madman. Despite his apparent bravado, Kenny was terrified.

"Well, Kenny Peters, I thank you for bringing this object to me. Now, if you would just hand it to me, then you will have done your duty and I will have what is so rightfully mine. Please?" The madman's voice dripped with sarcasm.

Kenny raised his arms slowly, and offered the package to the lunatic, who took it with as much care as if he were handling a newborn baby. Kenny kept his eyes focused on the mask, trying to make out the man's eyes behind it. And... he could. He saw those eyes, glistening through the wide slots in the mask, and in them he saw something almost like relief. Yes, he was sure of it now. There was relief, and if Kenny wasn't mistaken, there was genuine emotion, like a parent being reunited with a missing child, or a kid with their pet dog. It gave Kenny a brief moment of hope. *If he really has got what he wanted,* he thought, *maybe this will all end quietly. Maybe he'll set the girls free.*

That was more than Kenny could possibly hope for, and he was old, ugly and wise enough to know that good things rarely happened to good people. *What am I thinking? There's no way he'll let any of us out of here alive.*

Kenny had to do something. And he had to do it now.

Without taking his eyes off the deranged monster before him, Kenny flexed his fingers and wrists. He was a little out of shape, and was the first to admit it. Yet Kenny was a robust man, with strong shoulders and a powerful grip. If he could take the man by surprise, and get close enough to clutch him in a bear hug, he felt sure he couldn't be stabbed or worse, slashed with the sword/club-type weapon.

All about the timing…

He remained stock still, risking a glance down at Ridley, who stood halfway up the steps. He didn't know Kane's whereabouts, but guessed he was somehow out of commission. *If I could just incapacitate this son of a bitch then I can help Kane, and help lead the girls to safety and back to their families. Shit, I might even be a hero,* he thought.

All about the timing…

He glanced back at the psycho and peered again into those eyes. There was a change there now, a new expression in them to replace the emotional one from just moments ago.

What Kenny saw now was amusement.

The monster took a step back now as if anticipating Kenny's thoughts. "You should know this entire place is rigged with explosives. I have placed more than one-hundred devices at different structural points across the complex, all set to explode at the simple click of…"—he pulled from his pocket a small device with several buttons and blinking lights over its surface—"... of this detonator. With just a couple of clicks, this entire structure will be destroyed, and everyone inside will be destroyed with it. Of course, that would include me, but also you. So, if you were to attack me now you know what will happen. I suggest you do not." Quetzal stared down at Kenny, almost as if daring him to attack him. To do something. Kenny didn't. At least, not yet. He would not be the one responsible for killing these girls. He would wait.

"That is what I thought. You are sensible. But before the main event, there is something I need to do. If you would be so kind as to step over this way and take a seat on the stone chacmool here?"

Kenny felt the blood drain from his face. He knew without doubt what that meant. Quetzal would kill him. Yet, he somehow kept his composure and went along with the demands. He took a few steps towards the grotesque looking plinth, then paused, glancing down again at Ridley, who caught his gaze. She shook her head very slightly, her eyes wide, pleading, and it was obvious what she meant. *Do NOT sit down on that thing.* But what could Kenny do? The psycho told him he had the entire place wired; Kenny had to believe that was true. If he attacked him now, he risked the man setting off those explosives and killing them all. The fact Quetzal would die too would not be nearly enough compensation.

Son of a... What the hell should I do?

Then Kenny Peters had an idea.

Chapter Forty-Five

Danny Kane scrambled along a narrow stone corridor, almost blindly following the distant muffled sounds coming from far ahead in the cloying darkness. He was sweating profusely in the humidity of the tunnel and his shirt clung to his skin. There was no way of knowing in which direction he was heading, but as long as the passage continued, he had to believe it would eventually lead him to the right place, wherever the hell that was.

One thing he knew for certain was that danger awaited him ahead, and maybe lurked around every twisting corner he took. Now was not the time for fear, and he hustled on as fast as the claustrophobia-inducing passage and inky blackness would allow. He cursed himself now for not charging his phone in the bar at Kenny's... the phone's torch would have been a great help, and comfort, right now. He couldn't risk using the torch and draining his battery. The last time he checked he only had five percent. Besides, who knew what else shared these ancient tunnels with him... rats, tarantulas, snakes... probably all of them, and not one of them made his journey through the subterranean labyrinth any more pleasant. And did he really want to see them? *Sometimes*, he mused, as the saying went, *ignorance really is bliss*.

Danny focused on the girls who needed their help. He pushed on for what seemed like hours but was in fact only minutes, and paused. Was he imagining it? Was that a light ahead? He stayed still for a moment, unsure if his mind and eyes were imagining it. They were not. Far ahead, though it was almost impossible to tell how far in the dark confines of the passage, the faint flicker of a light illuminated the walls of the tunnel. That was both good and bad, he realised. Good, because now he could at least see where he was going and what other dangers lurked there with him. Bad, because although he knew he had to face up to whatever lay ahead at some point if he was to help, it meant he was probably getting close. He exhaled slowly, then sucked in a long and fortifying breath. He repeated the process, stealing himself for whatever was to come, and then he edged on into untold dangers, each stride taking him a yard closer either to helping those girls, or a yard closer to his own violent end.

Only time will tell, Danny knew, but time was not on his or anyone's side.

He reached the source of the light, a flaming torch attached to the wall. He thought about grabbing it, but spotted another one further along the passage and continued his progress towards it. He reached that one in a just a few seconds, and then another, until finally he emerged onto a narrow ledge, almost as if it were some kind of viewing platform.

What he saw next defied belief.

Standing atop an incredible internal pyramid was a hideously dressed character. On the giant's head was a feathered headdress, and covering his face was a mask that was in itself frightening. Coupled with the scene and the outfit and the... the fact he wielded a glimmering blade... it was truly the stuff of nightmares. Then the tableau took a whole new turn for the worse. Standing next to the madman was his friend, Kenny, and it looked for all the world as if Quetzal was about to kill him.

Danny hurriedly glanced around the vast chamber, and soon saw all the girls strapped to stone plinths, just like the ones he'd had seen on the news. Then he spotted Ridley; *Hiram must be nearby.* Yet, he couldn't spot him anywhere. *Is he hiding? Waiting for the right moment to make his move?*

Is he... is he dead?

Danny would not believe Hiram didn't have the better of this guy, whoever the hell he was, and quickly filed that notion under *most ridiculous thought of the day*.

So where the hell is he?

Danny didn't have time to wait for Hiram. He had to do something. And now.

Chapter Forty-Six

There had been very few times in Hiram Kane's life when he had felt totally helpless. Very few. At least as an adult. When Danny went missing at the Old Rec' that day when they were kids, he'd felt helpless then. Most of the time, through good sense, he managed to retain some form of control, no matter the situation or how high the odds were stacked against him.

Not now. Now, he was helpless, and it infuriated him. He had no real choice when Quetzal demanded he jumped down into the pit. He had known he was giving up any advantage he might have had, and he'd also known that in a way he was abandoning Ridley, not to mention the girls. But jumping into the pit was a better, safer choice than not doing it. The girls were the priority, not Kane's life. Definitely not his ego. With Ridley, he knew that as long as she remained standing, the girls definitely still had a chance.

Yet... he couldn't just stand there and do nothing. Accept defeat. Kane scanned the sheer walls of the man-made pit, its smooth stone interior glinting under the torch light far above. There were a few cracks, likely caused by residual water or humidity so far underground, but none seemed deep or wide enough for him to even wedge his fingers into. It was about fifteen feet to the lip of the pit. Just out of reach, tantalisingly close if he jumped. He had already made a couple of valiant attempts to leap and grab the edge, but despite standing at a fraction over six foot himself and although he remained in great physical shape —though the wrong side of forty—Kane simply couldn't reach.

With his teeth gritted and jowls clenched, Kane paced the pit... *more of a cell, really,* he thought, and grimaced. *What the hell can I do?*

Kane examined the smooth walls of the pit once more. If those tiny cracks in the walls of the pit were all he had, then they would have to do. Kane took a few slow, deep breaths. The only chance he had of climbing out of this prison was if he could centre himself and achieve a state of utter calm. Difficult under the circumstances, but not impossible.

Kane reached out and touched the wall in front of him, his fingertips brushing the stone. He closed his eyes and breathed deep.

Slowly, ever so slowly, Kane stepped closer to the rock wall, raising his arms and running his fingers up the surface. He could feel them now, the tiny cracks in the rock. *So small... so thin.*

His right hand, almost working under its own power, stopped at the crack he felt might afford a chance. A fraction bigger than the others, Kane worked his fingertips into the gap in the stone. Minute rock particles drifted out and showered the ground.

He had it, just enough of a grip to keep himself pinned against the wall.

Kane repeated the process with his left hand, his fingertips searching and searching until they found another, deeper crack in the rockface.

A wave of doubt suddenly filled Kane's head and chest. *What am I thinking? This is impossible.* Even if he could manage this climb, that madman up there would spot him as soon as he crawled out of the pit. Then that monster would kill him, or maybe murder Ridley.

Kane shook his head to dispel the thoughts. Not only were those young girls, including Rosa, in terrible danger up there, but so was Ridley. And Kane was helpless down here.

He had to keep up his attempt to escape, even if it was an impossible task.

With his feet still on the ground, Kane tested his grip in the rockface, lifting himself up a couple of inches. It was precarious, but if he could get some grip with his feet, then he could begin climbing.

Kane raised his left foot, sliding it up the rock wall. The edge of his boot snagged on something. He squirmed his boot into it until he felt he had some purchase. His muscles trembling from the exertion, Kane hauled himself up another few inches, head craned back as he searched for more handholds.

There...

To get to it he would have to let go with his left hand and reach up, stretching to grab hold. Kane wasn't sure he could support his weight with just one fingertip hold and one foot hold. *What other choice do I have?*

Kane took a couple of slow, deep breaths. Then, in one swift movement, he reached up and shoved his fingers into the tiny split in the rock face. At the same time, he hugged the wall as if it was Ridley.

For a moment he thought he had lost it, and that he was about to plunge to the ground. But no, miraculously he managed to cling to the wall, like a huge spider. His fingers stung, and though he didn't look, he was sure they were bleeding. He ignored the pain.

Carry on like this, pal, and you're guaranteed the next Spider-Man movie, he mused, grinning inwardly, a grimace its external counterpart.

Neck arched back, searching for those tiny cracks in the rock, Kane took another long inhale and hauled himself higher. Now he had no choice but to let go of his fingertip hold with his right hand. *Where's the next one?*

Kane let go, and ran his hand up the wall, fingers searching for fissures in the smooth rock.

His foot slipped out of its tiny foothold. Kane gasped as he was left hanging by one hand. His feet scrabbled across the rockface as he searched for a foothold. His right hand suddenly found what it was hunting. Fingers dug deep into the tiny crack in the rock, causing him to wince in pain.

His right foot found a shallow recess to support him. Kane hugged the wall, panting. He looked up and spotted several blood smears glimmering on the rock. The top of the pit was now only a few feet away. If he could find one more handhold and haul himself up, he could grab the edge of the pit and maybe pull himself out.

Kane searched the sheer wall, eyes probing for just one more split in the rock.

Yes… there!

It was the biggest yet. All he had to do was reach up with his left hand, haul himself up and then grab for the edge of the pit with his right hand.

Then he would be out. He just had to hope Quetzal was distracted, not noticing Kane escaping. If he could escape the pit and make a dash for a shadowy corner without being seen, he would have an advantage for the first time since this nightmare began.

Kane breathed slow and steady, readying himself for the final, punishing exertion.

He let go of his handhold and reached up with a grunt, fingers finding the split in the rock above him and digging in for purchase.

Without pausing, he continued the movement, pulling himself higher, reaching out for the edge of the pit with his right hand.

His hand smacked against the cavern's floor above him. Then the fingertip hold he had with his left hand began crumbling.

"No!" Kane huffed through gritted teeth. "No!"

The hold gave way and Kane dropped back into the pit, smashing into the ground on his back, and knocking the wind from his lungs.

A black despair washed over Kane, suffocating him with the realisation that he was trapped down there. He had tried climbing out, and he had failed. He could see no other route out. The reality finally sank in that the only way he was getting out was if Quetzal released him.

Kane sat up and brushed rock dust off himself. He looked up at the pit opening above him.

The worst part was, he didn't know what was going on up there. He could hear what Quetzal was saying, as he spoke loud and clearly, his voice carrying across the echoing chamber with the help of the hidden speakers. But as for Kenny and Ridley, well their status eluded him, and it was driving him mad. He couldn't even see anything other than what was directly above him; the flickering torch-lit shadows playing across the stone ceiling high above.

He cast his eyes about the floor of the pit, desperate for some spark of inspiration, even a weapon of some kind. He saw nothing, other than a few small rocks that had plummeted into the pit with him just moments ago, chips of the natural stone that now kept him prisoner. *Rocks?* He reached down and grabbed the biggest one he saw. It was modest, about the size and weight of a cricket ball, he realised.

Hmm. He tossed it in the air and caught it a couple of times, measuring the feel of the rock and testing its potential in his palm. He noticed his fingerprints, marking the rock in blood. Kane had a strong arm, despite a dislocated shoulder in his twenties that still gave him grief if he laid on it too long, especially on cold nights. But his throwing action remained solid, and given a target, he'd have a damn good go at hitting it.

Now I just need a target…

Chapter Forty-Seven

Kenny resumed his slow shuffle towards the chacmool. He figured he had just one chance to get this right. If he failed, he would be dead, and he would no longer have to worry. *But the girls...*

He reached the stone plinth and turned to face his adversary. He locked eyes with Quetzal for a long beat, and with a hint of a forced grin, he sat down. The stone was cool to the touch, which surprised him, but it felt good. His hands were clammy with sweat, and he needed them dry. He'd been a quarterback on his college football team, and he would tell anyone who asked he had the best arm in all Ontario. Perhaps that was an exaggeration, but his arm was indeed good, and his throws were once as accurate as they were powerful.

Kenny had come to understand something in the last couple of minutes. No matter what he did, he didn't think he could possibly make it out of the pyramid alive. Even if he successfully attacked Quetzal, knocked the weapon away, then he could still be stabbed with the knife. If he managed to evade the sword *and* the knife, it meant there was some distance between them, and Quetzal would then be free to detonate the explosives, surely killing them all. And if none of those things happened, and he missed with his attack completely, then the last thing he would ever see would be the madman standing over his decapitated head, likely with a twisted smile on his face.

So, Kenny understood that his death was imminent, and it both terrified him and, to his surprise, it stilled his nerves. He was actually calm. Kenny wasn't exactly an everyday church-goer, but he was raised Catholic, and he believed he was in good standing with God. He was well read up on the martyrs, Kenny's particular favourite being the second-century Justin Martyr. He took a breath, then said so quietly Quetzal had to lean closer to hear him, "... and we believe that those who live wickedly and do not repent are punished in everlasting fire."

"Did you... say something to me?"

Kenny nodded. "I said, '... and we believe that those who live wickedly and do not repent are punished in everlasting fire.' It's a quote by a martyr, a man executed for doing the right thing."

Kenny couldn't be sure, but he sensed the monster smile beneath his mask.

Quetzal said, "And do you think that is what I will do to you? Execute you?"

"It certainly looks that way from where I'm sitting, so why don't you just get on with it?" His voice was calm, but his heart now hammered so powerfully he was sure Quetzal could hear it.

"Well, I admit you are right. I have to practice, to get the technique right for—" He cut himself off, apparently realising his error.

"For what?" Kenny demanded. "Get your technique right for what?" Then with crystal clarity, Kenny suddenly realised what Quetzal had planned all along. He meant to kill Ridley. It was likely the reason he'd forced Kane into the pit he'd spotted.

Is he going to make Hiram trade Alex's life to save the girls?

Son of a… The mad bastard's going to kill Alex, and make Hiram watch.

Goddammit!

Chapter Forty-Eight

Danny scanned the scene, desperately seeking out his brother.

"Where the hell are you?" he whispered.

A buzzing sensation against his hip alerted him to a message on his phone. *How's that possible? Surely there's no signal down here.* In the depths of the earth below a massive stone pyramid, he was in shock.

Danny snatched the phone from his pocket and, shielding it with a cupped hand so as not to betray his presence with the glowing screen, he checked the message.

system_axg34^xos available
What the hell does that mean?

Danny noticed his battery was now down to two percent. Soon he would have no way of contacting the outside world.

Deciding he was wasting time, he shoved the phone away. *Wait a minute...*

From his hiding place, Danny looked up and out, scouring the cavern's ceiling for anything out of place. He

The Feathered Serpent

spotted it immediately; a small video camera, just visible in the gloom. He continued his search, and found another.

Of course... it has to be! The cameras weren't wired up, at least not that Danny could see, which meant they had to be communicating with the server via a Wi-Fi stream.

That's what *system_axg34^xos* was.

Danny grabbed his mobile and went into the settings. He was right. *system_axg34^xos* was already connected, and he had a Wi-Fi signal.

The battery was now down to one percent. If he was going to make a phone call, he had to do it now. Danny pulled up Hiram's recently added contact details. He thumbed the green connect button, praying his brother had his phone switched on and was also connected to the Wi-Fi signal.

One ring. Two rings...

Come on, Hiram, answer it!

Three rings. Four.

"Danny?"

"Hiram!"

"Where are you? How'd you—"

"No time for any of that... phone's about to die. Where are you?"

"I'm in a chamber beneath the pyramid."

"Yeah? So am I, but I don't see you."

"That's because I'm in the p—"

The phone died.

Danny looked at it in disbelief. Just one more second, that was all he needed. Now his phone was useless.

That's because I'm in the p— What did that mean?

Danny inhaled, then let it out slowly. He had to do something. He looked out across the chamber. Then he spotted the pit, and somehow he knew that's where his brother was. *That's because I'm in the p—* The pit.

"Shit!" *What the hell are we going to do now?*

Looking about the stony platform he now crouched on, Danny saw no obvious way down, not whilst remaining hidden. He recalled the long tunnel that had led him to his current position, and didn't remember any sign of an alternative route. No side passages. No doorways. He could either go all the way back and hope to find another way into the chamber, or take a chance and scramble and jump down into the open space below him. He felt sure he would be seen by the madman; the consequences of that didn't bear thinking about. Time was running out. It looked for all the world as if Kenny was about to be murdered, and Danny simply could not stand by and let that happen, despite what his actions might mean for the others. Time was up. He had to move, and now.

Kenny knew he had seconds left to do something. Seconds left to live. If he didn't do something right now he would die, and likely so would everyone else. He took a couple of rapid breaths and made his decision.

"Now or never, Peters," he whispered, and Kenny made his move. He sensed Quetzal behind him and waited a couple of beats longer until the man stood just a yard away. But when he saw a slow, shadowy movement arc across the floor in front of him, he knew it was the blade being raised, and he launched himself up and backwards, slamming into Quetzal's midriff. It took the monster by surprise and he faltered, the blow knocking him sideways and the blade swinging harmlessly past Kenny's head. They tumbled over, and from the corner of his eye Kenny saw the detonating device spill onto the floor, the red digital timer now glowing bright in the gloom. To his horror, the timer was counting down. *No!* He squinted hard, making sure he was reading it correctly.

02:59. He was. 02:58. 02:57. *Son of a…*

Kenny scrambled to his feet and dived for the timer. He had to stop it somehow, destroy it if he could, but as he reached for it he heard a wild roar of frustration as the macuahuitl blade came slicing down onto his wrist, his hand falling uselessly to the ground beside him.

Strangely, it didn't hurt, and Kenny looked on in awe as arcs of crimson blood spurted from his wrist, soon pooling all around him. He balanced himself on his knees and looked up at the monster before him. He tried to stand but couldn't, and resigned himself to his fate.

If I could just…

"I admire your bravery. But you cannot defeat me. I am Quetzal. A God. You are no match for me." Quetzal glanced down at Ridley, who stared back at him.

Ridley fought with every inch of her will power to stay where she was. She knew rushing at Quetzal now meant Kenny's certain death, and she was too far away to reach him before he finished Kenny off and snagged the detonator from the floor. She forced herself to wait, but she locked eyes with the monster through his mask and held them, daring him to come for her.

Out of sight, Danny seized his moment. He was powerless to help Kenny now, and his heart broke for his friend, clearly seconds from being slaughtered. But he saw his chance to enter the chamber unseen, and took it. He scrambled over the ledge and swung his legs down, reaching as far towards the ground as he could.

It was a big drop—about fifteen feet—but he had no choice. He said a silent prayer that he wouldn't break an ankle, and let himself fall, landing on the unforgiving stone below with a heavy thud. He remained still for a second, hoping he'd entered the chamber unnoticed, and mentally appraised his body for injuries. *Nothing broken. Good.* But he knew he'd sprained an ankle.

Could be worse, he thought, and crouched on one knee, ready to make a beeline towards the pit. If he could get his brother out of his prison, there was still a chance they could end this madness.

Kenny was losing so much blood that he wilted a little, and only his desire to do something good in the last seconds of his life kept him upright at all.

02:35. 02:34.

Images of his nieces flitted in his mind, and it gave him a last burst of energy.

Quetzal believed the man was just seconds from death, and looked down at him impassively. He would finish him off in a few seconds, but he was in awe at the amount of blood flowing from the severed limb. Absentmindedly he thought of the two girls he had already slain, and though there had been lots of blood then too, it was nothing compared to what he saw now. Then his latest victim fell forward, his body prone on the floor.

Kenny knew he had one last chance. He let himself fall forward, as if unconscious, strategically falling towards the detonator with his intact arm stretched out before him. The device was just two feet from his hand now. His good hand. His throwing hand. He took a couple of long shallow breaths; the last, he knew, of his life.

02:11.

In a sudden flurry of activity, Kenny crawled to his knees, snagged up the detonator in his good hand and swivelled, launching the device through the air towards the pit, praying to God that it survived the landing, and as he saw it spiralling through the air, the macuahuitl swung through the air too, catching Kenny clean in the throat and killing him before he even hit the floor.

Chapter Forty-Nine

Kane heard the commotion above but he couldn't see anything, though he feared the worst.

He stood there, frustration threatening to get the better of him, when he heard the unmistakable sound of steel crashing against stone, and he immediately guessed—somehow, he knew—someone had been killed by a sword. He took in a long, deep breath, when something glinted in the air above him, and he had to dodge sharply to his right to avoid the arcing projectile that thudded into the hard rock floor.

"What the...?"

Kane shook off his surprise and darted over to what appeared to be some kind of detonator, alarmed to see it counting down towards what he assumed would be bad news for everyone.

02:10.

"Two minutes ten seconds? Until what? Fucking coward has rigged the place to blow up?"

02:07.

Kane twisted the small device in his hands, searching frantically for a way of arresting the countdown, but there was nothing obvious. He sucked air in through his teeth, that feeling of helplessness once more weighty around his shoulders.

"Come on! Give me something to work with here, please?" he said to no one. At least, he thought it was to no one.

"What do you have in mind?"

Kane's eyes shot upwards. He knew that voice.

"Danny? "How the hell did you manage to get over here? "

"No time for that... let's get you out of there and stop this madness."

"What about this? It's a detonator I think... I'm sure... it's counting down to what must be something terrible. It says... one minute forty-five seconds left."

"Shit. Not good." That was an understatement, and despite the dire situation, both Kane brothers grinned.

Ridley had just watched Quetzal murder an innocent man, and she still wasn't sure how she'd managed to watch on without reacting. She knew it was wrong, but Ridley also knew that if she'd rushed to help she may have made things worse for the others. That old saying sprang to mind; what was it... *sacrifice the one for the good of the many? Jesus!* At least Kenny had dispossessed the deranged monster of the detonator; she had watched on as it arced over her head and disappeared right into the pit.

She was breathing hard now, torn between attacking the bastard or playing along with his scheme until the right moment arrived to take him out. She looked up, and saw the psycho watching her. He opened his arms wide now, as if to show he still retained all the power, and then he laughed. It was a loud, booming laugh, which smacked of both ego and insanity. Quetzal hadn't missed what Kenny had done, and had turned in time to see where the detonator had sailed to.

"That was a good idea, what your friend did," he called down to her. "But do you think I'm stupid enough not to have thought of every possible scenario?" He reached into a flap of his costume and pulled out what looked to Ridley like some kind of smartphone. "With a couple of touches on this device, I can cancel that countdown and activate a new one, no problem. In fact, I will do it now." He spoke loud, Ridley suspected for Kane's benefit. "This is not a game. I am in complete control of this situation. I do not want to destroy this ancient temple, nor most of the people inside here with me. I will now stop the countdown."

Danny darted out of view, staying hidden from Quetzal atop the pyramid and searching for something to help Hiram out of the pit. He scrambled behind one of the girls, who lay semi-conscious on her chacmool. For the briefest of moments he considered freeing her, but thought better of it. He thought if he released the girl, she may scream, or become hysterical, and inadvertently alert Quetzal to Danny's presence, and that would be worse for all the other girls. But, the leather straps that held her down against the plinth were exactly what Danny needed to help his brother.

He shuffled quietly along to the next girl, who was either asleep or unconscious… or dead. He didn't want to risk waking her for the same reason as before. He needed to find a girl who was awake, and if he could just make eye contact with her, relay to her the message he was there to help, maybe he could get the straps without causing hysterics.

And there she was, the fourth girl along the base of the pyramid, thankfully out of view of Quetzal, unless he suddenly went to the opposite side of the platform. This girl was a little older than the others, maybe fourteen, and she was awake. More than that, it seemed as if she was calm, and when Danny smiled at her and put his finger to his mouth to indicate silence, she nodded, an air of understanding about the situation clear to Danny.

Within a couple of seconds, Danny had untied the girl, who silently remained in place on the chacmool rather than flee and hide. *Smart girl,* thought Danny, and gently placed his hands on her shoulders.

"Espera aqui, esta bien?" he whispered to her. *Wait here, okay?* She nodded, and Danny quietly but swiftly made his way back to Hiram, well aware there was little time to waste. He would just have to take his chances Quetzal wouldn't see him, and hope Ridley was canny enough to delay whatever it was Quetzal had planned.

Chapter Fifty

Quetzal once more beckoned Ridley to the top of the pyramid, and after a moment's hesitation she slowly scaled the last remaining steps. When she reached the platform, she glanced around her. She couldn't fail to be impressed by the amazing structure within a structure, and she again marvelled at just how brilliant humans could be when they put their minds to it.

But the sub-human standing a few yards away from her now was putting his mind to an altogether different idea, and it sickened her. She still didn't really know—none of them knew for sure—what point Quetzal was trying to make, or what he sought to gain. Surely it wasn't as simple as claiming back the artefact? She understood he might desire it, and that they'd robbed him, rightly or wrongly, of any credit he may have deserved for discovering that amazing haul of artefacts beneath Teotihuacan. But killing people? Little girls? Nothing could justify such atrocities. Nothing!

So what was it driving him to this insanity? Ridley

glared at the creature before her, unable to know what the man looked like beneath the gruesome mask and huge headdress, or what expression he wore on his face. She suspected it was smug. He did indeed seem to hold all the power, and she knew she'd have to tread carefully in whatever she did, in case it sparked more danger for everyone, especially the girls.

"What is it you really want?" she asked, taking a few steps to his right. If she kept him talking, and if she could occasionally take a couple more steps, eventually he would be facing away from the pit. She hoped he didn't see through her ploy. "If you're man enough to tell me, that is?" She held his gaze, or at least the gaze of the mask, and he remained silent behind it for long seconds before he answered.

"I simply want what everyone wants. I do not think it is too much to ask. I should be a famous archaeologist now. A well-respected professor and an internationally renowned figure in the world of discovery..." He paused, and Ridley sensed where this was going.

"Like Hiram?" she suggested, though she already knew the answer. A few more steps, and Quetzal would be blind to the pit.

"Why not? Hiram Kane is no more of an archaeologist than I am. He discovered something famous and important at Vilcabamba. I discovered something famous and just as culturally significant here in Mexico. We are the same. Except we are not, are we?"

"Well, you've got that part right," Ridley said. Even though his face was covered with the mask, she could sense his sudden discomfort.

The madman stiffened, and glared at the Ridley through the mask's eyeholes. "What do you mean?"

"I mean, the big difference between you and Hiram Kane is that Hiram doesn't kidnap defenceless little girls and then proceed to murder them."

Ridley saw his eyes narrow. *If I could just snatch that mask off his head and destroy it...* She had a feeling he would not feel so brave and powerful then, with his face exposed to the world. If she got the chance, and the cameras were running and livestreaming to the world outside, that might even be the end of it.

"You think I want to do this?" Quetzal said. "I grieve over these innocent lives as much as you do; no, more even. And yet I have been forced into this insidious position by the world of academia, by the greed and selfishness of my peers."

"No, you've been driven to this by your own insanity, your selfishness, your greed, no one else's. Get your head out of your arse, and take a good look around. This is on you, and nobody else."

A deep, throaty chuckle erupted from beneath the mask. "Really, Alexandria Ridley, you have no idea of what my true purpose here is."

Ridley hadn't a clue what he was talking about now. If it wasn't about his fame and glory, then what was he up to? Ridley banished the question from her mind. She knew it was important to keep this lunatic talking for as long as possible, that nothing else mattered right now. It would give Kane a chance to somehow escape the pit and help her take this sick bastard down once and for all.

Quetzal paused again. He remained silent for a few seconds before talking a short step towards Ridley. In one hand he held the hefty macuahuitl, still dripping with Kenny's blood. In the other hand he held the small transmitter device, the object Ridley was far more concerned about. She could fight any man with any weapon. But she could not risk triggering a series of explosives that would mean certain death for all the girls, not to mention herself and her man, Kane.

"I have had everything taken from me, Miss Ridley, everything. You know that by now. I am not a bad man, but... well, it is time I had my moment in the spotlight. And what better way to do that than taking everything from someone else?"

"The girls?" asked Ridley.

"It is true, I have taken the lives of two girls, and I would be prepared to take all their lives if need be. But that is just an unfortunate side effect of my real plan. I needed to make sure I got what I wanted. First, my knife, which I found, and by rights is mine. They took it from me, and now I have it back. But that is also just a bonus."

"And the main thing? What's the thing that would make you truly happy?"

Another long pause, and then, "I want two things that belong to Hiram Kane..."

Ridley flinched, and the man took another step towards her.

"The head and heart of his beloved Alexandria."

Chapter Fifty-One

Danny made it back to within a few feet of the pit, apparently unseen. He drew his gaze upwards, relieved to see Quetzal now faced away from him. Danny had only known Alex Ridley for a few days, since she and Kane had arrived in Mexico to find him. But just in that short time, he'd come to know her as incredibly smart, and suspected she had deliberately turned Quetzal away from their activity at the pit.

He quickly and silently got to work. He had claimed almost twenty feet of the strong leather straps that had just a few moments ago tethered a young girl to a rock as if she was nothing more than livestock. Now he would put them to a much better use. He tied one end around his waist, and after another check to ensure Quetzal wasn't watching, he ran to the edge of the pit and threw the other end of the straps to Kane.

"Here, grab this!" he said. "Have you got the detonator? We need to figure out how to stop that countdown."

"It's already stopped," Kane said, and glanced up doubtfully. "I'm not sure that'll be strong enough."

"We have to try… now! Come on, pull yourself up."

Kane snagged the flailing leather straps and wrapped them tightly around his left wrist, leaving his stronger right hand free to pull himself up.

Danny took a tight hold on the straps. He wasn't sure if he'd be strong enough to hold his brother's weight for more than a few seconds, but if Kane could just get half way up, Danny thought he might be able to swing himself up and grab the edge of the pit.

"Ready?" Kane asked.

"Ready. And… pull!" He leaned back, planting his Converse trainers as firmly as he could against the stone floor. Unfortunately, the Aztecs were accomplished stone masons, and had finished the floor stones to a high-sheen polish, making it almost impossible to grip.

Kane pulled himself up a couple of feet, reeling the strap in to his left fist one handful at a time, so it was coiling as he climbed. His feet were planted firmly against the wall, his hiking boots offering solid purchase, despite the smooth walls. Suddenly Kane dropped down a foot, as Danny had slipped towards the pit, but he somehow wedged his foot into a slot between two flooring stones and arrested the slide. Danny took a deep breath and set himself to try again. This time they did better, and using the last of his energy, Danny pulled his brother to within just two feet of the lip of the pit. He held firm, and a moment later, Kane swung his arm up and clutched onto the edge of the pit as if his life depended on it.

"Have you got a good enough hold that I can let go of the strap and grab your shoulders?" asked Danny.

"I think so… only one way to find out. Do it."

Danny immediately dropped the strap, and a second later grabbed his brother under the armpits, and helped hauled Kane over the side. Both men stood and ducked out of view before Quetzal had a chance to see them.

"Erm... Thanks," Kane whispered.

"You're welcome. What else are little brothers for other than getting big brothers out of the shit?"

Both smiled, but Kane turned serious. "Right, we need a plan. Alex is in obvious danger, but we have to focus on these girls. Let's untie them and hustle them out of here before the psycho notices and blows this place apart."

"That's your plan?" Danny said.

"Have you got a better one?"

Danny ground his teeth in frustration. "No. Let's do it."

Chapter Fifty-Two

Ridley was torn. The monster standing before her held the detonator in one hand—which she had to assume was not fake—and the sword in the other. She felt certain she could defeat him if she attacked him, regardless of the weapon. But he only had to press one button, probably, and this whole place could crumble down on top of them, crushing the girls to death. She so desperately wanted to take him down, make him suffer for what he'd done to those innocent children. She just couldn't take any chances with the explosives.

Instead, she continued to go along with his instructions.

"Please, turn around and put your arms out behind you. Remember, just one click of the screen here and..."

"I know, I know. Just get on with it." Ridley was the last person on Earth who would let a crazy man like this tie her up, but what choice did she have? "Let's get this over with."

"You are very wise, Miss Ridley. Mister Kane chose well. But, I have chosen well too, would you not agree?"

To tie her hands behind her back, she knew Quetzal

would have to put down both the sword and the detonator. Ridley suspected he understood she wasn't stupid enough to risk it and attack him before he could activate the explosives. Ridley had considered just that, but she remained calm and let him think he retained all the control. He did, obviously, yet when it came to Ridley, she knew anyone who underestimated her did so at their your own peril.

A minute later, Ridley stood facing Quetzal, her hands bound tightly behind her back, apparently all hope lost of preventing what was about to happen.

"Please lie down on the chacmool."

Ridley glared at the mask for a few seconds, took a deep breath, then turned and walked slowly across the platform to the stone plinth, well aware that it meant Quetzal would now have a good view of the pit. She hoped Kane had somehow managed to escape from it already. If he hadn't, then she was as good as dead.

Ridley did as she was told, and laid herself down on the chacmool. The stone was cool to the touch, and she shivered involuntarily, unsure whether it was caused by the cold of the stone or the cold-heartedness with which Quetzal was going about his barbaric business. Either way, it was suddenly becoming a very real possibility she would die there in that dark chamber, beneath an ancient and remote pyramid somewhere in the central Mexican highlands. It was not a pleasant thought, though it was an altogether better prospect than being responsible for the deaths of those girls still alive below her.

With Ridley now in place on the chacmool, Quetzal felt certain he would achieve his success. He now tied her down to the stone, one loop of strap around her neck—which lay extended off the back of the chacmool's own head—and another length around her ankles, securing her tightly to the stone. He knew she would be uncomfortable. He did not care. She would not feel that discomfort for long.

Then, Quetzal paused, as her words floated back into his mind.

"No, you've been driven to this by your own insanity, your selfishness, your greed, no one else's. Get your head out of your arse, and take a good look around. This is on you, and nobody else."

Why did her words suddenly bother him? She was wrong; she was an ignorant woman with no understanding of his greatness. She was a pitiful human, prostrate before God. For that's what he was now; he was a God, a higher being.

And Gods could take whatever they wanted. Right now, he wanted Alexandria Ridley, and so he would take her.

Because, wasn't she rightfully his anyway?

Quetzal then glanced down to the pit as if something had caught his eye. "Have you escaped?" he whispered, and smiled. It didn't matter now. There was nothing they could do to stop him. He looked around at the stone plinths and noticed nothing amiss there. From his position, all the chacmools still held their girls tightly in place. They were lucky... their misery would soon be over too. He had finally decided that no one would be leaving this pyramid alive.

It is probably best for those girls anyway, he thought. Most of them were poor, most of them lived in dusty shacks with no carpet and no running water. The lucky ones might have an internal bathroom at home, but many would not. What future did they have? What could they possibly have to look forward to, in a world that does not care for justice and dignity and in a country where the menfolk leave their kids alone at night to be snatched so easily by… *by people like me?*

No, Quetzal had decided they would all die, and that they should thank him for it.

Then something really did catch his eye. A foot sticking out from behind a chacmool. He assumed it was Kane. *Right, I must focus.* He shook away Ridley's words and refocused on his mission. *Okay… where was I? Ah yes…*

He turned back to the chacmool.

It was time to take the heart and head of Alexandria Ridley. In doing so, he knew he would take the heart and mind of Hiram Kane.

Chapter Fifty-Three

Quetzal closed his eyes for a moment. This was it; the moment he'd been waiting a long time for. He knew the strategically placed cameras were filming everything, and from many angles; even if Kane wasn't watching on right now what was about to happen, Quetzal knew he would watch it later. And when he did, he would be watching a scene he would never ever forget as long as he lived. Nor would anyone else who saw it forget either. He'd make sure of that.

Quetzal took a step towards Ridley on the chacmool. "It is time," he said from behind his mask. "Miss Ridley, you are a worthy sacrifice. I am sure you are not a virgin... but no matter. You will serve my purpose very well."

The maniac stepped closer still. Slowly, Quetzal raised the macuahuitl.

Again, he hesitated. Doubt swirled through his crazed mind. *It shouldn't be like this,* he thought. He recalled all those years of disgrace and embarrassment, and all the planning since. *Here I am at the moment I've been waiting for, and yet...*

It was as though he was suddenly split into two. There was Quetzal, the avenging God, ready to sacrifice this woman and the children... And then there was Humberto Palomares. Not the Palomares who had been robbed of his rightful glory by his peers, but the young academic, taking his first hesitant steps into the field of archaeology. An innocent, who was appalled and terrified of this monster he had turned into.

It was as though the younger version of himself was pleading with Quetzal, begging him to put down the macuahuitl and set Alexandria Ridley free, to release the young girls, and to accept punishment for his sins.

"No!" Quetzal roared. "I will not be duped by you and your words! I am Quetzal, the mighty Aztec god, and these sacrifices are mine to take!"

Time seemed to stand still. The silence was deafening, and the only thing Ridley could hear was the sound of her own heart and Quetzal's ragged breathing just a few inches away from her head.

Quetzal had just yelled something incoherent about being a God, and now he stood over Ridley, poised to strike the macuahuitl into her soft flesh.

But something had changed in Ridley's mind. She was well and truly trussed to the stone plinth, and despite her toughness, and although she hoped Kane would have come to her assistance by now, he hadn't. She felt sure now; she was about to die.

And although she knew all that, knew exactly what was about to happen, she felt a sense of calm flood through her. Ridley had enjoyed a good life. There had been many ups and downs, of course; *isn't there always?* She'd been on many wild, fantastic life-changing adventures, both alone, and later alongside her man, Kane.

She had loved Hiram Kane since the first time they'd met, though she had kept that knowledge secret, even from Hiram himself, for more than fifteen years. Yet, she loved him, and she knew he had always loved her too. Her only regret was that she hadn't let him closer earlier, let him through the barriers she'd built all those years ago, when her parents had died and she'd had to learn to protect herself. It was not exactly regret... more of a wish that things had been different, that she had allowed things to be different. But there it was. People made mistakes in life, that was a fact. 'Anyone who never made a mistake never made anything,' Kane told her often. It was so very true.

So this is it... this is how it ends. Ridley closed her eyes, ready and willing to accept the fate that was about to befall her, knowing that in doing so, it would give both Hiram and Danny, plus the police, a fighting chance to stop the burgeoning madness. She was okay with it. It was just one more lost life. Quetzal had already killed at least two of the young girls. Her sacrifice now meant it might at least give the others a chance to survive. Thus, it was an easy choice. So she would not fight it now.

She had seen Kenny Peters die—slaughtered—right before her eyes, and it was gruesome. It had been over quickly, and he had died heroically, trying to prevent the psycho blowing up the entire place, and though it had been in vain, he had tried to do the right thing until the very last moment of his life. It had been a noble death. Ridley wasn't afraid of pain; she doubted she would feel any for more than just a few seconds anyway. *If I'm lucky. If not... Well, I'm Alexandria Ridley, and I can handle it. I can can anything.*

Though her eyes were closed, she sensed the lunatic edging closer still.

Any moment now...

Any mom—

Quetzal raised the macuahuitl high above his head. In doing so, he banished Palomares forever, buried him in a grave so deep he would never cause Quetzal to doubt himself again. Gods did not doubt, they did not falter; theirs was the final word. Theirs was the right to take whichever life they chose to.

Quetzal plunged the macuahuitl down in a slashing motion at Ridley, the swing powerful enough to separate her head from her neck in one smooth slice...

The crack of a rifle echoed through the chamber, and Quetzal staggered as a bullet slammed into his shoulder. The macuahuitl clanged against the stone chacmool. Thrown off course from its intended target, Ridley's neck, the blade narrowly missed slicing into Ridley's upper arm.

Blood flowed freely from Quetzal's shoulder as he dropped to his knees beside Ridley. For a moment he thought the macuahuitl might fall from his hands as the shock of realizing he had been shot flooded through his system.

Scarlet blood ran down his arm, over his hand and his fingers and onto the macuahuitl. Droplets of his bright red lifeforce fell from the blade and onto the cool stone of the chacmool and the stone floor beneath.

Quetzal's grip tightened on the macuahuitl. They thought they could kill him, but Gods could never be killed. *Do they not realize that? Are they so stupid as to think they could stop me with bullets?*

The Feathered Serpent

Quetzal lifted his head as manic laughter erupted from his mouth. The police officers led by Reyes came to a standstill as the echoes filled the chamber and chilled everyone where they stood. He placed down the ancient sword and withdrew from his pocket the second detonator. He spoke then, and his voice coming over the loudspeakers throughout the chamber was so cold and menacing it made everyone freeze in their tracks.

"Everybody... stay where you are! I am too smart for you... you... insignificant people. This detonator here will destroy this entire structure, including everyone inside it, and everyone within one hundred yards of the outside." He held it up, and with a flourish, Quetzal pressed a button. The timer began its relentless countdown.

00:59.

00:58.

"I have started the countdown, and I will blow this entire structure to hell in... fifty-five seconds. I admit, thought Mister Kane might have been more of a match for me. I am disappointed, but I was wrong. It was all a little too easy really, but then again, I suppose having the deaths of another twelve children on his hands was enough motivation to come running and do what I said." He paused and glanced about, hoping—and half expecting—to see Kane make one last valiant effort to attack him. Kane was nowhere in sight.

"So, I recommend that unless you want to die," he said, aiming these comments at the policemen, "you should all leave. You now have... forty-seven seconds. And do not think there is any way to stop the countdown. There is not. It will happen, whatever anyone does." Quetzal raised his hands, and showed everyone watching the remote-control device. "Let me give you an example." He flicked a button, and suddenly, projected large on the flat surface of the carved interior of the cave, a massive image shone down. It was a zoomed-in shot of a flashing device. Next to it was a red digital display. It too ticked down, in time with what the madman had said.

00:45. Forty-five seconds.

There were stunned expressions all over the chamber as everyone now truly believed the explosives were real.

"That is just one of almost one hundred devices. So you see, there is no chance at all you can prevent this from happening." He laughed again, and it was the unhinged laugh of a man who had gone completely insane.

00:37.

Chapter Fifty-Four

It went against all Chief Reyes's principles to sit around and wait for things to happen. That just was not the way he operated, and over the last fifteen minutes he had been growing more and more impatient. When Kenny Peters hadn't returned within quarter of an hour—half the time they'd agreed on—the Chief made up his mind. It was time to move in and take the child-kidnapping psycho out.

"Right, men. We have waited long enough. We are going in." He glanced at Stephy and Vicki, and before they could speak, he said, "No, you two are not coming in. You must stay here, do you understand?"

Vicki stood up a little straighter and glanced at Stephy. The two women nodded.

"Very good. Bueno." Reyes turned to his men, who all seemed eager to go inside the pyramid and get amongst whatever action they came across. They knew the missing girls were inside, young girls... daughters. And all bar none of the men had daughters of their own. They were ready. "Vamanos."

At the mention of his name, and the implied guilt of the girl's deaths, Kane's shoulders slumped and he closed his eyes. It seemed he had failed to save them, and yet again he found he had innocent blood on his hands.

Then he opened his eyes again. *No. I can't give up now.*

Kane and Danny glanced at one another. The police seemed unable to move, either from fear for their own lives, or fear of somehow being responsible for killing the children. It was a tense Mexican stand off. Kane might have found that amusing under different circumstances.

Quetzal laughed that booming, chilling laugh. "Watch and believe."

00:31.

"What should we do?" yelled Danny. "We have to do something."

"There must be a way... we have to get to that detonator," replied Kane, desperation in his voice.

00:27.

Inhaling, Kane breathed out and stated, "You take that side of the pyramid and I'll take the other. We'll meet in the middle and take this sick bastard down. Ready? Go!"

The two Kane brothers sprang into action as though they were a single being. There was no time to talk, or plan further. They simply had to act.

Kane sprinted around the side of the pyramid, only slowing slightly as he approached the chacmool. Quetzal was lost in his own madness, laughing crazily, still on his knees and with blood pouring down his arm and off the edge of the macuahuitl.

Kane glanced up at the countdown on the big screen.
00:19.

Ridley knew now that things had changed again, and because the countdown had already begun she had no need to lie there and wait for Quetzal to cut off her head. Not only that, but when the macuahuitl had smashed into the chacmool, it had frayed the edge of the rope tying her down. While Quetzal had been busy laughing to himself, Ridley had managed to exert enough tension on the damaged rope that it had snapped free.

Now she swung her legs down from the chacmool, surprising the monster with the speed of her movement. But he was fast, too, and snatched up the sword and brought it down hard towards Ridley with a wild yell. She ducked out of the way just a split second before the lethal blade slammed into the stone plinth, causing a shower of sparks to fly into the air like a mini firework.

Another reverberating rifle shot sounded, exploding and echoing around the chamber. This one missed Quetzal completely.

The madman stumbled as he lifted the vicious blade, and readied it for another swing at Ridley. Although she had freed herself from the stone plinth, Ridley's hands were still tied behind her back. She rolled away, squirming and struggling to climb up onto her knees so that she could run.

Then she spotted Kane.

00:13.

The Kane brothers tore up opposite sides of the internal pyramid, and two seconds later they emerged together onto the stone platform. The first thing they saw was Quetzal swinging his sword wildly at Ridley. He hadn't yet noticed the brothers, and they froze. Then, after one more swing, they knew they were too late.

00:09.

Ridley dodged, but because her hands were tied she stumbled and fell, and Kane knew without doubt her time was finally up.

"Hiram!" she cried out.

00:07.

"Hey! Hey, psycho!" the older Kane bellowed, desperate to distract the madman before he killed Ridley.

Quetzal looked up.

Kane lunged for him and ripped off the madman's mask, revealing one of the ugliest faces Kane had ever seen. Twisted with hate and bloodlust, Quetzal looked barely human anymore.

00:05.

The madman's face transformed into a psychotic grin, and he held Kane's glare for a long second.

00:04

Quetzal then unleashed a roar of such ferocity that every single person still alive in the pyramid at that moment heard it. It was long and it was loud, as if trying to attract the attention of the ancient Gods themselves. That was Quetzal's biggest mistake.

He swung his blade at Ridley's neck. But he'd roared for so long that by the time he swung the lethal blade down towards Ridley's neck Kane was upon him, throwing himself directly in the path of what would have been a fatal blow. Kane blocked it with his arm and swept the blade to one side where it clanged against the stone plinth.

00:01.

Kane could see the detonator in Quetzal's other hand, but understood he did not have a chance to grab it. He knew it was all over as he threw himself towards the love of his life... He never made it.

The Feathered Serpent

00:00. Time, zero.

An enormous, thunderous boom echoed throughout the entire complex. The ground rumbled from the massive shock wave, and huge chunks of jagged rubble crumbled from the ceiling as a layer of ancient dust filtered through the cavern.

Kane and Quetzal tumbled from the pyramid, the two men smashing to the ground as debris rained down upon them. In the thick dust swirling through the cavern, Kane saw Quetzal's blade spinning away across the ground.

Another explosion ripped through the further reaches of the cavern, setting the ground trembling beneath Kane's battered body. Kane wondered how many of the explosive devices had gone off. Surely with the amount of explosives Quetzal claimed to have primed, the entire place should have been destroyed by now, with Kane and the others dead and buried amid the rubble.

Kane dragged himself to his feet.

Danny and Ridley had both tumbled from the pyramid too, and lay nearby, both of them stirring, and sitting upright.

But Quetzal... *Where the hell is Quetzal?*

Chapter Fifty-Five

From a hidden perch high above the madness, Rafael watched as the police Chief and his officers successfully unstrapped all the girls and shepherded them towards the exit. He chuckled when he saw their dismay to find it now blocked after the ceiling had crashed down during the explosion. It was too dangerous to attempt an escape that way with thick waves of dust and falling debris assaulting them from all angles. The Chief and his men would have to get out of there another way.

Rafael searched the confusion below for his master. Quetzal had disappeared into the swirling clouds of rock dust. This wasn't how it was supposed to happen. Quetzal should have sacrificed Ridley by now, in front of a horrified Kane. That was to be his true victory.

Somehow it had all gone wrong. And now that cop and his men were emancipating the girls. Rafael knew he had to take action. The chief had met with failure on his first attempt to escape, yet Rafael knew there was another route out of the pyramid.

If the Chief and his officers were savvy enough, they would soon find it. Rafael could not let that happen. Even if Quetzal was dead—although Rafael refused to entertain that thought for more than a millisecond—Rafael could not allow those girls to escape. Because maybe, if Rafael could recapture the girls and then follow through with their sacrificial deaths, Quetzal might be resurrected.

After one last brief look around the cavernous chamber, Rafael began the descent from his hidden perch. He was young and agile, scurrying and scampering over the outcrops of rocks and hidden ledges like a monkey.

Once on the ground, he dashed through the debris left by the explosions, darting around and over chunks of rubble. The overhead arc lamps flickered in the clouds of dust, casting crazy shadows over the Aztec architecture. *What a fitting sight this is for a sacrifice or two,* thought Rafael. *It's like a vision of Hell.*

Rafael had guessed correctly about the Chief's intentions, and managed to get ahead of him. There was no doubt he was a smart man and a good leader, as he had already deduced where there might be another exit from beneath the pyramid. Yet, as smart as he was, he wasn't as clever as Rafael. It was the young man's intelligence that had first attracted Palomares to him, his master had explained.

But you are insignificant in the eyes of academia, Professor Palomares had explained. *You always will be. But join with me, and I will elevate us to heights you cannot imagine. I will make us famous throughout the world, forevermore.*

Now that plan was in danger of failing, and all because of Hiram Kane and his people. None of that mattered now. Rafael was going to fix everything.

Rafael found another hidden perch to await the police

chief and his men. Rafael had spent hundreds of hours in these caverns, wiring up the sound system and the cameras, setting up the recording devices and the Wi-Fi, that he knew every inch of it, and every hidden crevasse and hiding space.

Rafael heard the Chief, his officers and the terrified, sobbing girls, before he saw them. He shrunk further into the shadows. Rafael understood that on his own he was no match for the police, especially as they were armed. But if he could snatch even just one of the girls from them, Rafael was convinced that would be enough of a sacrifice to turn the tide, and to bring about the victory Quetzal sought so desperately.

Rafael watched as the policemen passed below him, every single one of them on high alert and their weapons held ready, while urging the little girls on. He waited until the last of the cops appeared from the clouds of dust, and Rafael's heart quickened with excitement when he saw the young girl with him.

Rosa!

That little chica had caused him so much trouble already, it would be poetic to snatch her again and sacrifice her on the chacmool. Rafael wiped the back of his hand across his mouth. He was trembling with excitement. It had been Rafael who had snatched Rosa from her bed after he'd witnessed the bungled kidnapping earlier that morning.

He wasn't going to let her escape again.

Rafael dropped from the ledge he was waiting on and landed feet first on the policeman's head and shoulders. They crashed to the rocky ground, but Rafael landed heavily on top of the cop. He grabbed the man by both ears and smashed his skull against the ground. Once, twice, and then a third time, at which point the back of his head exploded in a crimson spout of gore and brains.

Rosa opened her mouth to scream, but Rafael was on her before she had drawn breath, and clamped his hand over her mouth.

"Shush now, little chica," he hissed. "It is time for you to fulfil your destiny. Your sacrifice will change everything."

With one last glance behind to ensure he wasn't being followed, he scooped her up and ran across the cavern, disappearing into the swirling clouds of dust.

Chapter Fifty-Six

Kane, refusing to believe that Quetzal was finished, and determined to stop the madman at all costs, scanned the cavern for any sight of him.

Ridley had awoken from her brief unconsciousness and was staggering to her feet, almost losing her balance halfway down the steep-sided pyramid.

Danny was back up on his feet too.

As he scanned the cavern for any sight of the monster in the swirling clouds of dust, Kane spotted the police chief and his men leading the girls to safety.

Good. That was one less thing to worry about. Kane had confidence in them to do the right thing, no matter what.

"Where is he?" Ridley yelled, as another small explosion sent a ripple of shockwaves through the cavern's floor.

"I don't know!" Kane yelled. "But you must stay alert. He could be close and we wouldn't know it, not with all this smoke and dust blocking our view."

Ridley nodded, her face a mask of grim determination.

Although Kane would have preferred that she was a thousand miles from this danger, he was glad to have her here, watching his back.

Suddenly he saw movement in the shifting shadows.

"Hiram!" Danny yelled.

Too late, Kane spotted Quetzal appearing from the clouds of smoke like the evil monster he was, charging at him with the macuahuitl held high.

Kane attempted to throw himself out of the way of the charging madman, but the blade came swinging down with a sickening crash against the rocky ground. Kane grunted in shock as the blade bit into the flesh of his arm, and he rolled away before Quetzal could attack him again.

Quetzal disappeared back into the shadows.

As he scrambled to his feet, Kane suddenly felt lightheaded. On the ground at his feet were spattered drops of scarlet. His blood.

And his hand, chopped from his arm at the wrist.

An almost overwhelming nausea flooded through his torso as an icy knot clenched in his guts. How could he continue the fight with a missing hand, and losing so much blood?

Kane raised his arms to look in horror at the stump where his hand should have been.

And saw that both hands were still attached to his arms. His left forearm was bleeding from a nasty gash where Quetzal had sliced at him with the macuahuitl.

Kane looked down at the severed hand lying on the ground, and realized with a sickening finality that the hand belonged to Kenny Peters.

The nausea receded, replaced by a steadfast determination to avenge his new friend's mutilation and death. Kane's hands curled into fists, almost of their own will, as Quetzal appeared once more from the darkness.

Kane stood face to face with the psycho, blood spilling from the wound in his arm.

Ridley approached, followed close behind by Danny.

Kane held out a hand to stop them drawing any closer.

"Stay back," Kane growled. "I've got this."

Quetzal tipped his head back and laughed. "One of us will die today, but it will not be me. I know you do not doubt I can make that happen." Quetzal pointed to a small bank of monitors that Kane hadn't noticed before. "Oh, everything that is happening here today is being seen by millions of people all over the world. Right now. And if you think that was the last of the explosions, you are wrong. That was just one round, a warmup, if you will. There are more. Many, many more."

He held out another detonator in his free hand, raising it high as though it were a trophy.

Kane winced. "You've got to be kidding me. More bombs?"

"If you do not do as I say, the world will all know that you are responsible for what happens, not me. You will be held responsible for the deaths of all those innocent young girls. So I say again," he stated, and nodded towards Ridley, "one of you must die. And then... and only then, maybe the children will live, and you two get to be heroes."

"Enough!" Kane yelled. "This has to end now. Your twisted plan is finished, and those girls you intended on sacrificing... on killing... are being led to safety as we speak. Give it up, Palomares."

"My name is Quetzal!"

It was all Kane could do not to attack the crazed madman, his idiotic ramblings painful to his ears. But he clearly did have the power to do as he said, and Kane was not going to risk being the one to bring this entire structure down on top of them all.

Despite his brave words, Kane knew Quetzal had the upper hand here. He had the macuahuitl and the detonator. Kane had nothing.

"So, the girls are free, are they?" Quetzal said, his eyes flicking from side to side, as though he was searching for them. "It does not matter; they have served their purpose. You, and your beautiful woman, on the other hand, shall be their surrogates. You shall die in their place. Isn't that what you wanted?"

Kane ground his teeth together. One false move and this could all be over, including his and Ridley's, and Danny's, lives. Kane had already lost Kenny; he didn't want to lose any more friends or loved ones.

"Nothing to say?" Quetzal raised the blade.

Kane bent low into a crouch, ready for whatever came next.

Chapter Fifty-Seven

Ridley half turned to Kane, who was starting to look weak from a loss of blood, which was continuing to pour from his wound and gather in slick puddles on the ground. She knew he would die if they let the wound continue to bleed out. He had to have hospital treatment, and soon.

Keeping a wary on Quetzal, she grabbed Kane's hand. "Hiram... For once it's time to save yourself. Go now... go with Danny and help get those girls away from here. It's whay we came, isn't it? Believe me, I can deal with him." She flicked her head towards Quetzal. Then her gaze settled on Kane's eyes, flickering from both pain and worry. "Go. Please..."

Kane wasn't through yet. "No... it's me he... me he wants."

"Hiram... come on, please!" his brother yelled from the base of the pyramid.

"Listen to me," Ridley whispered. "You and Danny have only just reunited. You have so much lost time to make up for. This will all be for nothing if you don't get out of here now."

Ridley turned her gaze to Quetzal and saw a sickening grin spreading across his twisted face. He obviously no longer cared who was to become the ultimate sacrifice, and was glaring at Ridley with some kind of sick bloodlust. *Ugly inside and out,* she mused.

"I can't… can not let you do this," Kane managed to say, reaching out with some effort and placing his good hand on her shoulder.

"It's okay," she responded, not taking her eyes of Quetzal. "Everything's going to turn out fine. Trust me…"

She heard a sharp intake of breath from Kane. He'd caught on that she had a plan. It wasn't a particularly good plan; in fact it was truly awful. But it was a plan.

She felt Kane relax a little behind her.

"Be careful," he whispered.

"I will."

"I love you."

"I… I love you too."

With that, Kane offered the tiniest hint of a grin and released his hand from Ridley's shoulders.

"All right then, Quetzal, or Palomares, or whatever the hell your name is now," Ridley hissed, no longer even trying to pretend she was afraid of him. Quite literally, she was not. "Come on, big man… where do you want me?"

Quetzal huffed through a smile and indicated the pyramid rising up behind him. Parts had been destroyed in the massive explosions, but the structural integrity remained largely intact. "On the altar of course. Where else can we offer up such a special sacrifice to our worldwide audience?"

"Yeah, well, make sure the camera gets my best side, okay? If I'd have known I was going to be on TV today I would have taken more care with my makeup this morning. Maybe worn a fucking dress."

As she ascended the pyramid, Ridley took a last look over her shoulder at Kane. He was sitting on the ground, his brother supporting him. Kane was growing weaker by the minute. Ridley had to finish this. And she would, very soon, of that she was certain.

Chapter Fifty-Eight

Vicki and Stephy had waited a couple of minutes after the Chief had led his team inside, then followed behind at a safe distance back. There was just no way either woman was going to wait and not lend a hand in some way.

Once they'd been discovered, Reyes had not seemed surprised and had just grunted something in their general direction.

Since then they had been helping Reyes and his men evacuate the girls from the cavern. They were at the back of the line of men, with Rosa and one of the cops, when Vicki had noticed one of the girls ahead of them fainting. Both Stephy and Vicki rushed over to help the cop.

"Rosa?" Stephy called.

The only answer was a rumble of rock as a part of the cavern collapsed somewhere. Stephy turned to Vicki who was helping the cop pick up the young girl as she began to revive.

"You go ahead," Stephy said. "I'll go back and join

Rosa, she might be a little scared on her own with that other cop."

"Good idea," Vicki said. "See you outside."

Stephy headed back into the swirling clouds of dust. "Rosa!"

And then she pulled up short when she saw the cop lying on the ground, blood and brains leaking from his head.

"Oh my God, no!"

She kneeled down beside him and checked for a pulse, although she knew it was hopeless. And then she looked up at the passageway disappearing into the darkness. This man was dead, but Rosa was still alive. Someone had taken her. It couldn't have been Quetzal, he was still up on the altar as far as she knew.

Stephy glanced behind her, wondering if she should go back and alert Vicki. There was no time, she had to find Rosa.

Stephy hauled herself to her feet and dashed down the passageway. If whoever had taken Rosa was carrying the little girl, that would mean they were weighed down and probably going at a slower pace than Stephy. There was a loud rumble overhead, and Stephy skidded to a halt. Something was crashing towards her, but she couldn't tell where it was coming from.

Then the clouds of dust in front of her began to swirl in a maelstrom, like thunderclouds massing in a time-lapse movie. Stephy dived for cover just as a mass of rock and rubble smashed to the ground, and crashed through the spot she had just been standing on.

Stephy threw her hands over her head and tucked her chin in. After only a few moments the roaring stopped. Stephy looked up and saw her path ahead was blocked.

The Feathered Serpent

"No!" Stephy hauled herself to her feet and approached the wall of rubble. A sense of dismay welled up inside her, and erupted in a wail of helplessness. They had been so close to rescuing Rosa.

Stephy looked up, and her spirits lifted just a little. There was a gap where the boulders met the passage ceiling.

And it looked just big enough for Stephy to crawl through.

"Come on, Stephy, you can do this."

With those words she began climbing, taking her time to find handholds and footholds that wouldn't crumble away at the first moment she placed any weight on them.

Sweat poured down her face and she had to blink it out of her eyes. The muscles in her arms screamed in protest, but on she climbed. She would not let Rosa down.

At the top of the wall of rocks blocking the passageway, Steph found the gap she had planned on crawling through was smaller than she had thought. Stifling a cry of frustration, she set about dragging rocks away, and making the gap wider.

And she tried not to think about the seconds ticking past, and how Rosa's captor could be anywhere in the cavernous chamber by now, and Stephy might never find them.

As she scrabbled at the rubble, the hard-edged rocks caught her fingernails, ripping bits of them off. Blood splattered her hands, but Stephy kept on digging until the hole was wide enough that she could pull herself through.

She reached out her arms and hauled herself through the gap, coughing and choking in the dust. As she pulled herself through to the other side, the rubble began giving way, sliding in rivulets down to the ground. Before she realized what was happening, Stephy was tumbling down the rockfall until he smashed into the ground on her back.

For a moment she lay dazed, bright stars exploding in the darkness. Then she pulled herself upright and shook her head. This was no time to be lying on the ground, no matter how dazed or concussed she was. Somewhere out there was a little girl, and she was in desperate danger.

And Stephy wasn't going to let her down.

Chapter Fifty-Nine

At the top of the pyramid, Ridley turned to Quetzal. Ridley wasn't the tallest of woman; at five ten she wasn't the shortest either. Yet, the madman stood watching her from a few yards away towered over her. Although much of his height was from the ghastly feathered headdress he had put back on, she sensed a reasonably large man beneath the costume. Probably six foot at least, and of medium build. Ridley knew she was more than a physical match for almost any man... she'd bested Kane on the tae-kwon-do mat in sparring on numerous occasions, and like her, Kane was officially a master of the sport. Now, she had the small matter of this unhinged, unstable psycho to deal with.

She stared at him now, the disdain and hatred she felt seeming to be the opposite of his attitude. Despite being once more hidden behind the grim mask, she sensed an air of amusement about him, the way his arms hung loosely at his sides, and the way his shoulders seemed relaxed, as if his imminent victory was assured and only a matter of time. She had encountered all sorts of sordid, dangerous criminals in recent times, and the men were all heinous for differing reasons. The one thing they all shared, however, the one flaw that made them the same, was that they all believed they were stronger and smarter than Ridley, simply because she was a woman. All bar none of them had been wrong.

She took a challenging step towards Quetzal, ensuring there was no trace of fear in her eyes and no falter in her confident step. She didn't fear him. She was confident.

"You will never get away with this," she stated as if it were a simple truth. "Never. Even if you kill us all, you will not get what it is you crave. Is it fame? Attention? Whatever it is, you will not get it, I promise you that. You will still be nothing. You will stell be a no one." She took another step forward; Quetzal remained motionless.

Quetzal had replaced the mask he had been wearing earlier. It seemed to give him strength, somehow able to embolden him. Ridley was convinced that beneath his mask he was smiling. He believed this was his moment on the world stage. That nothing could stop him now, even if the girls he'd had kidnapped were now being hustled to safety.

Ridley knew she had an advantage, and this idiot had no clue about it. For most of his life, Palomares had been an academic, a professor of ancient antiquities. He hadn't suffered through the trials and tribulations that Ridley had experienced. He wasn't tough, not like she was. And he'd never met anyone quite like Alexandria Ridley before.

She took another deliberate step towards him, and this time she saw him falter. It wasn't much, just the slightest movement, but she caught it.

No doubt about it… Humbert Palomares was intimidated by her.

"I admire your courage, Miss Ridley. But you are wrong.

Very wrong. Perhaps I once was nothing. Perhaps I was a nobody. But not any more. Soon, all the world will know my true name, the name of Quetzal. And I will be as famous... more famous... than my ancestor."

Ridley sensed the man's shoulders widen, and he seemed an inch or two taller now. He really believed in everything he was saying. "And who is this ancestor?" Ridley asked, her tone deliberately mocking. This was good. She had to keep him talking. "Who is this *famous* ancestor you speak of?"

Quetzal now took a step forward, and then another, until he and Ridley were just a few feet apart.

"A long time ago," started Quetzal, "this flawed country had a revolution. And at the heart of that revolution was the bravest man this nation has ever known. Emiliano Zapata, hero of the people and the one true founder of modern Mexico. Zapata is my ancestor. For a long time no one has believed the truth about my esteemed heritage. I have been shunned and discredited and shamed. Now that will all change. I will have my moment. I have retrieved the beautiful priceless artefact I discovered. And I will regain my rightful family name. And with all of those things finally in place, I will claim my rightful position in the history books of this country. But for that I will need your help. So please, Miss Ridley, do the right thing and save those girls. Take to your knees on the edge of the platform."

Ridley nodded. He seemed to have forgotten what Kane had told him; that the girls were being taken to safety. The madness was consuming him. Ridley knew it would be his undoing.

She had expected this was his plan all along. She glanced down at the floor of the chamber below far below. The police and the girls might not have yet found a safe way out of the structure, and as long as they were still at risk from more explosives, she had to proceed with extreme caution. She knew she was to be sacrificed, and although she couldn't see them, she knew a series of cameras were watching their every move. She was to be beheaded, and she was to have her heart ripped from her chest on live television. Then, when she was down, this monster would remove his mask and reveal to the world his so-called true identity.

She hated even the thought of letting that happen. It was madness to even consider what she was plotting.

Yet, for the first time in her life, she would let a man do what he wanted to her. It was her only chance to save the girls, and in turn, save Hiram.

Ridley took to her knees as he had demanded.

She knew what she had to do; Ridley also knew she had only one chance to get it right. Get it wrong, and her death would be in vain. Then, like her, everyone else in that pyramid would die.

She could not let the pyramid at Canãda de la Virgin become a massive tomb for dozens of innocent people.

Just eight feet away, a dead man stirred.

Chapter Sixty

Stephy stumbled through the darkness. Somewhere in the chamber she could hear Quetzal ranting, but his voice echoed around the cavern, making it difficult for her to pinpoint where he was.

Quetzal wasn't Stephy's concern right now. Although worry about her friends gnawed at her insides, she knew she had to keep her mind focused on rescuing Rosa. Hiram and the others would look after themselves. They would find a way of defeating Quetzal. And, she believed the other girls were now safe.

There was just Rosa to think of.

Stephy had no idea if she was headed in the right direction anymore. The rockfall obstructing her way had taken too long to get through. There was no other choice but for Stephy to trust her instincts and to keep going.

Stephy paused when she heard a scream. Where had it come from? The scream had quickly been stifled, so quickly in fact, that Stephy was now doubting that she had heard it at all.

No, she had to trust herself. The scream had come from somewhere on her left, and maybe above her too. In the flickering, yellow/orange glow of a flaming torch on the wall, Stephy noticed a set of steps roughly carved into the rock.

Now she had a choice to make. Follow the path on, or climb the steps up?

Stephy closed her eyes. *Come on, girl, you can do this. Which way?*

Stephy opened her eyes, her decision made.

Up.

Stephy scrambled up the steps, hugging the wall to her left and all too aware of the probably lethal drop to her right. Higher and higher she ascended until she arrived at a platform overlooking the enormous chamber.

Stephy gasped at the sight below, suddenly revealed to her as the clouds of dust shifted in a breeze of unknown origin. Ridley was kneeling on a platform on the pyramid, and Quetzal was looming over her. In his right hand he held a vicious-looking blade high and ready to swing down and kill Ridley.

Kane and Danny were at the bottom of the pyramid, and Kane looked as though he was injured badly. *Where the hell's Kenny?*

Stephy looked away. Even though there was nothing she could do to help Ridley, the guilt of leaving her new friend at the mercy of that madman ripped through her heart.

Rosa. She had to concentrate on finding and rescuing Rosa. That would be what Ridley and Kane would want of Stephy, and what they themselves would almost certainly do.

Stephy ran along the platform until she arrived at another set of steps carved into the rock wall. And now she could see Rosa, struggling in the arms of a man who was carrying her higher up the steps.

The sight of that little girl, fighting to free herself from that bastard, galvanized Stephy, renewing her determination to rescue her. With no regard for her own safety, ignoring the precipitous drop to her right, Stephy sprinted up the steps.

The man turned and spotted her, his face twisting into a snarl of hatred.

Stephy dug into reserves of energy she didn't realise she still had, and surged up the steps. She smashed into the man, knocking him on his back. Before he could recover, Stephy punched him in the face. Blood splattered from his nose and he cried out. Stephy punched him again, letting the absolute fury she felt surge through her. How dare this man kidnap young, innocent girls for his own twisted desires? Stephy would kill him before she let him hurt anyone ever again.

Stephy raised her fist to deliver a third and final knockout punch when she heard Rosa scream. Stephy twisted around to see what was happening. The young girl had fallen off the edge of the steps, and was clinging to the rocky ledge while her legs kicked out over empty space.

Stephy let go of the man and reached out to grab Rosa before she slipped and fell to her death.

She never got the chance.

Quetzal took a step forward towards Ridley, who knelt down at the very edge of the pyramid's uppermost platform. In one hand he held the magnificent ancient weapon, the macahuitl. In the other hand he held a small electronic device Ridley knew was the master detonator that could bring down the entire complex. She had long ago decided that the only chance to help the girls was to accept Quetzal's next act without protest. If she let him kill her, then it might be enough for him to let the others go. That's what she had decided then. It is not what she was thinking now. Kane was right... she had one more ace left up her sleeve.

Even that would likely not be enough. Ridley did not believe in miracles. However, she needed one now. Quetzal stood tall just a couple of feet behind her. He muttered a few words in some language Ridley didn't understand, but knew it wasn't Spanish. Probably some ancient Aztec dialect, she guessed.

Quetzal gazed over to where he knew the main camera was recording him from, confident his tech friend was streaming this all to millions of screens all across Mexico and beyond. *Just another minute,* he thought, shivering with a wave of unadulterated excitement, *and I will reveal to them all who I really am.* Then Quetzal raised the blade for what would be the final time.

Quetzal took a few deep breaths, and paused. A single bead of sweat dripped from his forehead into his eye and he squinted, the stinging sweat a mere annoyance at the moment of his glory. He focused once more on the admittedly brave woman before him. *Shame,* he thought. *Then again, not really...*

"It is almost time, Miss Ridley. Are you ready to do your duty?"

"Get on with it... if you're man enough?" Ridley hoped taunting him might delay him further. It didn't work.

"Just a couple more seconds. But I warn you... if you

try anything and I drop this detonator, you will kill everyone in this pyramid. Is that clear? Do not move."

"Yes, yes. I get it. Now, swing that fucking blade or I'm going to walk out of here and take your so-called glory with me. Do it," she yelled. "Do it now!"

A final grin beneath the mask, and at last Quetzal swung. But, that single bead of sweat had blurred his vision, and in that exact moment, and trusting the timing to her survivor's instincts, Ridley dived forward. Clutching the edge of the top stone step with her left hand, then pivoting, she grabbed the ceremonial knife that Quetzal had demanded they bring to him. Ridley had spotted it minutes earlier, lying forgotten where the madman had placed it after taking it from Kenny.

With a sharp twist to her right, Ridley narrowly avoided the macahuitl, and it clashed against the stone altar. Quetzal's eyes widened behind the mask as he spotted the dagger in Ridley's hands.

Quetzal lunged for her, his hand outstretched to take the dagger back.

Ridley ducked and shot forward. With all her strength, she plunged the ceremonial dagger into Quetzal's stomach. The madman doubled over. His hot breath exploded over Ridley as she leant into the knife, shoving it deeper and deeper. Quetzal's wheeze turned into a gurgle. Ridley swept the knife up, cutting through his flesh and his insides.

Quetzal's legs buckled, and he dropped to the stone platform on his knees. Blood poured out from the wound in his abdomen, and Ridley knew she'd slashed his insides into ribbons. Then almost as if in slow motion, Quetzal tumbled forward, his body cartwheeling wildly down the steep steps of the pyramid.

He was dead, although even in death he clutched at the prized ceremonial dagger. That was good. What wasn't good was that the live detonator was now arcing skywards, tumbling, glinting under the flicker of the fiery torches and angling away and far out of her reach. There was no way she could scramble to her feet and catch it in time, and she covered her head and braced herself for the imminent and deadly explosion.

Chapter Sixty-One

Kenny Peters was dead.

Except he wasn't.

The lethal macahuitl blade had cut a wound deep into his neck, and would have looked to anyone who might have seen it to have been a fatal blow. In fact, to many it likely would have been. Kenny though was a tough man. A Canadian of mixed Scottish and Serbian heritage, Kenny had ancestors that had survived ancient bloody battles. Kenny was made of stern stuff. And he hadn't died.

While Quetzal was threatening Ridley, Kenny had somehow awoken from unconsciousness and had enough wits about him to analyse the scene playing out around him. He knew he didn't have enough time or strength to tackle Quetzal, but out of the maniac's view he had hauled himself first to his knees, then to his feet, and had started to make his move when the mighty macuahuitl descended towards Ridley's neck. But she had rolled away, and attacked him with something, although Kenny couldn't see what it was.

But Kenny had known about the detonator, and luckily spotted it spiralling high into the air, and even more luckily, it was arcing in his general direction. Plucked from some deep and previously unknown reserves, Kenny found the strength for one last act in this life before finally succumbing to his injuries, and he rushed a couple of steps towards the edge of the platform and launched himself head first off the pyramid's summit towards the detonator, knowing in that split second that if he failed to catch it he would die, and if he succeeded in arresting the detonator's fall, he would still die.

Kenny strained every sinew and reached out his arm, and for a heart-breaking millisecond he knew he wouldn't make it. Then the detonator slammed into his hand and he curled his strong fingers around it as his body flipped so his back was adjacent to the stone steps of the pyramid. Such was the force of his heroic leap that he finally hit the stone steps close to the base of the structure, only a couple of yards from Danny.

As Kenny hit the unforgiving stone, Danny heard a horrific crunch, and knew immediately that Kenny's neck had snapped, and he lay crumpled against the steps, all his limbs in unnatural positions except one.

The hand that clutched the lethal detonator, the small device that was just a second or two from killing everyone within that ancient structure, was pinned tight up against his chest. Kenny was dead.

Yet his heroism had just saved at least two dozen innocent lives.

Ridley scrambled over to Kenny and snatched the detonator from his grip. There was no time to grieve over Kenny at this moment; she had to cancel the countdown before the remaining bombs exploded and collapsed the chamber on top of them.

However, when Ridley looked at the detonator, she saw the numbers were frozen at two seconds to zero. Somehow, Kenny had stopped the clock.

Ridley looked down at the man she had known only a few hours and tears welled up in her eyes.

Kane staggered up beside her. "He was a good man."

"He was a hero."

"We will make sure everyone knows that," Kane said.

Chapter Sixty-Two

Rosa screamed as the man kicked out at the woman who had been chasing him. The sole of his boot connected with her head with a satisfying crunch.

The woman had been reaching out to grab Rosa and pull her to safety, but now she was tumbling down the stone steps like a rag doll. Rosa squeezed her eyes shut as she clung to the step. Tears squirted from between her eyelids. They weren't just tears of fear, but guilt too. Guilt that it was because she had screamed and distracted her rescuer that the woman was now probably dead.

The man grabbed Rosa and pulled her back onto the stone step. His nose was swollen and bruised, and blood flowed over his mouth and dripped from his chin.

But his eyes, they were alive with a mix of hatred and what Rosa thought was excitement.

He lifted Rosa and carried her up the remaining steps to a narrow walkway.

Rosa squirmed and kicked in her captor's arms, but the

man with the narrow eyes and a mean mouth was too strong. Stronger than Rosa, that was for sure.

"Stop struggling or I will slit your throat open right now!" he hissed.

Rosa let herself go limp, the fight suddenly disappearing from her exhausted body. Too much had happened in her young life over the last twenty-four hours. First of all she had been rescued by Hiram Kane from the man attempting to kidnap her. Then she had been snatched from her bed by this same man, before witnessing the brutal, gruesome deaths of two other kids around her age. And then, just as she thought she was safe with Chief Reyes, she had been taken again.

Now as she looked down from his hiding place on the horrible display below, Rosa knew she was going to die. Quetzal might be dead, killed by that kind woman Alexandria Ridley, but she knew that would not stop this man. He had already told her he was going to use her as a sacrifice.

This time no one was coming to her rescue. Hiram Kane was wounded, and Ridley was already with him, tending to him. Rosa knew that they all thought she was safe with the other girls and Chief Reyes.

No one had any idea that she was about to die.

"Come with me," he whispered, his hot breath in her face.

He dragged Rosa deeper into the shadows. One sweaty hand was clamped over her mouth, keeping her from crying out.

He darted in and out the natural recesses along the edges of the huge chamber until they arrived at a ledge. She saw more of the the flickering lamps and her terror renewed.

The man threw Rosa on the stone ledge. She gasped with pain as her back slammed against the hard surface.

She watched as he rushed to the edge of the ledge and raised his arms high. In his right hand he held a blade. Rosa recognized from her lessons in school; it was some kind of special knife used to take the skin from sacrificial victims in ancient times.

Her blood ran cold at the sight of it.

"Hiram Kane!" the man yelled.

Kane grunted with pain as Ridley wrapped a makeshift bandage around his forearm. She knotted it tight, and Kane grunted again.

"Sorry," she said.

"Forget about it. You killed that monster and saved us all."

"Let's not forget about Kenny," Danny added.

"Yeah, he was a good man." Kane looked at Kenny Peters' body, his arm still outstretched from where he had caught the detonator. Kane would make sure everyone knew how brave the Canadian had been, and how he had sacrificed his own life to save the others.

Then his gaze turned to Quetzal, lying facedown in a pool of blood only a few feet away. How ironic that he had been defeated with the artefact he had been so obsessed over.

"Hiram Kane!"

Kane jolted, and looked up at the sound of the his name being shouted, and saw a man high above, bathed in the light of several glimmering oil lamps, and waving his arms to get their attention.

"Hiram Kane!"

"Isn't that the receptionist from our hotel?" Ridley said. "What was his name, Rafael?"

"I think you're right."

"We paid for our room, didn't we?"

Kane ignored Ridley's attempt at a little levity in the madness.

"Hiram Kane!" Raphael yelled again, then he ducked out of view.

"Maybe he's coming down to talk to us," Danny suggested.

"No wait, he's there again, and he's…" Ridley gasped. "Oh no."

Kane stiffened, and the knot in his guts tightened.

Rafael held a struggling Rosa in his arms.

Ridley clambered to her feet. With his good hand, Kane reached out to her, and Ridley helped him stand too.

"Let Rosa go! It's over now!" Kane yelled.

"It is just beginning, Hiram Kane," Rafael shouted. "With this last sacrifice I will resurrect my master, Quetzal, and he will be immortal. Then nothing will stand in his way."

Rafael raised one arm, and in his hand held a shining dagger. Ridley gasped at the sight.

"We have to help her," she whispered.

"They're too far away," Danny hissed. "We'll never make it to them in time."

"Put the dagger down, and let Rosa go!" Kane's firm, bold voice echoed through the chamber. "In your heart you must understand you can never get your master back. All you will have done is murdered a young girl."

For a moment it seemed as if hesitation passed over Rafael's features. He lowered his arm, the ceremonial dagger now hanging by his side.

Kane watched him intently, his jaws clenched tight.

Then Rafael raised the dagger once more, his face transforming into a rictus of hate.

"Oh my... he's going to do it." Ridley's hands flew to her mouth.

"Rosa!" Kane yelled. "Koshi Suriyoku! Koshi Suriyoku!"

Rafael looked down at them, clearly confused at the foreign words.

Rosa's face remained expressionless, then she suddenly sprang into action. She did exactly what Kane had told her, dropping into a squat, then stepping to her right, placing her left foot between Rafael's feet, hooking her foot behind Rafael's ankle and throwing him to the ground.

Rafael rolled towards the edge of the stone platform. As he seemed to grasp what was about to happen he reached out to grab Rosa, but missed. With a short, sharp scream, he tumbled to the ground, limb over limb before crashing into the unforgiving bedrock with a sickening thud.

He did not get up again.

Chapter Sixty-Three

Kane looked up at the little girl. "Well done, Rosa," he called to her. "Are you okay?"

"Girls kick ass, right?" Rosa yelled.

"Right!" Ridley shouted back. "Can you find your way down here?"

"Si!" Rosa shouted, and disappeared from view.

Ridley held the detonator up and looked at it.

"You just can't let go of that thing, can you?" Kane said.

"If I do I'm afraid the countdown will start again. I won't be happy until we are all safely out of this place."

"I know what you mean, but I believe it's over now. You can let go of that thing, Alex. It's not going to start up again on its own."

"I'm not so sure." Ridley walked over to Quetzal's body and looked down at him. "What the hell possessed him to come up with this sick plan?" She turned her back on the body. "I will never understand people like him, and the depths of depravity humanity can sink to."

"Hiram! Alex!" Rosa appeared, running towards them.

Kane and Danny turned as one to greet her, but then Kane heard a sucking, gurgling noise behind him. He spun around, and was confronted with Quetzal. He had felt certain the psycho was dead, but somehow the madman had survived Ridley's attack.

With one hand he was attempting to hold in his intestines, hanging in glistening loops from the gash in his stomach. Somehow even more shocking to Kane than seeing a dead man standing, was that Quetzal's other arm was locked around Ridley's neck, and in that hand he held the detonator once more, the display frozen on two seconds.

His thumb hovered over the activation button.

"It seems I will have the final say, Mister Kane. The last laugh, perhaps?" Blood spilled from his lips as he spoke. Ridley flinched in his grasp, but Kane sensed she dared not struggle too much due to the proximity of the detonator.

"You've got a warped sense of humour, Palomares," Kane stated, as he frantically wondered if he had enough time to dash over to Quetzal and overpower him.

"I am Quetzal. I am a god. And now, you *will* bow down before me!"

Kane was sick of hearing madmen spouting rubbish and wanted nothing more than to attack the bastard. But Ridley, Danny, Rosa, the other children... Everything seemed too risky.

Yet nothing was riskier than doing nothing. He met Ridley's gaze, who fixed her eyes on his as if to say, *Whatever you're thinking, fucking do it right now!*

Kane nodded, inhaled, yelled "Duck!" and pushed off like a sprinter and in less than two seconds he was on Quetzal, smashing his forearm over Ridley's head into the man's windpipe with such force it knocked him off his feet. The detonator dropped to the ground with a clunk and Kane froze. But Ridley didn't hesitate and was on him in a flash, and in a moment Kane would likely never forget, he watched on as Ridley grabbed Quetzal's protruding entrails in both hands and tugged, spilling them out onto the stone ground in a pile of steaming blood, tubes and gore.

Rosa screamed and ducked behind Danny, clutching his legs. Danny scooped her up into a hug and held her tight, turning her face away from what was left of her tormentor.

"I think he's dead now," Ridley said matter-of-factly. She poked at the body with her foot. "Yep. He's dead." She turned to Kane. "Now we can we get out of here!"

Kane nodded, and shook his head as he retrieved the detonator from the ground. The digital display that had just a moment ago declared two seconds was blank. Kane could only hope that was a good sign.

"Hiram! Danny!"

They all turned at the sound of the voice. Kane stiffened, ready to fight once more, even though he abstractedly through he recognised the voice.

Stephy Loren emerged from the shadows, bruised and limping, and clutching her left arm close to her side.

"Stephy?" Danny yelled, incredulous. "What the hell are you doing here?"

Despite the obvious pain she was in, Stephy grinned. "It's a... well, it's a long story. Hey Rosa!"

"Stephy?" Rosa's voice was soft and questioning, as if she couldn't actually believe who was standing there in front of her.

Danny put Rosa down and she charged over to Stephy and wrapped her arms around her in a hug as big as her little arms would allow.

Danny walked over too. "Seems like the two of you have

a story to tell. But first…" Danny looked at his brother. "Now can we get out of here? Please?"

Right at that moment, Rosa screamed!

Epilogue

Two Days Later

"What the hell's this world coming to, eh?"

Danny turned sharply upon hearing that voice, and it was a welcome sound indeed. "I don't... I just can't... holy shit, you're alive," was all he said.

Kenny Peters lay there, more or less unmoving other than the very gentle rise and fall of his chest, almost imperceptibly. Other than the fact they'd just literally heard him speak, it would be hard to believe. He had been so badly smashed up, it more or less defied logic that he wasn't dead.

"I... I don't feel very alive... I feel like... an extra in 'The Greatest Hits of Scott Stevens and Rob Blake'." Those names were met with largely blank looks. "Ah... sorry... hockey players... ice hockey... violent bastards."

"Mate, I'm just so glad you're back with us. We all are."

"Yes, we are," added Kane, still somewhat in shock.

"Totally," said Ridley, as a few tears of relief leaked

from her eyes. "We thought... well, it didn't look good. Honestly, we thought you were dead."

Kane exhaled. "We were just about to leave the chamber, when Alex spotted you were still breathing."

"Well, folks, I'm glad you didn't leave me behind. Anyway, how do I look?" he asked, holding up his bandaged left arm, its hand missing due to the fight with Quetzal. "Least I still got my good one, eh?"

There was some gentle laughter, but beneath that deceptive sound Kane sensed an awful sadness in all of them. Kenny too. Kane suspected Kenny thought his sacrifice had been worth it. Kane would agree. It was much less of a sacrifice than those made by the poor girls who'd died at the madman's hands, not to mention the unimaginable psychological damage he'd inflicted on those who had survived.

"I mean, really... what's the world coming to when someone is driven literally mad by society and resorts to... to this,"—he waved his bandaged stump in the air—"to make his point?"

Over the last few days they had learned the truth about what had happened to Quetzal, or as they now knew, Professor Humberto Palomares, to have caused his angst.

Standing or sitting around Kenny's hospital bed right then were Hiram and Danny Kane, Alex Ridley, Kenny's girlfriend Sandra, and Chief Reyes, as well as Stephy Loren and her husband Nelo, and of course Vicki Allen. None of them had mentioned it, but Kane doubted any of them had any regrets Professor Palomares had died beneath the pyramid at Canãda de la Virgin. He had done terrible things to those poor girls, slaughtering two of them and forever mentally damaging the others. But despite that, Kane sensed that they each probably had a little sympathy for the man Humberto was before everything changed.

Quite simply... he had been let down by a social system so flawed people couldn't even be themselves. So Humberto Palomares was a little different to some people. He was homosexual. So what? He was eccentric and socially awkward. Equally, so what? None of those were crimes. By all accounts he had been a super-intelligent and very talented individual. Sadly, Kane had learned some weaker people were threatened by such things.

There was also the issue of Palomares's claim to be related to Mexican revolutionary Emiliano Zapata. To Kane, the sad part of that was that it was actually true. Apparently, the man had found no way to prove that claim, and his family didn't back him up either, which was a constant source of frustration to him.

So for those reasons and many more, Humberto Palomares had been let down his entire life.

Humans are fallible creatures. Kane knew that as well as anyone. They often teetered on the brink of madness and some are unable to maintain control when it seemed the entire world is conspiring against them. That, in essence, is what had seemingly happened to Professor Palomares. And in the end, he could not handle it. Slowly the system wore him down and he lost control. It was that madness that triggered his breakdown and his rapid descent into obvious madness that ultimately cost the lives of two young girls, and almost another ten, not to mention the injuries sustained by Kenny Peters, Danny, Stephy and Ridley. Kenny's were the worst, but they would all survive, and for that Kane was grateful. Kane himself was not unscathed, though he knew his worst injuries were those that couldn't be seen.

Of course, Humberto had lost his own life, but if he could still communicate, could somehow manage to speak from beyond the grave, Kane imagined he would say that his life had been taken long before the events beneath the pyramid. Humberto had been killed many, many months before. And the man, the creature known as Quetzal that died two days ago, had been created by the very system that killed Humberto. He would tell you that he too was a victim, Kane was sure, a flawed product of an irredeemably flawed social system. Would he say he was sorry for what he had done and what he had tried to do? Well, Kane, and the world, would never know that.

It had been yet another series of harrowing events in Kane's turbulent life. Yet again he had survived, but this time he knew it was more through luck than anything else. Between them, they had managed to keep Quetzal from massacring all those other girls, and all had somehow lived to tell the macabre tale. It wasn't always the case when Kane was involved. In short, this time they had won.

And yet it didn't feel like a victory. How could it, when two girls had been killed in such a barbaric manner? Slaughtered, their lives sacrificed just to a prove a point. It was a senseless waste of life. Kane was not guilty. He had done nothing to cause their deaths. And he'd been given no chance to prevent them. Yet guilty was exactly how he felt now as he looked at Kenny Peters, in good spirits, despite the clear and obvious pain he was in and the fact he'd lost a hand.

Kane had done nothing to cause any of this, and yet he knew as he stepped out of the room and walked out of the hospital to get some fresh air that he would never get over it.

Never!

"Want to talk about it?"

Kane turned to see his brother standing there watching him. Kane grinned a little, but the smile didn't stick around long and wasn't even close to reaching his eyes. "Not really, Danny. What is there to say? Two girls are dead, and you... well you could have died and I've only just got you back in my life. I—"

"But I didn't die. Neither did you, or Alex. Kenny lived. Despite his injury, terrible as it was, it'll take a lot more than a missing hand to keep a good man like Kenny down. Ten girls are alive today, including Rosa, because of what you've done."

"What we all did," corrected Kane. "We all did what we could... but if I had only worked out the location a little quicker, maybe we'd have prevented—"

"No," Danny cut in. "He didn't give you a chance, remember? The first girl... that was before we could have found out where he was keeping them. Right? Hiram?"

Kane didn't answer for a full minute as they stood staring out over the magnificent evening vista of San Miguel de Allende, the parroquia a stunning centrepiece of what seemed to Kane to be a truly magical city.

"I suppose you're right," he said at last, then added, "You *are* right." Kane turned and looked into Danny's eyes. "It's good to have you back, Danny. You know, I wish it was under better circumstances, obviously... but it's so good to have you back in my life."

"Hiram, listen to me, please. I am so very, very sorry for what I have put you through for all these years. I know my words can never change what I've done, but I want you to know I will never leave you again, never. And now I have a favour to ask."

Kane smiled now. "Of course, anything… what is it?"

"Right. Okay, well, when you leave here, are you going home to Cuzco or to England?"

"Well that depends…"

"Depends on what?" asked Danny.

"Well, whether I go to England or not would depend on you?"

"What do you mean?"

"I'll go to England on one condition… you come with me."

Danny seemed to fight hard to hold back the tears that threatened to spill down his cheeks, but he failed and Kane watched as they flowed in torrents, glistening under the glare of the dying sun to the west. Kane stepped close and hugged his brother and held him tight in that embrace for long minutes, his own tears dampening his cheeks. When both men's tears finally subsided they stepped apart and looked at each other. Smiles crept onto both their faces.

"You know what?" Kane said, inhaling and gazing out at the sunset. "England does sound good right now. Good, and peaceful." He tapped So, yes, bro, let's agree to go home, eh?"

Danny wrapped his arm around his brother's shoulder, and the two of them walked back into La Rojo Cruz Hospital, Kane believing that the world would be a much calmer place now this latest in a long line of tragedies was over and that his long-lost brother was finally back in his life.

That's what he believed. Kane had been wrong before.

Next in The Hiram Kane Archaeological Thriller Series

vinci-books.com/samurai-code

Hiram Kane is thrust into a deadly yakuza feud as Japan's most lethal storm ravages the land.

In the midst of Japan's deadliest storm, Hiram Kane launches himself into the rescue mission, only to cross paths with a retiring yakuza boss bent on settling a score with an ancient enemy. Soon Kane finds himself trapped between duty and survival. With time running out and the body count rising, Kane must decide if he will stand firm in his principles or compromise to save lives.

Turn the page for a free preview…

The Samurai Code: Prologue

A battlefield near Kyoto, Honshu Island, Japan

April 25th 1185

Ravens cawed and stabbed at each other beneath a full moon, fighting over chunks of human flesh.

Ghostly wraiths of mist billowed in the darkness, as if blown by Futen, the Japanese god of the wind, carrying with it the stink of rotting corpses. Shattered, torn bodies lay strewn across the muddy, blood-stained earth. Spilled guts and crushed bones bore grim testimony to the recent battle. After long days of brutality, it was over at last.

The main conflict of Dan-no-ura had raged wildly in the inland sea, not far from Kyoto. The ground skirmishes were just as terrible; thousands had died. And yet, although the fighting was over, the killing was not.

Beyond exhaustion, Katsu Hanzō stumbled. The physical and mental exertions of the arduous battle had edged

The Feathered Serpent

him to the brink of collapse. Through squinting, bloodshot eyes, Katsu scanned the battlefield. Before him lay acres of churned up muddy ground strewn with fallen samurai, both the dead, and those still dying, most noisily. He was among the few survivors. Today he didn't feel lucky. To die in battle was a great honour, if you died with dignity and courage. His own body had been sliced often, his arms, back and chest crisscrossed with deep, bloody wounds.

Yet destiny had spared him, and he knew why; Katsu had one last duty to fulfil.

He was hurting, agony searing both within and across his body. Though, he would not show it—not here, not in front of his enemy. This same enemy that had slaughtered his father and brother. Their destroyed bodies lay somewhere to the south, where the tide of the bloody battle had finally turned in favour of the Minamoto. It was they, the hated samurai clan from the north, who now encircled his master.

Twenty yards away, Takamochi Taira stood tall, calm and still. He was defeated, and the enemy was closing in around him like a human noose. But he was calm. Takamochi knew what must be done. As his second in command, so did Katsu Hanzō.

The leader of the Taira clan took one last look around. He surveyed the fallen warriors, his own and those of the enemy. A deep, slow sigh escaped his lips, and he wondered inwardly if it had all been worth it. Was it ever? Takamochi's gaze rested on the young warrior waiting in solemn quiet.

He bowed to his second, long and slow. Katsu returned the respect. Then, at last, Takamochi slowly dropped to his knees.

The ravens squabbled, their raucous calls piercing the

silent world as he whispered poetic words heard by no one but himself:

> *I'm glad to die*
> *in spring, beneath*
> *Blossoms of cherry,*
> *while a springtime moon*
> *is full.*

Takamochi breathed in slowly, held it, then exhaled even slower. He repeated that process several times. Next, he carefully positioned his white kimono on the filthy ground before him, and readied himself. He closed his eyes and moderated his breaths even further. To an onlooker the breaths would have been imperceptible, such was his calm. Takamochi sensed his trusted *kai-sha-ku-nin*—his assistant, Katsu—move closer and position himself alongside. As the metallic swoosh of Katsu's samurai sword being withdrawn from its sheath announced the moment, Takamochi opened his eyes for the final time.

He pulled out his own short, ceremonial *O'tanto* dagger, its handle bound tight in worn brown leather. Takamochi admired the weapon, feeling its weight as he thought about his next action. His final action.

Narrowing his eyes as his heart rate slowed, the slightest trace of a smile curved his lips. Calmly, slowly, Takamochi turned the blade towards his own stomach and gripped hard.

It was time.

The Samurai Code: Chapter One

Hiram Kane considered the city of Hiroshima to be a symbol of human endurance. The way it had risen again after its total annihilation in 1945 was awe-inspiring. Yet, he also lamented the fact that humanity still hadn't learned the myriad lessons the devastating atom-bomb attack should have taught.

Instead, he knew the world was more like a vicious cycle, one cruel and violent act followed by another. *What was it Gandhi said?* he mused. *An eye for an eye makes the whole world blind?*

As he explored the city after speaking at a conference, Kane came upon the infamous twisted wreck of the A-Bomb Dome. The former exhibition hall was the only significant structure left standing in Hiroshima after the bombing, and its enigmatic, warped steel frame was left in place, remaining to serve as a tangible reminder of the perils of war and the merits of peace.

After a few restorative Asahi beers at a riverside cafe to

help alleviate his somber mood—and a few coy glances from the youthful male and female staff members who seemed interested in why the tall foreigner was visiting their local hangout—Kane headed back to his hotel as rain began to fall. While he was packing and changing for dinner before his short journey to the island of Miyajima in the morning, something on the television caught his eye. He felt his stomach clench at the scenes playing out on the local news channel, that seemed to be something akin to an ultra-realistic disaster movie. Reporters were battling just to stand upright against the high winds, reporting from beside what looked to be the dangerously bulging banks of an out-of-control river.

Kane didn't need a translator to understand the severity of what was happening. The storm had hit central Japan with frightening speed. It was typhoon season, but no typhoons had been forecast. This one appeared to be a freak storm that had taken everyone by surprise, not least the residents of the city being shown on TV: Hofu, very close to Hiroshima.

Close enough, in fact, that Kane now became aware of the same strong gusts right outside his window. The camera flashed to the river again, and a quick Google search informed Kane it was the Saba River that flowed through central Hofu. His whole body was suddenly firing and alert. The danger of such powerful water was visceral for him. His mind darted back to when he was just eight years old. Playing near a river with his friend Evan back in his home village, he had attempted an unlikely handstand in an attempt to impress his mate. He had over-balanced and fallen backwards into the fast-flowing water and plunged under, his legs quickly tangling in the submerged fronds of stoneworts algae. The more he had struggled against the tidal flow and the weeds, the tighter their clutches became.

He had panicked and was unable to think clearly. If his friend had not dived in and helped dragged him out of the water, he would not have lived to grow up and explore the world as he had.

It was the memory of that terrifying experience, the scariest event of his life at that young age, that prompted his next decision. So, just half an hour later, Kane was on a train bound for Hofu, certain the city would soon need its own rescuers. The swollen, brooding clouds outside the train window painted a dire warning across the darkening sky, but hiding in comfort while people suffered so much nearby was simply not something Kane was prepared to do.

After arriving in the city, he took a short taxi ride and was soon checking into to a small ryokan, a Japanese traditional inn, as close to the Saba River as he could get while ensuring his accommodation was high enough to escape the expected flood waters. The otherwise serious-faced receptionist gave Kane a curious look from beneath raised eyebrows, as if to imply he must be insane to have turned up in Hofu just as the storm of the century was about to hit.

She's probably right, he thought, and caught himself grinning knowingly. The grin soon faded.

Sitting on his futon on the tatami flooring in his stylish yet spartan room, and watching the dated television, Kane knew that the red swirl on the map represented the peak of the approaching, ever-burgeoning storm. He glanced out of the window, but neither destruction nor panic were yet visible. Just twenty minutes later, the evidence on the television was no longer required. The spiteful storm was growing louder outside the thin walls of his accommodation, assaulting the building with a constant roar akin to the pounding of ocean surf.

Traditional wooden ryokan have paper interior walls and sliding paper doors set beneath an ornate tile or carved wooden roof. Kane soon discovered that, even when inside, outside noises could not be escaped.

Before long, Kane could hear objects thudding into the walls. He guessed they were tiles or plant pots, broken branches, and one metallic clash even suggested a bicycle. With his nerves starting to fray and the room seeming to grow darker with every passing minute, he reached out and flicked on the lamp beside the futon. The place was immediately plunged into total darkness as the power went out. Then there was a sudden, violent ripping and crunching noise and Kane momentarily froze as the ryokan's roof was torn clean off like a giant scab, then he dove for cover as rain and jagged splinters of tile and wood cascaded onto Kane's face like bullets finding their target.

The brute force of the wind had escalated tenfold in mere minutes, bringing unprecedented chaos to the city of Hofu and beyond.

Kane sprang into action. He ran to the balcony to see if other buildings had been destroyed and if anyone needed help. He spotted there were people hustling about on the streets who had not made it home in time before the strom hit. Others had seemingly left their properties for fear of being crushed, and they were now under threat from the heavy objects that tumbled down the road like clothes in a dryer. Cars were flipped over like pancakes. Lamp posts, felled like saplings. Road signs zinged through the air like lethal ninja stars hurled by mythical giants.

Kane shrugged into his jacket and pulled on his boots, then quickly made his way out of the swaying, teetering ryokan that seemed on the brink of total collapse, and headed down to the river. What se saw when he arrived made his heart leap into his throat and his guts twist into knots.

The Samurai Code: Chapter Two

Muddy water raged past with such power and ferocity that the very ground shook, and Kane had to stiffen his limbs and stretch out his strong arms to stop himself falling in and being swept away to a rapid death. It wasn't just the filthy, swollen river that threatened. Clouds roiled above in a black vortex, promising more misery. Across the wild surface, the wind gusted like the breath of vexed, forgotten gods.

Others had not been strong enough to prevent themselves from falling in. Gurgled half-screams reached Kane from all directions. They reverberated off the buildings opposite, some with frightening clarity, others little more than a pitiful wail. The cries for help merged together like a tortured choir, but Kane couldn't make out from which bobbing, floating bodies the sounds came, such was the ferocity of the out of control river.

Kane knew he had to act. And fast. There were plenty more brave volunteers around him, ready to aid the rescuers. But panic had incapacitated many of them, and nowhere near enough was being done. As he glanced around, he understood that people were simply too afraid—or too shocked—to help; too many seemed stunned into inactivity.

He beckoned to a man standing on the bank and clutching a rope. The man was frozen to the spot, his face pale and his eyes wide with obvious fear. Kane's Japanese was limited and hard to recall right now, so with a series of frantic hand gestures he communicated his plan. Kane then grabbed the rope and in seconds he had tied it around himself. He attached the other end to the thick trunk of a massive fallen tree, its exposed gnarly roots clawing at the sky like the fingers of a dying man. After a quick check of the knot's strength, Kane gestured to the other man that he should reel him back in as though he were a fish on a line. The man hesitated, and Kane looked hard into his eyes, trying to impart the strength and confidence needed for the task.

"*Tasukete! Tasukete!*" came a desperate cry from the river. *Help! Help!*

Kane looked upstream and, scanning the surging torrents, he caught the briefest flash of red surging towards him amid the peaks and troughs of churning brown. An instant later, what looked to have been a red jacket suddenly disappeared.

"Dammit!" Kane grunted. He kept searching, his eyes darting across the surface of the maelstrom. After several anxious seconds, the jacket reappeared, a dozen yards closer and nearer to the bank.

That is it. Got to move now!

Kane stepped back, took a few deep breaths and without another thought he launched himself into the deadly river.

His world turned black as he tumbled beneath the

surface. The sheer power and gut-wrenching force of the flow was even greater than he feared. He stretched out a long leg, desperate to brace against something solid below. But the river was at its highest level in half a century, its surface a series of raging whirlpools.

Kane, a strong swimmer and experienced scuba diver, remained calm. With a flurry of powerful, confident strokes, he surfaced several yards upstream, emerging in the path of the helpless little girl in red. He wrapped her in his strong arms, but her flailing limbs dragged them both under the surface. Choking on the filthy river water, he fought the powerful current with all his strength. With exertion burning in every muscle, he pushed up and broke the surface.

He looked down and saw that the girl slumped unconscious in his arms. Water ran over her like a tidal surge, plastering her hair to her face. Keeping both heir heads above water as much as he could manage, Kane kicked hard for the nearest bank. Their bodies jerked and twisted in the rapids, spinning this way and that, first away from the bank and then back again. Then, just as it looked as if they might finally reach the shore, a fierce undercurrent sucked them dangerously away. Kane just managed to keep his eyes above water, but he was battling the full force of the river to try and drag the girl to the surface.

As Kane finally brought the girl up for air, he could see the man on the bank had planted both feet into the earth and was hauling on the rope with all his strength. He was joined by a woman, who had apparently seen what was happening and sprung into action. They pulled again and again until the thirty yards of played-out rope was now twenty. Fifteen. After more heroic effort from all involved, just five yards of heavy saturated rope were left. The woman looked into Kane's eyes, wide and hopeful over the frothing water. The violent river yanked Kane and the girl away once more, almost dragging the two rescuers into the surging water.

With desperation evident on their faces, the man and woman managed to wedge themselves amongst the tangled roots of the ancient tree, scratching and scraping their shins on craggy bark. Finally secure, they pulled on the rope as if it were their own child on the end. It was someone's child, and Kane would not let her go. He could not.

Yard by yard, inch by agonising inch, the pair hauled Kane and the girl closer to the bank. Finally, the river relinquished its death grip. With the last of their ebbing strength, they dragged the sodden people onto the bank.

The little girl flopped pale and unconscious onto the muddy ground. Lying on his back, Kane gasped for air. Even in his exhausted state, he noticed the anguish in the eyes of the man holding the rope, who seemed to be muttering a prayer, imploring some higher power to spare the child's life.

The woman immediately knelt next to the girl and cleared her airways of debris, pulling clear a length of choking, clogging weed. Then she clamped her mouth over the girl's and began to pass life-giving oxygen between their bodies.

Within seconds, the girl's weak lungs blasted water out in a sludgy, brown spray. Her eyes flickered open. She was deeply shocked and clearly confused, but alive.

The woman carried the girl across the stodgy mud to the nearby road, where ambulances and first responders waited to transport the storm's victims to hospital.

The remaining man, who had assisted Kane from the start, held out a hand and smiled weakly, helping Kane to get up off his back. Kane had recovered enough energy to sit up, and the two men shared a silent moment of gratitude and admiration. They hadn't yet spoken a word to each other, but Kane was not surprised when the man looked into his eyes, leaned in a little and with something like hope glinting in his own eyes, said, in English, "Again?"

With a slow nod and the barest hint of a resigned grin, Kane climbed to his feet. The two men shook hands firmly and briefly. After scanning for life amid the troughs and swells of the roaring flash flood, and checking the knots on the rope, Kane turned to face the river then launched himself into its terror once more.

Over the course of the next three hours, Kane and the man took turns risking nature's wrath in order to save the lives of eighteen men, women and children. In a rhythm of diving, grabbing, swimming and pulling, they had saved more people in one day than most would save in a lifetime. They had worked in vital unison but hardly spoken. There was no time for talk or pause.

Only later, after the surging flood waters had abated and the river had calmed to something like its usual placid state, Kane and his new friend slumped down on their backs to rest. Both their minds and bodies were exhausted and battered from the previous harrowing hours. It was only after several minutes that they could exchange a few words.

"Naki," the man said, turning to look at an exhausted Kane, who nodded.

"Hiram. Hiram Kane."

Rescue support workers brought them warm blankets and steaming bowls of miso soup. They slurped in silence, neither possessing the energy to communicate in second languages. What was there to say? Both men had done all they could do. They'd done what they had to do. Kane had not thought twice about putting his own life on the line to help others, and after his initial reticence brought about by shock, Naki had clearly shown his inner courage and strength. That shared bond was far stronger than stuttered words.

After confirming with the rescue team there was nothing further they could do to help, Kane accepted their final nods of gratitude and got to his feet. He and Naki scrambled up the banks of the Saba River, finally edging away from danger.

Naki led Kane to his car, parked a half-mile from the destruction zone, and invited Kane to go with him to his home. Kane gladly accepted the offer, and fifteen minutes later, he found himself standing beneath a hot, revitalising shower. He was safe from nature's fury and, though he didn't fear death, he was grateful to be alive.

But as the clean water pounded his skin and washed away the dirt from the river, it failed to wash away the vivid memories and the haunting sounds of the suffering. Kane was devastated. They had helped save many people. And yet, others had not survived. Tears of sadness and frustration suddenly began to fall, mingling with the running water. Kane took every single lost soul personally.

In that moment, Hiram Kane was sure he would have traded his own life to save just a few more.

Grab your copy...
vinci-books.com/samurai-code

About the Author

Englishman Steven Moore grew up by the seaside, thus his first true joy was the great outdoors. His innate love of travel and a degree in anthropology, archaeology, and art history, help inform his fiction writing. Steven also loves painting, photography, and both playing and watching sport.

The travel bug bit the now perpetual nomad early, and to date Steven has lived and worked on five continents, and visited almost seventy countries. Steven combines an age-old writing adage; Write what you know, with his own mantra; Write where you know, and sets most of his novels in places in which he has either lived or spent an extended period of time.

When not on the road, Steven divides his time between Norwich, UK, and San Miguel de Allende, Mexico, which he shares with his rescue cats Ernest Hemingway and F Scott Fitzgerald (Ernie and Fitz), and his rescue puppy, Charles Dickens. Oh yes, and his beautiful travel writer wife, Leslie.

A lifelong love of food, wine, and beer, have demanded a new-found love of yoga and hiking in order to fend off the imminent arrival of middle age.

Acknowledgments

I don't know of any author who can finish a book of any kind without a lot of help and support, and I'm certainly no different. The assistance I've received for this novel and all my books has been both necessary and invaluable.

So, a quick shout out to these lovely folks—I couldn't have done it without you.

My gratitude to Anja Peerdeman, Michael Rhew and Tim Birmingham, my crucial BETA readers. Any remaining mistakes are my own. Thanks, guys.

I also want to thank the incredible team at Vinci Books for believing in me and supporting me on my journey. I appreciate you all.

And as always, to the one and only Leslie, my unstintingly supportive wife, I say thank you.

May you always be you!

Thank you! Gracias! Tlazocamati! (Nahuatl)

Steven